THE WAGES OF SIN — IS DEATH

Father Hines stood in front of the confessional. He reached out and touched the warm wood, and when he did something plucked far back in his head and he felt he was inside the box.

Sweat poured from him and soaked into his white robes. He looked down at his hand and saw a crucifix, and he tried to draw strength from it but could not. It was useless, nothing more than a lump of worthless metal.

But in his other hand there was steel which could be put to use. As he brought it up the glint of the honed edge of German steel shone, reflecting a light that was not there.

He brought the blade closer, the shrieks of a thousand million pleading angels in his ears, the knowledge that he had lost the Kingdom of God swelling in his brain with an agony that knew no bounds. When the blade touched his neck, he pulled down hard on it, wincing just once as it sliced through his flesh . . .

Confessional

Jack Olesker

LEISURE BOOKS NEW YORK CITY

To my darling wife, Dorissa—
the sweetest spirit
this lucky man has ever
known.

A LEISURE BOOK®

MARCH 1990

Published by

Dorchester Publishing Co., Inc.
276 Fifth Avenue
New York, NY 10001

CHAPTER 1

Throughout the 90 minute drive north into Wisconsin, it had been snowing. In fact, snow had greeted Father John Hines the moment the 747-B he'd come in on had dropped beneath the clouds.

O'Hare International Airport teemed with thousands of delayed travelers. The storm savaged most of the Midwest and a good portion of the East, creating havoc for the airlines. O'Hare's transient population bloated in response. Snack shops and bars were packed to capacity, and the lines at TWA, Delta and United stretched with weary travelers waiting to be told the bad news.

Although he could think of dozens of places he'd much rather be than O'Hare, Father

Hines was at least grateful he was incoming. He didn't know how fortunate he was. Half an hour after his Eastern flight from Miami had landed, planes were being diverted. Two hours after that, that most rare of occurrences would take place—O'Hare would be completely shut down.

Wisely, he'd carried his two pieces of brown Hartmann luggage onboard. As he struggled down the concourse, his briefcase wedged under his arm, he wondered if it had been so wise after all. A glance at the chaos that was Baggage Claim would have told him he'd made the right decision, but there was no need for him to take the escalator down in that direction.

Instead, he walked into the sprawling ticket area and set his luggage down. Father Hines unbuttoned the black topcoat he had not worn in four years, pulled a handkerchief from his pocket and mopped his brow. It had been 82 wonderful degrees when he left Miami. How was it possible for things to have changed so quickly, he wondered.

He thought about pulling his coat off but decided against it, realizing it would be one more thing to carry. To confound matters, he was starting to perspire. He was struck by the absurdity of sweating when it was 18° outside. When the pilot announced the temperature after they touched down, there had been a communal groan on the plane. John merely closed his eyes and fought against the impulse

4

to curse, even if silently. He'd lost that fight.

The priest was assessing the difficulty of finding Tom Conforte among the masses swirling around him when a voice called out, "Father Hines?"

He had a Polaroid of Tom that the boy's father had sent him after they talked on the phone last week ("He'll pick you up at the airport, Father."). The gangly 18-year-old standing in front of him looked nothing at all like the photograph. His hair was a much lighter brown and longer than in the picture. Two months of Wisconsin winter had paled the tan the boy had been so proud of as he stood before the camera in June.

"Tom?"

Tom Conforte grinned and held out his hand. "Hope you haven't been waiting too long."

"Not at all. I just got here. It's amazing you could find me so quickly in this crowd."

"To tell you the truth, Father, you're the fourth priest I've talked to."

John laughed, then said, "We should get going. The snow looks like it's getting bad."

"Here," Tom said, reaching for his luggage, "let me take that."

John let him take one piece, then picked up the other along with his briefcase. "Where's your car?"

"Out front, unless the cops towed it. I told them I'd only be a second, but your flight was late."

The blue Ford Mustang was still parked in the temporary loading zone, a thin sheet of snow blanketing the windshield. John was glad he hadn't taken off his coat, as a blast of arctic wind slashed through his topcoat as soon as he had cleared the sliding electric doors.

Traffic was worse than anything Miami had to offer. The snow, the slush and the gunk slipping and sliding across the windshield as Tom drove were all disgustingly new to John. Not totally new, actually, but he'd been in Miami for close to ten years, with one brief trip north for his father's funeral, and the mind tends to forget those things it doesn't care for.

An hour and a half later traffic thinned. They'd crossed the border into Wisconsin. White whisps of snow slid like quicksilver on the highway. Passing trucks kicked up billowing funnels of snow, leaving them engulfed for a moment in a mass of white as they passed.

"It's a small church," Tom said almost apologetically. "Not what you're used to down in Miami, I'm sure. Nettleton's a nice town—small, but nice."

"I get the feeling you don't like small."

Tom smiled, glancing sideways at him. The priest sitting in the passenger seat seemed pretty sharp to him. He'd better be, Tom thought, if he was going to make it in Nettleton.

Tom guessed, correctly, that he was on the

good side of 35. That would be both an advantage and a disadvantage. Youth would give him a shot at attracting younger parishioners, and that was something the church would have to do if it was going to function more than the ineffectual one Father Dreiband had run.

Personally, he liked going to church. It gave him a good feeling, but codgers like Dreiband took all the fun out of it. The old priest had always been so straight. Tom couldn't remember him smiling in the 15 years he'd been in Nettleton, always acting as if being a priest was such a somber deal.

But Father Hines didn't look like a priest. He was tan and tall and had a full head of curly black hair. He seemed to have all the qualities Father Dreiband had lacked. For the past 60 miles he'd kept up a steady banter about sports and school and Wisconsin. The priest admitted he'd never been to Wisconsin before, but he knew quite a lot about Nettleton. Tom was impressed that he'd done his homework.

But the man's youth would put other people in the town on guard. It was hard enough for an outsider to come into the community and be accepted, let alone a young man who was taking a position of religious authority.

It wasn't going to be easy for him, especially when you thought about what had happened to Father Dreiband.

"Well, I like the big city," Tom admitted. "I

come down to Chicago once in awhile with my friends."

"Nettleton's a little too quiet for you?"

"There's not a whole lot to do. Know what I mean, Father?"

John nodded.

"Not that I don't like Nettleton," Tom added quickly. "I've lived here all my life. My folks lived here all their lives, too. I just wish there was more to do."

"Dances and things like that?"

"Right."

"Maybe there will be."

Tom flipped the wiper blades to high, the snow slashing down in sheets now. "Huh?"

"I think it's a church's responsibility to minister to the whole community, including the young. There's no reason we can't sponsor a dance occasionally. Maybe get together a softball game and other activities."

"Hey, that sounds great, Father." He had been right, Tom thought. This guy was going to be okay. After a second he added, "I'm glad we've got someone like you coming to Nettleton."

Someone like me, John thought.

He leaned back in the seat, sighed and said, "I only wish I could be coming under better circumstances."

A frown creased the corner of Tom's mouth. He squinted, peering through the windshield. Then he turned off the heat. It was getting too hot in the car, and he was starting to sweat.

'Yeah," was all he said.

The priest looked out the window into the swirling, taunting white that was the Wisconsin countryside.

Under better circumstances! That wouldn't be hard to manage. Circumstances couldn't possibly be any worse for a priest coming to a new parish.

"It's not an easy mission you're going on," Bishop O'Donnell told him after the compulsory small talk had been tended to.

Sitting in the plush, wood-paneled office of the Bishop, John Hines fought against an almost irrepressible urge to plead with the Bishop to change his mind and not transfer him out of Miami.

How could they do this to him? He'd been with Miami's St. Mary's Church for ten years and knew he had been good for the church. Attendance had swollen and he felt a good part of the reason was his pulling power.

It was a feat to increase church attendance anywhere, but in Miami it was a miracle. Not that the city was any less religious than any other city, but it was a resort town catering to conventioneers and vacationers. Most of the hotels provided services for their patrons in the hotels themselves, and who really worried about going to church when there was the sun and the tennis courts and the ocean?

St. Mary's Church was located in affluent Bal Harbour, and although there was a sizable Catholic population, the church had been suffering from the general malaise organized religion as a whole had been going through since the early sixties.

John helped change all that. He was custom-made for Bal Harbour. He fit in with the people. In high school he had been an excellent golfer, and he found Miami offered magnificent golf courses. When word got around that there was a scratch golfer in town who happened to be a priest, he became something of a local oddity.

When it was discovered that he confined his preaching to the altar, the doors started opening for him. Bankers, real estate tycoons and entertainers were intrigued, and he often found himself filling out a Wednesday foursome. Most of his Catholic golf partners reciprocated by attending church services, many of them for the first time in years.

John was a natural for preaching. His sermons were filled with hope and optimism, rather than fire-and-brimstone. Many of the congregation drew pride in having him as a social friend as well.

There was nothing in all of this that John considered wrong. Sailing on yachts and deep-sea fishing were merely perks of his service to God. That there were priests in the seething Cuban barrios of Miami who were living little better than tenement dwellers was something beyond his control.

As time passed he gained a certain celebrity. Bishop O'Donnell took note of this, but he also took note of the now bursting Sunday morning Mass. If it caused the Bishop some pause to hear of John dining at The Forge, he also took into account that St. Mary's Church's coffers were filled to an all-time high.

So the Bishop's decision to transfer him to a small town in distant and frigid Wisconsin came as a complete shock.

Why, why?

There weren't many reasons a priest could be transferred, though certainly one of them was health. If a physician dictated a change of climate for health reasons, then it could usually be arranged. If a clergyman had a certain specialized talent—say a fluency in Spanish or a strong medical background—he might petition for a relocation to a diocese where those particular talents could be put to greater use.

But most transfers grew out of the needs of the Church, rather than petitions of the clergymen. Of these, the death of a priest and the need to replace him was the most common. Sacred Heart in Nettleton had suffered such a loss.

That in itself was not so unusual. Like all mortals, priests grew old and died. So the death of a priest in a small Wisconsin town would have been unremarkable except for the manner in which Father Dreiband had died.

"No," Bishop O'Donnell continued, "not an easy mission at all."

John kept the even expression on his face,

determined not to betray himself, but there was something that the older man read. Though frail and confined mostly to administrative work, O'Donnell was still a keen observer of humanity.

"I expect you'll be sorry to leave Miami, John."

"I go where the Church commands, Your Holiness."

"True. But you must have some feeling on the matter."

He hated statements like that. They weren't really questions, but you had to answer them all the same. Bishop O'Donnell was particularly adept at this sort of inquisition.

"I confess I've formed an attachment to Church of Mary over the years."

The Bishop leaned forward, folded his hands and placed them on top of the enormous desk he sat behind. "And you've done a good job here, John. I don't often have the pleasure of telling a priest that." He smiled slightly. "One of the nice things about old age is that you can be candid. Most of the time priests come and go and leave little imprint, especially in this city, but you've been special, John. You've done a fine job here."

Then why did he have to leave for some desolate—

He caught himself, turning against his thoughts.

I'm a priest. How dare I question my Church? How dare I question the wisdom of my Lord? There is a Divine purpose in this. I am needed elsewhere, and Christ has seen to it that Bishop O'Donnell makes the change. I am ashamed. I am contrite. Forgive me, Holy Father.

"Thank you. I'm eagerly looking forward to the new assignment."

Bishop O'Donnell unfolded his hands and leaned back in his leather chair. "Perhaps you won't be so eager when you learn the details." Sadness came into the Prelate's voice as he said, "The priest of Sacred Heart, Father Malcolm Dreiband, died last week."

John crossed himself instinctively. "I'm sorry to hear that."

Bishop O'Donnell's blue eyes blinked, the heavy lids folding down and holding for a moment as he contemplated the pain of what he had to say. He looked up at John. "He committed suicide."

It was one of the few times in his life that John had been totally surprised, totally caught off guard. He felt his mouth fall open stupidly. In that moment he understood how his mother had felt when he announced on his nineteenth birthday that he wanted to become a priest.

"Suicide," he managed to say.

"Yes. A terrible affair, John." The Bishop shook his head gravely at the thought. "Imagine the effect such an act has had on the community."

"What could possibly drive a priest to

commit suicide, to deny himself the Kingdom of Our Lord?"

"Indeed." O'Donnell peeled rimless glasses from his face. "A complete loss of faith. And what could cause that, in a man who had been a priest for thirty-two years, is beyond me."

"There was no explanation? No note?"

"Nothing. I won't go into the details, John." He pushed the folder across the table to him. "It's all contained in this report. You'll also find a police report in there. I'm afraid it's grim reading, but you should familiarize yourself with it. It's best you know all the details before you get to Nettleton."

The Bishop stood, picking up his glasses as he did. "Nettleton has suffered a great loss. They need young blood up there. The town needs healing, John. I trust you to do the job."

John rose and nodded. "Thank you."

As Tom Conforte's blue Ford Mustang passed the highway exit sign for Nettleton, Sheriff Doug Koester looked up from his desk to see Deputy Russell Patterson open the door of the sheriff's office.

Sheriff Koester squinted for a second, having difficulty seeing anything in the storm that raged beyond the open door. Then Russell tumbled in from the snowbank, slapping the mantle of flakes from his brown sheepskin jacket. The deputy pulled off his Stetson, another clump of snow falling to the ground where it began to melt. By the time he closed the door a puddle was forming around him.

"Christ, it's a fucking mess out there."

"Yeah, well you're making a fucking mess in here."

"What'd you want me to do, Doug, take my coat off before I got inside?"

"Don't see how you could accumulate so much snow just walking across the street from Brenner's Grill."

Russell unbuttoned his coat and hung it on the rack, watching as the snow melted and dripped from it. "You try taking a stroll out there tonight."

"No thanks."

"Never seen it like this in all my life."

"That's 'cause you're just a young shit. You should have been around in forty-eight. *That* was snow."

Russell glanced at his boss. There was a smugness he could read even through the jowls that sagged expressionlessly on Koester's face. Russell knew he would have preferred having an older man for his deputy, someone he could relate to, someone who didn't have a college degree.

It was a continuing bone of contention between the two men—Russell's degree in Criminology. The sheriff never spoke of it outright, but Russell knew it gnawed at him all the same. He also knew that Doug Koester was a dying breed—a sheriff without a degree. Koester believed in the flying-by-the-seat-of-your-pants school of law enforcement.

Most of the time that was good enough. It was sure good enough to get the balding, pot-bellied Koester reelected year after year. Russell would be the first to admit his boss knew his job well. After nearly 40 years in the profession you amassed an incredible amount of experience. What bothered Russell was that there were simply better and faster ways of doing some of the things Koester did.

Russell wanted computers put into Nettleton's four police cars so they could patch in to the State Police computers up in Madison. Koester had vetoed the idea. "Not that often we have to worry about escaped fugitives roaring through Nettleton on a rampage."

Russell also wanted to update the department's armaments, but Koester voted him down on that one as well. "Can't think of many things you need more than a .45 or a riot gun for."

It was a strange statement for a man like Koester, who was more than content to use physical force when it was needed. For that matter, Russell thought at the time, Koester was known to use physical force even when it wasn't called for.

There had been a particularly ugly incident about six years back. A couple of college kids from Minneapolis were on their way down to Fort Lauderdale for spring break. They were hitting 78 when they passed Nettleton. It was just their bad luck that Doug Koester happened to be crossing the highway overpass at that exact moment.

If Russell had stopped them he would have brought them in to Hal Buchanan, Nettleton's Justice of the Peace, had them pay a fine and sent them on their way. If they were locals, or even in-state, he probably would have just given them a ticket. But out-of-staters, Russell knew, had a tendency to take the ticket, say "Thank you," tear it up and then say "Fuck you." Still, all they'd end up with was a fine if he had stopped them.

But it hadn't been him that night.

It had been Sheriff Doug Koester.

And Sheriff Doug Koester had had an argument earlier in the day with his wife, Essie, and Sheriff Doug Koester, truth be known, had downed four Buds after Essie stormed out of the house.

There was no crime in a man having a couple of beers, even a sheriff, before he came to work. There *was* a crime in belting your wife across the chops, as he had done, but that was another matter altogether. The problem was the combination of the brews and the argument and Essie walking out of the house, and here were these long-haired kids on their way down to Florida where they'd probably get laid by young chicks who were more gorgeous than anything Koester could ever hope for.

When they were both pulled onto the shoulder, Koester stayed in the four-wheel

Bronco with the Nettleton Police Department insignia on the side. He pulled the mike off the radio, switched to PA and said, "Get out of the car and keep your hands in sight."

The driver of the car, a 20-year-old, was the calmer of the two. "Just stay cool, Freddy. We got nothing to worry about."

Sitting next to him in the Camaro, his pimple-faced friend said, "Nothing to worry about, shit."

The metallic voice echoed again. "I said, get out of the car . . . *now!*"

Koester watched as the driver's door opened. The kid started to get out. Not a moment too soon, the passenger side opened. When both of them were out of the car he spoke into the mike again. "Hands on the roof of the car."

After they'd assumed the position, Koester climbed out of the Bronco, his black lead-core night stick in his hand. One part of his mind considered unsnapping the strap on his service revolver, but even through the haze of the beers he realized that was bullshit. More than that, it was dangerous. He knew the beers were having a mild effect on him. The chances were one in a million that the kids were actually dangerous, but if they were he didn't want one of them to have the chance of grabbing his piece.

"Other side," he said to the driver.

The one kid turned toward him. "Huh?"

"Get on the other side with your friend.

You're exposed to traffic out here."

Everything was going to be all right, the kid thought. He walked around to the protected side of the car, next to Freddy, and put his hands on the roof.

Koester walked along the shoulder and stood behind them, his feet spread apart. To the driver he said, "Let me see your driver's license."

The driver was a smart kid, he thought. He was moving real slow, no jerky moves. He pulled his license out of his wallet and handed it to Koester.

"This your car?"

"Yes, officer."

"You got the registration?"

"Yes, sir. In the glove compartment."

"Where you headed, boy?"

"Florida. We're on spring break."

Koester peered into the backseat of the Camaro. Two pieces of new luggage sat on the seat. "You got anything in there you shouldn't have? Firearms, alcohol, drugs?"

"No, sir," the driver said.

"Open the door."

Freddy turned around, speaking to Doug for the first time. "Wait a minute. You got no right—"

The impact of the nightstick in his belly caught the words in midsentence. Freddy's eyes bulged, then rolled back into his head as the air burst from his lungs. He tried to shield his stomach with his hands, but he was unable

19

to move them. The boy had no idea anything could hurt so completely, could paralyze so quickly.

Koester watched as Freddy leaned back against the Camaro and slowly slid down the side of the car to the ground. He glanced at the driver, who still had his hands on the roof of the car. He was still looking straight ahead.

Real smart kid.

"Your friend is kinda stupid, ain't he?"

"Yes, sir," he said, his voice cracking.

Koester looked down at Freddy, who was still reeling in agony. Then he turned back to the driver and asked, "What's your name, boy?"

"Carl. Carl Lovitt."

"Turn around." When Carl turned, Koester saw that the corner of his mouth was twitching. Fear was a good thing, he thought, kept you out of trouble. "You know, I couldda shot him and been within my rights." That was stretching it a bit, but Koester figured the boy was in no position to argue. "You don't turn quickly on a law officer."

"Yes, sir."

"You help your friend up. Then we're gonna take a look inside the car. Unless *you* got some objections?"

It would have been difficult for Koester to have found a worse subject to vent his anger on. The boy's father was a rather prominent lawyer in Minneapolis. All hell broke loose when he found out Koester had used a nightstick on his son. Charges probably would have been brought, except for the half ounce of marijuana the sheriff's illegal search of the luggage had netted. All things considered, everyone decided to call it a wash.

Word got around, though. It usually did in small towns like Nettleton. For awhile there was some grumbling. No one knew for sure that Koester had been drinking, but he was known to drink and his arguments with Essie were no secret either. A lot of people were able to put two and two together.

It was forgotten by election time, though, and he won handily against Craig Abbott, Nettleton's leading lawyer.

Now, six years later, standing in the sheriff's office while a hellish blizzard raged outside, Russell Patterson remembered the incident. A mental file cabinet opened in the back of his brain and he didn't like what he read inside: Sheriff Doug Koester—62 years old, Caucasian, moderate-to-heavy drinker, harbors a strong dislike for the younger generation and people more educated than himself.

Russell pushed the disturbing images out of his mind. He was overstating the case, he decided. Wouldn't he be a little on guard if he'd been the sheriff of a town all his life and along came a man young enough to be his son—his grandson, for Crissake—who was ready to annihilate him with a college degree?

Maybe not.

"Saw Warren Conforte earlier."

"Yeah?"

Russell sat down on the other side of the partner's desk he shared with Koester. "Said he's a little worried about Tom."

"Why's that?"

"Tom drove in to Chicago to pick up the new Sacred Heart priest."

"Tonight?"

Russell nodded.

"Helluva thing. Why'd he drive in on a night like tonight?"

"The plane was coming in from Florida and—"

"Then they should have stayed overnight in Chicago. Them roads are going to be a mess tonight. State Police are thinking about closing them down altogether."

"Maybe he did decide to stay in Chicago."

"Nope," Koester said, "not Tom Conforte. That kid would slide down a ten foot razor blade naked just to show how fuckin' brave he is. He'll try to make it. I just hope he doesn't go and get himself killed. That's all we'd need."

"He'll probably be all right," Russell said.

Past eleven, Warren Conforte thought, looking at his watch for the umpteenth time. He made the mental calculations again. Tom had left before five. It was only an hour and a quarter drive down to Chicago. Give or take an hour for snow, he was still two hours overdue.

Warren spent those two hours—and the one before them—pacing the anteroom of Sacred Heart. He had determined that there were 31 linoleum squares to the length of the chamber and 12 to the width. Hours ago he computed out how much the job of laying the flooring had come to. In his mind he calculated the construction costs of each part of the church—the roof, the rectory, the altar. He didn't know the exact cost, but he was certain he was pretty close. Inflation was a factor, since his construction company had built the church 16 years ago.

It was a good job, an expensive job. As a member of the church board, Warren had been careful to keep his costs down. He even had cut his profit in half, though he didn't bother to tell anyone. With all of that, he still had made a nice profit. All told, it took his men the better part of a year to go from excavation to ribbon cutting.

He recalled his pride that Sunday morning when the formal dedication was made. Father Nicoletti, who was rector of another Catholic Church over on Oak Street, presided at the ceremonies. Through it all, Warren could sense how pleased the priest was.

The ceremony completed, the congregation entered the church. Father Nicoletti delivered a touching sermon that day, although Warren couldn't recall the gist of it. The choir never sang sweeter. Sun broke through the towering stained glass windows that depicted scenes from the Resurrection and the Creation, all blue and yellow and red. Warren had personally supervised setting those massive windows, and seeing the completed work made his heart flutter with excitement. Molly, his pretty brunette wife, sat beaming next to him, squeezing his hand. Young Tom hadn't figured out everything that was happening, but he sat up straight next to his mother.

Warren broke out of his train of thought. It didn't seem possible that he was in the same place he had been thinking about. This church, which once held so much joy for him, had become something else. The tragedy of Father Dreiband, who had come after Father Nicoletti had left, had been a personal loss for Warren. He was close friends with Dreiband, and for him to go that way was inconcievable.

It had been doubly painful, coming as it did so shortly after the loss of Warren's youngest boy, Frank. One day the boy had just disappeared, and all the dogs and search parties in the county couldn't find him. Young Frank had been an altar boy at the church, and Father Dreiband was crushed by his disappearance. The priest lapsed into a deep depression, and though Warren didn't want to admit it, he thought his son's death might have contributed to the priest's decision to take his own life.

Even now, at this moment, the church seemed to be stirring disquieting feelings within him. Warren felt a prisoner, forced to wait out bad news. Tom was far overdue, and as his anxiety built, Warren could feel the walls he had helped build begin to close in on him.

As the demons of parenthood taunted mercilessly at him, the headlights of Tom's Mustang raked across the front of the Sacred Heart, unseen by Warren Conforte.

John had had a few nervous moments during the ride up from Chicago, none of them being Tom's fault. The boy was a fine driver, but with the roads iced over like they were and the snow all but blinding them, John was on edge during most of the last half of the endless trip.

He was relieved as they pulled up in front of the church.

"Here we are, Father." Tom shifted into Park and turned off the ignition.

"Your house is right out back, Father. There's a connecting hallway in the church. We could have pulled around to the house, but I thought you'd want to take a look inside the church first. If you want we can—"

"No," John said, reaching for the door handle, "you were quite right. I do want to have a look at things first."

Tom looked at the light coming from under the door of the church. He'd seen his father's car as he pulled into the church parking lot, and he said, "My dad's inside. I'll bet he's pi . . . angry."

They got out on opposite sides of the Maverick. "Maybe you should have called him from Chicago."

"Yeah, I guess I should have." Tom pulled the luggage out of the car, and they walked toward the church.

This is a strong man, John thought when he saw Warren Conforte. There was a resemblance between him and his son, but his face was rougher, more weathered. He was ruddy-complected, even having been in the church for so many hours. It was a face that was accustomed to working outdoors.

Relief showed on the man's face as he held out his hand. "Father Hines, I'm Warren Conforte."

His grip was as strong as John's. John felt a man's handshake was a good first measure. Nothing put him off quite as much as handshake that felt like a dead fish.

"It's a pleasure to meet you, Mr. Conforte. Tom's been talking nonstop about you all the way up here."

This was not completely true, but Tom was grateful for the attempt at bailing him out. "I'm sorry we're so late, Dad. The traffic was unbelievable."

"The phone lines weren't down. I called your mother four times and—"

"I'm afraid it's my fault," John offered. "We got to talking about football and things. I want to apologize if we caused you much concern."

Warren frowned. He disliked being backed

into a corner, and that was exactly what the priest was doing. How could he say anything to a priest who was apologizing to him? Maybe it quashed his anger at Tom for the moment, but it would have been better for him to stay out of it and let a father correct his son, Warren thought.

"Well, let's go in," Warren said. He pulled open the wide double doors of the anteroom, and John saw his new church for the first time.

John walked past both of them, taking in the church. It wasn't as big as St. Mary's Church down in Bal Harbour, but what it lacked in size it made up for in feeling. Tall, polished beams vaulted skyward. A long nave halved the church, and on either side 36 birch pews sat empty and waiting for Sunday morning.

As John continued walking down the nave he took in the chancel at the front of the church and bent to genuflect. Warren and Tom also crossed themselves. John was surprised by the size of the sanctuary and that, by extension, the church could have such a sizable choir. There was room in the chancel for a good 30 choir members.

The pavement lights were dimmed at the altar, but he could still see vases on either side. Ivory-white altar candlesticks stood like sentinels.

He passed the chancel rail and stepped up onto the altar. The high altar and frontal were fashioned from polished oak and were as fine as any he'd ever seen. He looked up at the crucifix behind the high altar. It was gleaming bronze, and even in the dim light it was magnificent, some ten feet across.

My church, he thought. My congregation.

A wave of shame swept over him as he recalled his earlier reluctance to leave Miami. How could he have been so self-consumed? How could he have fooled himself for so many years? The work of the Church wasn't conducted on sailboats or in the clubhouses of country clubs while sipping Perrier with a twist of lime. The work of the Church wasn't merely to build the size of the congregation. If it was, then what difference would there have been between him and a carnival barker?

Somewhere along the journey from receiving his vestments after lying prone on the cold concrete floor of St. Mark's on his final day of seminary and the Fourth of July last summer he'd spent hauling in a marlin, he had lost sight of his true purpose.

Standing in the empty church in Nettleton, he rediscovered himself. This church, these people who had suffered the loss of their spiritual leader and needed healing, this was the core of his service to God.

As the shame left him, a feeling of goodness and beginning took its place. He turned to Warren and Tom Conforte and said, "It's a fine church." As they approached the altar, he said, "I didn't expect anything like this."

"Dad built it," Tom said simply.

"He . . ." John caught an image of himself staring at the boy in disbelief. He turned to Warren. "Did you truly build this church, Mr. Conforte?"

"I did, Father. How about calling me Warren. Mister makes me feel too old."

"But what a marvelous thing that you built this church."

"Well, I had some help from my construction team and—"

"Come on, Dad. You were here every day. The whole town still talks about how hard you worked on the church."

Warren wrapped his arm around the boy's neck and mussed his hair, all the anger he had felt at him dissipated. What had the anger been, really, but concern that the son he loved was in danger, had plowed off the road somewhere and was in a ditch?

Warren broke into a smile. His son was proud of his old man, and that was something a lot of fathers would given an arm for nowadays.

John said, "You've done a wonderful job, Warren. I'm proud to be the rector of this church, and I'm proud to count you among the congregation."

"Thanks, Father Hines." He patted his son on the back and said, "Tom, why don't you take the Father's bags back to the rectory."

When Tom left them, Warren said, "It's really more than just living quarters back there, Father. It's a complete home. A one bedroom home," he apologized, "and a bit on the cramped side at that, but it's a real home."

John came down from the altar and stood next to the man, sensing there was something on his mind by the way he wouldn't make eye contact with him. Suddenly the church seemed to have grown cavernous and, as the emotional distance increased between him and Warren Conforte, John felt some of the warmth escape, felt the chill of the winter storm outside starting to make him cold to the bone again.

"I'm sure I'll be comfortable," John said, adding with a forced smile, "once I get the heat turned on."

"Yeah, I'll have to show you how to do that." After a long silence, Warren looked him in the eyes and asked, "Do you know why I met you here tonight, Father Hines?"

John felt off-balance, the way the man was suddenly looking straight at him. It was unnerving, and he fought for control. These were strangers, and he knew it was going to take some time until he got to know them. But here was this man, alone with him in the church, looking deeply into him and about to make some terrible revelation.

"Well, I imagined it was so I would feel welcome."

Warren nodded. "That. Yes, that." He looked away again. "But something else, too."

"Go on."

Warren's voice was softer when he spoke

again. "I guess you know about Father Dreiband."

"Yes, I know all about it."

Warren's glare turned on him so quickly that John actually stepped back a half-pace. "*All* about him?"

"I know he committed suicide. That was a terrible thing, Warren. I know it must have come as a great blow."

"Do you know how he killed himself?"

He had read the police report, which hadn't painted a pretty picture. Apparently Dreiband had slashed himself with a straight razor.

"Yes, I—"

"No," Warren said, cutting him off, "you can't know how he killed himself. Even if you read about it or someone down in Florida told you about it, you can't know how he killed himself."

Warren Conforte took him by the arm and began walking to the side of the church with him. "I can tell you how he killed himself, Father Hines, because I was the one who found him."

John stiffened at the pronouncement, understanding now why Warren had met him here tonight. It was to be an orientation.

"I found him in there," Warren said, pointing toward the wall.

John followed his gaze and saw a tall, brown-stained confessional booth. As he walked closer he saw the intricate carvings on the front doors of the booth. They were reliefs of saints and angels and clouds carved into the wood.

"It's magnificent," he said, examining the confessional more closely. "What breath-taking workmanship."

"I've always thought so," Warren agreed, off the track for a moment. His tone softened as he said, "It's one of the few parts of the church I had nothing to do with. George Hayward did the work. Carved the whole thing himself. A real craftsman, that one."

"More an artisan, I'd say."

"Yeah."

Something in Warren's voice hinted at animosity, but John decided not to pursue it.

"Anyway," Warren continued, "that was where I found him. I was down here to check out some water leakage we'd been having. Nothing serious. As I was walking around I smelled something bad. I couldn't pinpoint it, but it was bad. I did my work and was about to leave when it hit me what it was. Dead deer. Dead meat. Blood was what it smelled like."

John shifted, his legs cramping on him now. It had been a long day, and Miami was light years away. He wanted to go and unpack, be anywhere except with this man and his tale of death and the suicide of a priest.

"It was coming from under there," he continued, pointing to the confessional. "As I walked toward it I could see blood was coming from underneath the door. It'd pooled right out front. I didn't want to think, but I knew I had to look inside."

John's eyes were riveted on the confessional. He felt pain in his chest, and he gasped as it struck him that he wasn't breathing. He felt the veins on either side of his head as they pulsed. He looked quickly at Warren, glad that the man's attention was turned toward the booth and not him.

"When I opened the door I saw Father Dreiband sitting inside, the razor still in his hand. The front of his robes were soaked with his blood. Only he hadn't sliced his wrist like you'd expect. He'd slashed the razor across his neck. Cut his carotid artery was what Doc Brannigan said he'd done."

John winced at the image and turned away, bitter bile rising in his throat and souring his mouth.

Warren's voice suddenly was back to everyday normality again. "I'm sorry, Father. Maybe I shouldn't have told you the story. I almost didn't, but I figured you'd want to know how it was. You'd hear rumors about it sooner or later anyway, and I thought it would make you more a part of the community to know the whole story instead of hearing it in bits and pieces."

It was a strange offer of friendship Warren Conforte had given him, but John recognized that that was exactly what it was. He also recognized that the man was right. If he hadn't known the details he would have been at a disadvantage. He would have jumped right into the confessional like it was nothing, and the townsfolk would look at him pityingly (Poor fool doesn't know). Better to have a look at the dirty laundry upfront and share in it with everyone else. No skeletons in the closet—or in the confessional.

Conforte would spread the word that he knew the story, and that would be the end of it. Well, if not the end of it, then at least one less hurdle to negotiate.

As they walked back toward the nave, John said, "I know how difficult it must have been for you to tell me the story, Warren. I appreciate your making the effort and the thought that went into it."

Warren nodded silently. They stopped at the center of the church and John asked, "What kind of a man was Father Drieband, Warren?"

"Tormented," was all the man said.

John shivered again. It was a shiver that had nothing at all to do with the blizzard raging outside the church.

CHAPTER 2

That Friday when he arrived in Nettleton, John slept straight through the night. Warren Conforte's story about Father Dreiband's death had upset him, and he was almost certain he would dream about it.

He hadn't.

The long day of traveling had left him completely drained. As if his brain knew what he needed, dreams were blocked out, and he slept a solid eight hours, waking up at the disgraceful hour of nine o'clock.

It was a pardonable sin, he thought, as he walked from the bathroom, a towel still wrapped around him. He dropped the towel, fell to the floor and pumped out 50 push-ups as he had done most every morning since he was 18. No one would ever be able to accuse Father John Hines of being out of shape.

Dressed, he picked up the silver key Warren had left him the night before; it fit the front door of the church. When he was finished with breakfast, he would unlock the church door and throw the key away. Churches were not meant to be locked at any time.

He explored the well-equipped kitchen, opening four cupboards before he found the one that contained cups and saucers. The kitchen was fully stocked with groceries, and before long he had a pot of Folger's percolating.

It was probably Father Drieban's coffee. How could a man go about normal business like buying groceries when he knew he was going to kill himself?

A knock at the front door jolted him from his morbid thoughts. John padded through the dining room, the living room and into the small foyer.

"Small," Warren had said. The house wasn't that small at all. It was more than adequate for him. The living room was painted a soft taupe color, and the furnishings were sturdy Early American. A plaid upholstered sofa squatted in front of an oak-manteled fireplace that promised to warm the blistery nights ahead.

Although the dining room he'd just walked through was on the small side, it was still large enough to entertain three quests for dinner. That was sufficient. There would be no large dinner parties here—not in Nettleton.

Maybe that was as it should be. Maybe a priest had no business giving dinner parties or sailing on yachts or slathering on Hawaiian Tropic Sun Tan oil. Maybe this was the Lord's way of telling him he'd better do some hard thinking about what a priest's purpose was.

He made a mental note to spend more time in the chapel in contemplation. How long had it been since he had meditated? Too long.

John opened the door and looked at the woman standing on the front step. She was attractive, in her early thirties, brunette hair framing either side of an oval face. Something in the face was sad, announcing that it had seen pain in its life and that pain had been bad.

She had a boy with her. Was it her son? Most times parents and children match. You could tell they belonged. That was not the case with the woman and the boy, and it struck him as strange. He was 12 or 13 and was wearing a bright orange ski jacket that begged to be taken to a snowball fight. An unruly lock of bright red hair peeked from under the sailor's cap pulled down over his ears. Buck teeth pushed his top lip back so he always looked as if he was just about to speak. His hands were jammed into the pockets of the ski jacket, and he stood with a confident stance that was in stark contrast to the frail impression one got from the woman.

"Father Hines?" she said.

"Yes?"

"I'm Jill Gregory." She put her hand on the boy's shoulder. "This is Evan, my son. We brought you a little welcoming present." She held up the small box she'd been holding. John hadn't even noticed it, so intently had he been studying the two of them.

"It's a coffee cake," Evan said. "Mom baked it herself."

"Hush."

John grinned as he stepped back from the doorway. "Won't you please come in? This is so nice, Mrs. Gregory."

As mother and son walked into the house, Evan said, "Mom doesn't like it when people call her 'Mrs.'"

"I'm a widow," she explained.

"I'm sorry to hear that." John closed the door and showed them into the living room.

"That's all right. It's been awhile. Quite awhile." She looked around the room like a real estate agent getting a feel for a house. "It feels strange to be here."

"You've been here before?"

"Yes, when Ned died. Father Dreiband was . . . He was very kind to me during that difficult time." Then she seemed to snap out of her train of thoughts. When she turned around she was smiling, and John was stunned by the change in her. It was as if another woman had taken her place. "I smell coffee brewing."

"I've just made a pot. You'll join me, of course."

"I'd like that, Father."

Evan asked, "Can we have some of the cake?"

"Evan," she scolded.

"Of course we can have some cake." He walked with the cake box toward the kitchen. "Why don't you get comfortable, while I take care of preparing things?"

"Do you work in Nettleton?" John asked as he poured more coffee.

"Yes. At Brenner's Grill. I don't have to," Jill said quickly. "Ned left me well off. He had a lot of insurance through the Teamsters Union. He was a truck driver."

"I see."

"Paid off the house. But what am I going to do, sit home and watch *General Hospital* all day?"

"No, of course not." John looked at Evan sitting with a dish on his lap, finishing the last of his cake. He noticed a small pouch attached to the boy's belt. "What have you got in the sack, Evan?"

"Marbles, Father."

John smiled at Jill. "Funny how boys never tire of marbles."

Jill looked at her son fidgeting in the rocking chair. He'd finished two pieces of cake and two glasses of milk and had had quite enough of all this.

"You want to go outside and play, honey?"

"Yeah. Is that okay?"

"Sure. Go on. I won't be long. I'll just finish this coffee and then we'll go. You still want to go over to K-Mart with me, don't you?"

"Yeah," Evan said, but already he was out of the chair and pulling on his coat.

After he'd left, Jill smiled. "He gets antsy sitting around."

"What young man doesn't? How old is Evan?"

"Thirteen."

"He seems a fine boy."

She laughed a high laugh. "You aren't around him like I am. Still, he's better than most. It's not easy raising a son in this world."

"Very difficult."

"Especially with Ned gone."

"I can imagine."

"Father . . ." She hesitated, looked at the coffee cup, then back at John. "I hope you don't mind if I come to you once in a while for advice."

"Jill, that's what I'm here for."

"Sometimes you have to talk to a man, get his point of view. Father Dreiband was good at that sort of thing." She sighed. "I don't know, maybe if Evan'd been a girl it would have been different. But he's not and it just makes it harder for me to understand him sometimes."

"Listen to me," John said with sincerity.

"Any time you need help or you just want to talk, you feel free to call me or visit."

She brightened then. "Thank you, Father. I'll do that."

In the backyard, Evan was playing in the snow. The storm had dumped six inches on the already heavy snow that had accumulated during February.

He ran zigzag paths in the backyard, running straight into drifts, liking the way they slowed him down against his will. The backyard here was great, much bigger than his. Their house was bigger, but this backyard was better and he'd take a backyard any day. Who needed all those little rooms anyway?

He wasn't sure about this new priest. Dreiband he had been sure about. Dreiband was easy to figure. It hadn't surprised him that the priest killed himself. Evan had heard all about it from the kids at school. The teachers tried to hush it up, of course, and old man Fortmann, the principal, had given this jerky lecture about how Father Dreiband had been such an upstanding citizen and all.

Well, upstanding citizens don't slash themselves to pieces, do they?

He smiled at that idea. It showed how stupid Fortmann and the teachers were, trying to make everyone believe it was okay, that nothing bad had happened. But something bad *had* happened. Dreiband had cut himself open like a lake perch, and pretending that he didn't only made the rest of them look dumb. Old Fortmann had done everything but say the priest had died while trying to take a Nazi machine gun nest. It was really dumb.

Maybe it was kind of surprising that Dreiband had really gone and slit his own throat. That took more guts than Evan thought the old coot had.

Pills would have been more his speed.

Evan stopped running and slashed his finger across his throat. He started gurgling, clutching at his neck and trying to imagine how it felt to feel warm blood spilling over your fingers and knowing that you were a goner for sure and that you'd eaten your last bowl of Shredded Wheat.

"Yuk," he said aloud, thinking it must have been a mess.

But if it was surprising that Dreiband had killed himself in that way, it wasn't surprising that he had killed himself. Everyone in town knew the guy was off the deep end. The sermons he'd been giving the last few months before he'd slit his damned throat were as weird as they come.

Not that his sermons were ever good in the first place. Not that Evan had ever been able to stay awake during an entire Sunday morning Mass. But during those last months he started getting really worked up. "It's like he's some sort of Billy Graham or something," he'd heard Deputy Patterson tell Lynn Spitler's mother in Dave's Grocery one day.

The funny thing was that once old Dreiband started with those intense sermons of his, it was the first time Evan actually did manage to stay awake on Sunday mornings. It was a kick watching everyone's reaction while Dreiband turned red in the face hollering about "divine retribution from Almighty God for the evil each and every one of us commits in our sinful lives."

It was a kick. He'd look back and see row after row of frozen faces staring up at Dreiband, and man, the whole church was like a crypt it was so still. All you needed was for someone sitting next to you to cough and you'd jump out of your seat you'd be so shook.

Yeah, you just knew something was going to happen to the guy. He was heading for Trouble City. Off the damned deep end.

Evan tried to make a snowball, but the new snow was no good for packing. It was this powdery stuff that just fell apart when you tried to ball it. It was too cold. He looked toward the sky, at the gray pallor that had hung over Wisconsin for four months and still had two more to go.

Sun was what you needed, a little heat to melt the snow so it would pack better. He dropped the snow from his hands.

But this new guy Mom was in there talking to was a whole different kind of priest. He was young, and Evan didn't even know that they made priests that young. The guy could be somebody's brother. He looked at you when he spoke, and he seemed kinda nice. You had to watch out for that kind of guy. They were the kind who would try to fool you into thinking they were okay. They'd talk to you about baseball or the Boy Scouts or how bad the new snow was for packing just so you'd let your guard down.

That was all you had to do—let your guard down. One little word about how you liked playing with your dick in the bathroom and they'd be over you like Hooker over a pusher. They wouldn't be such great guys then.

Evan turned as he heard something from near the red brick garage at the far end of the backyard. He cocked his head as he listened, trying to decide what it was. Then he started walking toward the sound. As he got within throwing distance of the garage he decided it was a bird. Since there were no trees around he figured it might be up on the garage roof.

Only it wasn't.

It was on the ground, in the snow.

He started running toward it once he saw it. It was a dark brown bird, and it hobbled away as it saw him coming, the chirping getting louder.

If you didn't want me to find you, what were you chirping for in the first place?

He played a game with it for a couple of seconds, pretending that he wasn't fast enough to catch it. The bird bought it, hopping around like it thought it had a chance to get away—but it didn't. Its right wing was busted from when it had flown blindly into the side of the garage during the snowstorm. Each time it tried to flap away it fluttered back down into the snow and settled into the drifts.

Evan didn't know the bird was that badly hurt, so he was worried it might actually be able to fly away. He decided to stop playing the game and reached down to pick up the bird. Before he picked it up he took off his gloves. He was worried for a second because he thought the bird might bite him, but then he thought the little thing probably didn't have any teeth, and even if it did, it didn't look like it had enough strength to do any damage.

He dropped his gloves into the snow and picked up the sparrow. It fluttered in his hands for a moment as Evan cupped them around its wings. The bird sensed that it was captured, but more importantly it responded to the heat of the boy's hands. Heat was something it needed almost as badly as food after a night in the snow.

Evan brought it closer to his face and looked at the tiny black eyes that stared back at him. "Cold, huh?" The bird chirped in response, but it was a quieter chirp than when he had been trying to escape.

A smile played at the corner of Evan's mouth as he winked at the sparrow. Then he squeezed his hands around the bird tighter, then tighter, then tighter still.

The bird let out a shrill chirp in the moment before its body was crushed. Evan was sure he heard a gasp of exhaled breath as the thing died. What was definitely neat was the feeling of the bird crumbling in his hands. It felt like it wasn't a bird at all, but something made out of toothpicks. The little bones snapped as he squeezed, and the beak opened and closed over and over and over again, no longer able to make the chirping sounds.

Evan opened his hands then and looked at the dead creature. It looked smaller than it had before. There was no blood or anything, but Evan was pretty sure he had hurt it badly before it died. It was a shame it had died so soon. He wondered if it had died *too* soon.

But then he knew it hadn't because he felt the tingle. It began low and it was like he had to pee, only he knew he didn't have to because he'd gone to the bathroom just before they left home. He kept looking at the bird and the tingle grew and pretty soon it was pulsing and spreading and was more than he could bear and he smiled all over as the golden shafts split outward and inward from his groin. He shuddered in that moment of culmination, closed his eyes and delighted in the sensation.

The bird dropped out of his hand into the snow. It wouldn't be found until spring, and even then it would only be the gardener's lawn mower that would find a decaying skeleton and slice it up into pieces that no one would see or know about.

"Evan, Evan," Jill called as she stepped out of the back door.

He turned and looked toward her. She was far enough away so that she couldn't see the dumb lust on his face, and he wasn't sure she would see it even if she were closer. That was the problem. It was always over so quickly.

"Yeah, Mom."

"Come on, honey. We're leaving now."

"Okay," he said. He glanced back at the hole the bird had made when it fell from his hands, and he whispered, "Bye-bye."

About 20 minutes later, just as Jill Gregory pulled her red Pacer into the parking lot at K-Mart, George Hayward reached for the lighter on the nightstand and fired up a Camel. It was his habit to smoke right after sex and lately he'd been smoking one hell of a lot.

Cindy Breslauer, stepping into a pair of black silk panties he'd bought for her, was the reason. George watched as she pulled the panties up over her firm ass. At 21, she was at the age when she didn't have to exercise to look good. Hell, that was just how he liked 'em.

"Turn around, girl, and let me see your tits."

Cindy turned automatically, and George was rewarded with a view of her high, jutting breasts. The nipples were still erect from the heat of their lovemaking. She brushed back a long strand of blonde hair and took her sweater off the chair.

He was crude and rude, she thought. But he was also the richest man in Nettleton, and she enjoyed driving around in his flashy burgundy Cadillac and eating at the country club he belonged to just outside Oshkosh. She liked being noticed when she walked into a restaurant on his arm, and if people spoke about her and speculated about what so young a woman was doing with a 51-year-old man, then so much the better.

There were times when she liked the fact that he was crude and rude. There were times when she liked the fact that he pawed her and treated her like dirt. It was exciting and animal, and she didn't have to act phony like she did when she visited her mother and father. She knew where George was coming from; there was a sort of disgusting honesty in the way he was. Sometimes she could get off on that.

But not always. Not most of the time.

Most of the time she felt used. The watches and clothes and other little trinkets he threw her way only made her feel like a whore, and Cindy knew she wouldn't be with George Hayward all her life. There was only so much of that you could take before you said to hell with his fancy house and his fancy car.

She wiggled her skirt up over her hips and

, caught a glimpse of herself in the mirror. She thought the image was what her mother must have looked like when she was her age. That scared her because she knew she would grow up to be what her mother was—a housewife. She'd marry Willie Gilbert or Stuart Karchmer and she'd wind up pregnant and popping Swanson frozen dinners into the oven for the rest of her life.

That was why she was having a fling with George. If she was going to be miserable the rest of her life, she decided she'd at least have a little while where she knew what it was like riding around in a Cadillac.

"Get that cute little butt moving," George said from the bed. "It's damned near eleven and the store should be open."

"I'll be open before eleven."

"Damned right you will. Saturday's a good day for business."

As if he really needed the income from his woodcraft shop, she thought. He had all the money he could handle, more than he could ever spend. The bedroom they were in was bigger than the living room in her parents' house, and the house itself was a rambling 11-room colonial that looked alien in Nettleton. It belonged in Washington, D.C., or Beverly Hills or someplace else where rich people lived. Not in Nettleton.

As she thought about George and her own chances of ever enjoying anything near what he had, her anger bubbled to the surface. She rarely challenged him, but he had just finished ravaging her and she was feeling hurt both physically and emotionally. He'd used a belt on her, all the while insisting that she loved it and making her say that she did, so she now found the courage to strike back at him.

"You don't need the damned store open. You don't need the money."

George stared unblinking at her. He wiped a hand across the grey stubble on his chin, his jowls shaking as he did. He tried to think about how to respond to the girl. Fucking her had taken a lot out of him. If he were younger he would have sprung out of the bed and lashed her one, but he wasn't young and he was overweight. The mere effort involved in hoisting 235 pounds out of the comfortable bed didn't seem worth the effort, and he'd had his fill of whipping her anyway.

"Think you're smart, don't you?"

She turned her back on him as she slipped on her brown pumps.

"You think I'm too tired to beat your ass, don't you? So smart, Missy." He yawned dis-interestedly. "Well, maybe you're right. You caught me in a lazy mood, so I'm gonna let it pass."

Cindy turned around to look at him triumphantly.

Then he smiled and said, "But next time you come over I won't be feeling lazy, and you can bet that wet little pussy of yours that I'll remember." He laughed out loud, as if he'd just understood the punch line to a joke.

"That's it, isn't it? You want to get that little ass beaten, don't you, honey? That's why you're trying to get me riled. Don't worry none, girl. I'll take care of you next time. I'll sure take care of you."

Cindy picked up her purse and hurried from the bedroom. She ran down the stairs, almost afraid he'd haul himself out of the bed and come after her. As she came to the bottom of the landing she was suddenly conscious of all the parts of her body that hurt—her nipples where he'd pinched them savagely, her shoulder where he'd bitten so hard that teeth marks had turned blue, her buttocks which still bore the red welts from his belt.

She looked up the long winding staircase and could hear him still cackling away in his bedroom, rolling with laughter. She envisioned the fat, black-eyed, balding monster, spittle at the corners of his mouth, hysterical at the bind he had her in.

At the top of her lungs she screamed, "Fuck you, you bastard!" Still he laughed, so she shouted, "Fuck you!" again. Now the laughter stopped. She reached in her purse and took out the key to Hayward's Woodcraft Shop and flung it across the marble-floored foyer. It clattered to the corner and came to rest against his baseboard.

"I quit," Cindy bellowed. "Here's the key to your goddamned store. Take it and shove it up your ass!"

Then she turned and quickly left the house.

It was nearly 7:30, and it was pitch black outside. John was beginning to wonder when Alan Landano, the towheaded altar boy who had been working all day in the church, would be picked up by his father.

Russell Patterson, who John learned was the deputy sheriff in Nettleton, had delivered him at two o'clock.

"He's a good worker, Father," Russell had said, his arm resting on the boy's shoulder.

"Thank you for delivering him, Russell."

"All part of being a councilman, isn't it?"

"I certainly don't mind having a law officer as a councilman of the church."

Russell watched as Alan went to begin his chores. "Glad to help out." Then he lowered his voice a bit and said, "You know, Alan's adopted."

"No, I didn't."

"Henry and Edwina Landano took him from an orphanage up in Eau Claire." He shook his head. "What they didn't have to go through to get him. But they love him and they give him a good home." Russell buttoned his jacket and said, "When you get settled in you should drop down to the office, and I'll introduce you to Sheriff Koester."

"Is he a member of the congregation?"

Russell laughed unintentionally, then caught himself. He rested his hand on the butt of his service revolver. "Not hardly, Father.

He's what you'd call a lapsed Catholic."

John nodded grimly. "Maybe we can do something about that."

"Don't plan on it. Not with Doug."

"You never know."

"I've got to be going. Alan's dad will be by to pick him up around six-thirty or seven."

The 12-year-old was, as the deputy had promised, a hard worker. Most of the day was spent taking inventory. Most dismaying was the shortage of supplies for the Eucharist. There were only a few dozen Communion wafers and hardly any wine to be found. For a moment John's concern rose about Sunday Mass, but then Alan discovered a box containing wafers stored in the sacristy.

"A good thing you found them," John said. "You saved me a trip to go begging for wafers from St. Andrew's."

"Maybe you'll take it easy on me then, Father."

"Take it easy on you?"

"Yeah. Father Dreiband always had me saying so many Hail Marys and Our Fathers. Gosh, I never thought I did anything so bad."

"We'll see, Alan. You'll go to confession tomorrow morning and we'll see."

"Yes, Father."

As they walked back toward the altar, John was satisfied that everything was ready for his first Sunday in Nettleton. He'd resigned himself that this was not Miami. He was not going to see strong attendance at daily Mass.

He knew there would be days when he would be alone saying Mass. These people had to work nine-to-five jobs, and the years of struggling to make ends meet during an economy that was just beginning to recover had taken their toll.

But he could hope for good attendance on Sundays. Tomorrow would provide a good turnout, he felt, if for no other reason than curiosity. So he had to be prepared to put on a good show.

Not a show, you imbecile. You're not an organ grinder or a mime. When are you going to get over this entertainment thing?

As he stopped before the altar, John asked, "Do you happen to know Evan Gregory, Alan? He's about your age."

"Yes, Father, I know him."

"He visited earlier with his mother. Seems like a nice young man."

"Yes, Father."

John was satisfied the candles were perfectly straight in their holders. He stood away from them and gave the altar one final inspection. Something was wrong, but he couldn't quite decide what it was. It struck him that it was too quiet in the church.

He turned and looked down at Alan standing before him. The boy was looking down at the ground, his hands stuffed into his pockets. He had stuffed them there so Father Hines wouldn't see that they were shaking.

*　*　*

It was dark, much darker than it had ever been in Miami.

And it was quiet, much quieter than it had ever been in Miami.

Father Hines lay in the bed, knowing it was too late an hour to be staring at the ceiling, too late for a priest to be awake on a Saturday night with Mass just a short time away.

But he could not sleep.

Friday night sleep had come to him easily, like a ministering angel who knew he needed to be physically replenished.

But that was no angel. That was jet lag.

But tonight there was no jet lag. Tonight was the first real night he'd spent in this strange bed in this strange town, and tonight sleep would not come.

Opening Mass jitters!

He smiled at the thought. An altar boy had calmed him years ago by cracking that joke. It was the first Mass he was to perform after he'd received his vestments, and he had a bad case of the jitters. The joke had done the trick.

But this wasn't the first Mass he'd ever given, and it wasn't the first time he'd been assigned to a new church either. What damnable circumstances to come under, he thought. That was the problem. He wasn't afraid of the congregation or the parishioners. He knew he had the charisma to carry the day, to win them over, to become a part of their community, to make it his community.

It was just the circumstances. It was Father

Dreiband. It was the curse left behind by a priest he'd never known that was keeping him staring at the ceiling in the dark, and he disliked Dreiband for it.

Images and thoughts shot through his mind like phantoms, and he knew they needed to be confronted or they would continue to weigh on him. But how did you confront phantoms?

John rolled over onto his stomach, pulled the blanket tighter around him and reached for sleep's embrace again. But it eluded him. He was almost there when the sound of a pack of snow sliding from the eaves of the house brought him out of it. He heard the snow land on the ground with a dull thud and opened his eyes again.

You wouldn't be bothered by a sound like that in Miami, because it would have to fight against the sounds of distant sirens or nearby traffic, and the sound would lose and you'd be able to sleep. But in Nettleton the sound of snow slipping from the eaves was enough to keep you awake because that was all there was, and because it was all there was, it was significant.

He rolled onto his back again and sat up.

It was not the sound of snow or Father Dreiband that was keeping him awake.

It was the confessional. If the idea of a priest committing suicide was difficult to grasp, then the idea of him committing suicide

in a confessional booth was beyond compre-
hension.

Why in the confessional? Why commit so
unholy an act in so holy a place? Why commit
that terribly damning sin in a confessional
and flaunt it in the Lord's eyes?

It was warmer in the church than it had
been when he arrived the night before, but it
was still cool. It was close to three o'clock and
outside the temperature had dipped to near
zero. A cruel Canadian wind, which had
originated in the Arctic, was savaging most of
Wisconsin and fighting mightily against the
furnace Warren Conforte had taught John
how to operate.

The pavement lights were on around the
base of the altar, bathing the church in a soft
light that extended as far as the third pew.
Beyond that the pews were in almost total
darkness. There was no moon out tonight, so
even the stained glass windows looked like
nothing more than blank holes.

As John opened the door and walked into
the church from the corridor that led back to
the rectory, he almost stopped.

Go back to your bed. What are you doing
walking around the church this time of night
in your pajamas? What if someone came in
and saw you?

But no one was going to come in, he thought
as he closed the door. Everyone was sleeping,
everyone in Nettleton except him and maybe

the deputy . . . what was his name? Patterson. Russell Patterson. John wondered if he had the night shift. He thought about going back to the rectory and calling him on the telephone. (Hello, Russell. This is Father Hines, the new boy on the block. Just thought I'd call you at three in the morning because I can't sleep because I've got the damned heebie-jeebies.)

John frowned at the profanity, but it brought home how much this was getting to him. Profanity, even in thought, was an indication of excessive emotions to John. So it was good he was alone in front of the first pew at three in the morning. It was just as well to deal with it now and get it behind him.

He walked up the nave, his black leather slippers soft and quiet on the carpeting. By the time he reached the eighth pew he was in darkness. He stopped, turned to his right and looked at the confessional at the end of the row. He could have as easily walked to the aisle that ran along the outside of the pews. It would have been an easier, quicker walk to the booth. Now he'd have to sidestep along in front of the oak bench.

He eased into the pew, shuffling along to the right, his eyes fixed on the confessional. In the haze it was nothing more than a large form that loomed before him. He squinted, trying to see it better.

As he continued moving down the pew he felt his heart begin to pound again. His temples throbbed, and the smell of wood filled his nostrils.

Damnit, he was scared.

Then his legs stopped moving. He hadn't made a conscious decision to stop walking. Something else had made it for him, some secret part of his mind—the same secret part that told you not to sleep with your arm hanging down over the side of the bed when you were a kid because you just knew that there was something hiding under the bed, and if you slept with your arm hanging down it could grab you and pull you under and eat you.

He shook his head at the stupidity of it.

But when he looked at the confessional again he was startled by the fact that he could see it very clearly now.

My eyes are adjusting to the dark, and I'm closer. That's all it is.

The confessional looked larger now that it was dark and there was less to contrast it against. It looked very big.

He forced his legs to start walking again, adult logic winning out against childhood instinct.

"All right," he said aloud, walking faster, "let's get this over with so I can go to bed already."

Then he was at the edge of the pew and the confessional was only six feet from him and it was very, very big now. At this distance he couldn't see the details of the carvings, nor could he make out where one ended and the other began. But he could see the surface where they were uneven. Slowly, in the faint light, the carvings began to move, as if coming to life.

John stood, transfixed, watching the carved figures as they began to move faster, as they danced and jumped in the air, frolicking. They spun and clapped their hands, and their faces laughed at the revelry that overtook them. He could hear their laughter—mad, insane laughter. And then the carved figures jumped off the confessional and began dancing on the floor right in front of the booth.

That was when he turned away and shut his eyes. As soon as he did, the laughter and voices died. A ringing took its place, and he shook his head for a moment. When the ringing disappeared he felt a sheet of nausea wrap around him as his stomach tightened.

John opened his eyes, holding the edge of the pew for support against his dizziness. He blinked again and looked back at the confessional. The carved images were back where they belonged, back on the front wooden piece.

It had been shadow and light playing tricks. That's all it was. Carvings don't dance, and they don't laugh. Again he thought, this is stupid.

He walked away from the edge of the pew and stood right in front of the confessional. He reached out and touched the warm wood, and when he did something plucked far back in his head and he felt he was inside the box.

He was sitting on the bench, his throat tight, his hand holding cold steel, his mind ablaze with self-loathing. The window dividing the confessional was pulled closed and he knew that the most important thing in the entire world was that that screened window remained closed. Nothing could be worse—not even dying—than having that window open.

The smell in the booth was almost too awful to believe. It was like nothing he'd ever smelled before, a foul stench that turned his stomach and sickened him. His tongue felt swollen and thick, and the taste of it was that of carrion being torn apart and chewed by a predator.

Sweat poured from him and soaked into his white robes. He looked down at his hand and saw that the cold steel was a crucifix, and he tried to draw strength from it but could not. It was useless, nothing more than a lump of worthless metal.

But in his other hand there was steel which could be put to use. As he brought it up the glint of the honed edge of German steel shone, reflecting a light that was not there. The light was from his mind, and the light was realization.

He brought the blade closer, the shrieks of a thousand million pleading angels in his ears, the knowledge that he had lost the Kingdom of God swelling in his brain with an agony that knew no bounds. When the blade touched his neck, he pulled down hard on it, wincing just once as it sliced through his flesh. Hot pain buckled him in two as his skin opened like an envelope parted by a letter cutter—first flesh, then tissue, then arteries. Then the blade finished its descent, striking hard bone.

John reached for the door, threw it open and looked inside.

The harsh rasp in his throat was the sound of reality, explaining that he was just a priest standing alone in his church the night before his first Sunday Mass, staring into an empty confessional booth.

He rested on the jamb, his chest still heaving. John looked at the dark brown leather upholstery on the bench inside. It was a bench he would spend many hours sitting on, hearing the minor and not-so-minor sins of Nettleton. Now he could sit on the bench. Now he could hear the sins. He'd driven his own fears out. He'd opened the door and seen that the hideously disfigured, decaying corpse of Father Malcolm Dreiband was not crouched inside waiting to spring on him for trying to usurp his authority.

It wasn't a coffin.

It was just a place where a sad man had committed a final desperate act. Beginning tomorrow it would be a confessional again.

John closed the door and walked up the aisle toward the door that led to his house.

But as he did he didn't look back, and he tried very hard not to think about the carved wooden figures on the front of the confessional.

CHAPTER 3

Jill Gregory scraped the remains of the scrambled eggs and bacon from Evan's plate and hit the button for the Disposall. The blades whined for a second, then died as she flicked the button down into the off position.

As she washed the dish she had a faint twinge of guilt that Evan had eaten before going to church. Of course she hadn't, and she would have preferred that he didn't either. But he still had six months to go before he was finished with Catechism and could begin taking Holy Communion. She supposed it was all right.

It had been different when she was young. Her mother had never let her eat before church, even before her confirmation. Evan was a boy, though, and boys were always hungry when they woke up, so she'd allowed him this childhood indulgence.

She put the dish in the cupboard and wiped off the orange Formica countertop. One more glance around the kitchen satisfied her that it was neat.

Dishes were never stacked dirty in Jill Gregory's sink, nor in the dishwasher. Ned had surprised her with the GE dishwasher one Christmas, but she hardly used it when he was alive. After he died, she never turned it on. There was something disgusting to her about the idea of dishes sitting in the dark cavern with decaying food on them. All sorts of germs could breed. Hot water wasn't enough to clean them. Nothing could cleanse the dishes. They had to be scoured under scalding water, at once and by hand, if there was any chance of getting rid of the germs.

As she walked from the kitchen she called, "Evan, hurry up will you. We've got to get to church."

Thick green shag covered the living room like newly planted sod. Beneath it were hard-wood floors which she had once heard were considered elegant. Not to her. Carpeting was easier to keep clean, and it looked cleaner, too. The carpeting was clean because Jill rarely used the room. It was reserved for only the most special of occasions and certainly off-limits to Evan most of the time. An invisible rope ran around the room, protecting the furn-

70

ishings that were doubly guarded by thick plastic covers that had taken on a faint orange tinge from the years of sunlight.

Jill usually took the hallway on the other side of the room when she wanted to walk from the kitchen to the stairwell at the front of the house. Today she was in a hurry, though, and when she got to the stairs she was a little irritated that Evan was late and had forced her to cut through the living room.

"Evan," she repeated with more urgency in her voice.

"Coming, Mom," the voice from above answered.

Church wasn't something you were late for. That was a hard, firm rule. It had been instilled in her at an early age, almost one of her first memories. "You just don't show up at the House of the Lord late," her mother had told her the first day she was to give confession.

Six years old, with an angelic face and fine straight flaxen hair, Jill stood in her mother's bedroom in a frilly pale blue dress that matched her eyes. She had begun Catechism just a week earlier, and now she was to give confession.

Jill knew she couldn't stall forever, and she knew Mother would be angry and win in the end anyway. But having to go into the dark box terrified her, so she had holed up in the bathroom forever. Finally, Father had rapped on the door and, in that low voice that said

71

he wasn't taking any nonsense, simply said, "Now, Jill."

It had been enough to get her to open the door. When she opened it she couldn't look up at him. He was a giant, and just looking up at her father was enough to cramp her neck. The thought of the giant striking her, though he never had, was enough to compel her to do his bidding.

"Get dressed," he said. "Your mother doesn't like to be late."

Her mother tied the blue bow in her hair, giving her a final inspection in her bedroom. "There. You look perfect, Jill. Father Thyssen will be so pleased."

"I don't care about Father Thyssen."

"Don't ever say that again." Mother bent before her, her voice gentler. "He cares about you. He likes you."

"I'm scared."

"What are you scared of?"

"I don't want to go in there with him." She looked at Mother, knowing tears would come if she did and hoping against hope that tears would work. "Why do I have to go in?"

"It's confession, Jill. We went all through this before."

"But the other kids don't have to go. Ellen Ogden says you don't have to go until you're confirmed, until you're twelve and . . ."

Mother stood back up, buttoning the high neck of her dress. "You'll have just that many years of practice on her."

"But I don't want—"

"Don't you want to be a good Catholic?"

It was a loaded question. She knew that much. She couldn't tell Mother she didn't want to be a good Catholic.

Mother looked down at her, seeing the tears welling in her eyes. "Jill, it's never too early to begin following a holy path."

Jill slowed the Pacer as she pulled into the entrance of the church parking lot. She'd never seen anything like it. The lot was crammed with cars. People were streaming into the church as if Armageddon was upon the world. Jill looked at them for a moment, then turned to Evan sitting next to her.

"Will you look at that."

"He must be giving away umbrellas."

"Don't be funny, Evan."

"Sorry."

"I've never seen such an outpouring."

"They're curious is all."

She pulled into the lot, looking for a spot. "It's certainly heartening to see people attending church again."

"You think it'll last?"

"I hope so, Evan."

Inside, all but the final six pews were filled. Evan scanned the church for his buddies. He spotted Mike Kopernik and Chucky Hamilton, but they were sitting further up toward the front and couldn't see him.

He settled into the pew, beginning the vital

task of guarding his mother's coat while she went to the ladies' room.

After a few minutes, Jill returned to her seat in the pew. Behind her, Elmer Fortmann stood talking with Russell Patterson, something about Tom Conforte and the good job he was doing as quarterback at Jefferson this year. It was making her sick, listening to the school principal go on and on about Jefferson's chances for a divisional title like it was just the most important thing in the world.

For a moment she was taken with the idea of turning around and saying, "Excuse me, Russell, but did Principal Fortmann happen to mention how he tried to feel me up in his office last year?" That would fix the bastard.

She closed her eyes, trying to bring back the scene. When she did, the desire to reveal it trickled out of her because it wasn't what you could call a clear-cut case of a dirty old man trying to cop a feel.

She'd had to come to school because of some trouble with Evan. He was a fighter (probably got it from his father) and was forever getting into scuffles at Jefferson. He'd been feuding with one boy all year, and it had finally come to a showdown. Evan bloodied the boy's nose and kept hitting him even after the student had given up, so Jill had to see Fortmann about it.

Jill was all right through most of it, but finally she'd broken down and begun crying in the principal's office. Wasn't that stupid?

Crying in the principal's office like she was 12 herself. Fortmann hadn't expected that, and when she went on about how hard it was for her to raise a child alone he had come out from behind his desk and put his hand on her shoulder to try and comfort her.

When he did that Jill stopped crying. She spun out of the chair, stood up and shot him one of those get-your-damned-hands-off-of-me looks. Fortmann was as shaken by it as she was, and to this day she wasn't quite sure if he was upset because of her reaction to an innocent gesture or because he was afraid she would spread the word around town that he'd tried to cop a feel.

"Did you hear me, Mrs. Gregory?"

She shook her head, turned back to look at the principal standing there in your basic brown suit and asked, "I'm sorry, did you say something?"

"Yes. I said Evan seems to be doing much better this year."

"At school?"

"Yes," Fortmann said. "His grades have picked up, as I'm sure you can see from his report cards."

"I think he's finally getting into his studies."

Effusively and loud enough for others in the confessional line to hear his praise, Fortmann said, "But you must take some of the credit. I'm sure you're enforcing good study habits at home."

Jill warmed to the idea of people realizing

she was a good mother. He had scored a direct hit on the chink in her armor, and any animosity she felt for him disappeared.

He was probably just trying to be nice that time in his office. Principals can't afford to go around squeezing widows' tits.

"Well, that," she granted, "and I think he's starting to mature."

"A's in English and Chemistry. Quite a change from this time last year. You should be proud of him."

She allowed a smile. "I am, Mr. Fortmann. Thank you."

Then, from behind, the awful door swung open.

Mostly, until she was nine, Jill had pleasant dreams and very few nightmares. There was the occasional threatening snake or marauding lion if her father indulged her in one too many hot dogs at the annual Memorial Day picnic or just at the onset of a bout of flu. But she had fewer of these than most children her age.

At nine that changed. They were not just nightmares. They were night terrors. She would wake screaming and shrieking, and it would always be her father who would come rushing into the room. It would always be her father who would turn on the lights and take her in his arms and comfort her until she calmed down enough to go back to sleep.

Sally Crandall just didn't hold with coddling

the child too much. "You'll spoil her," she always told Otis.

"But you can't just let her scream like that, Sally."

"She'll go back to sleep if you leave her be."

Otis couldn't leave her be. Her cries cut him like a sickle through harvest wheat. He was soft and warm for his daughter, maybe doubly so because his wife was cold and distant to him. She'd never been the kind of woman you could wrap your arms around, but in recent years she'd grown more stand-offish.

Otis Crandall was a big man—six foot four and over 200 pounds. He was all muscle. During the war he'd seen action—more than he'd cared for—in the South Pacific. He had been at that hell called Iwo Jima and miraculously came out of it unscathed. But that jungle carnage had sobered him. So much death, so many bullets, so many tears. Seeing people's heads and arms blown away before his eyes had left an indelible brand of horror on his brain.

But even that hadn't frightened him as much as his daughter's screams. Iwo Jima had been something that was happening to him. There was death, but if you were brave or lucky or both you might get out alive. You had something you could do about it. This was happening to his daughter, and holding her and telling her everything was all right did nothing at all to make everything all right.

When he ran into her room and threw on

the lights, Jill would be writhing in agony beneath the sheets, as if some hideous white monster were trying to digest her before his eyes. And when he grabbed the sheets and pulled them from her he discovered they were as soaked as sailcloth after a day on Lake Michigan. From head to toe she was covered in sweat, her hair shiny, tangled and matted.

Sally would hear nothing of him taking her to see a psychologist in Oshkosh. What if it got out? And besides, who ever heard of such a thing—a child going to a head doctor? Otis had almost decided to take her anyway, when the night terrors stopped abruptly.

They stopped one September when she was 11. Otis had gone up to Madison for the annual reunion of his combat brigade. Sally never attended such things, being put off by the drinking and carousing which were distasteful to her sensibilities. In truth, he was grateful that she didn't go with him. There were times when he needed to be away from his wife if he was to live with her at all.

Jill was in the middle of a dream that was not that unpleasant. Certainly it wasn't a night terror. She was riding in a car with the windows up, and it was hot. The radio was on, and it was daytime. She was sitting in the backseat and was a bit uneasy because no one was driving the car. It seemed an odd thing, but not terribly disturbing.

That was when she felt the fists begin to beat on her. She looked frantically around in the backseat of the Oldsmobile, but no one was there. They were ghost hands pounding on her shoulders and arms, but the pain was real. The pain was so real she woke from the dream.

"Hands under the sheets! You've got your filthy hands under the sheets!"

She looked up, past the flurry of unrelenting fists, and saw Mother. Only it wasn't Mother. It wasn't anyone she knew. The woman who had Mother's face was purple with rage, her face twisted and contorted by demons that clawed at her insides.

"Why are your hands under the sheets?" she screamed.

Jill looked down and saw that Mother was right; her arms were covered by the sheets which were pulled up around her neck. The pain was real and oh, so bad. Her arms felt swollen and too heavy to lift, but still Mother pummeled her.

Jill struggled to pull her arms from beneath the covers, but they were tangled in the mass of blankets. "Ow! Mama, please, please don't hit me! It hurts!" Hot tears scalded her face as the beating continued.

"No, no, no, no!" Mother screamed, punctuating each shout with a punch.

Jill rocked back and forth on the bed, unable to escape the attack. Finally, she managed to get her arms free. As she pulled them from beneath the offending covers, Mother finally slowed down. Jill didn't know if she stopped because of exhaustion or the bluish welts that ran up and down her daughter's arms.

Hysterically, Jill covered her head with her arms and wailed, "What did I do? Why are you hitting me, Mama?"

Mother slumped to the bed, sat on the edge and bent her head, shaking it sadly. "Don't you ever put your hands under those sheets again. I won't have a daughter of mine giving in to the carnal lusts of self-abuse."

"Mama, I wasn't do—"

"Don't lie to me, girl!"

Jill shook on the bed from the force of Mother's shriek. She backed away from her, banging her head on the pine headboard. She brought her legs up and wrapped her arms around them, cowering.

Mother's eyes narrowed. "Don't you lie to me," she seethed. "You hear?"

Jill nodded tentatively.

"You listen to me, Jill." Mother drew deep breaths, her rage ebbing. "I don't like to hit you. It hurts me." When she reached out to stroke her daughter's hair, Jill cringed and Mother withdrew her hand. "But you have to learn what's right and what's wrong before it's too late."

"I know what's right and wrong, Mama."

Mother shook her head. "No, you don't. Don't say you do. If you did, then it would be too late for you because what you did was wrong." She stood and looked down at Jill, her voice ragged from shouting, her chest tight. "Keep your hands on top of the sheets when you sleep. Don't ever let me catch you like you were this morning again. If you do there'll be another lesson. Understand?"

Jill nodded again, but Mother hadn't seen her. She'd already turned and left the room.

"Bless me, Father, for I have sinned."

"When was your last confession?" Father Hines asked Jill through the screen.

"Last month, Father."

"How have you sinned, my daughter?"

The nightmares stopped because Jill rarely slept long enough to dream after that. It was not the last time Mother beat her. It took awhile to learn the trick of sleeping lightly.

For a time she tried setting the alarm clock an hour earlier, but that didn't work. Father wanted to know why her alarm was going off at five o'clock every morning, and she couldn't tell him, couldn't explain to him, because after all it was her fault Mother had to beat her. She had made Mother beat her because she was bad, and she didn't want Father to know she was bad, especially the way she had been bad.

Sleeping light was the answer. Jill would never sleep for more than an hour straight and, as morning grew closer, the intervals of sleep grew shorter and shorter, so by dawn she was only catching five minute cat naps.

In time she forced her subconscious mind

to keep her arms on top of the sheets and her sleeping routine became unnecessary. By then it was too late, though. It had become habit, and she slept that way all the nights of her life.

Sally Crandall was pleased. After a month of tribulation, her daughter had escaped from the lust that preyed on her.

It wasn't until she was 13 that the true test came.

Sally made a habit of picking Jill up at Jefferson each day. One had to be careful with the world the way it was. It wasn't the same as when Sally had been growing up. There was so much more sin and temptation. No one was safe, and it was all a mother could do to provide some modest barrier of protection. Picking her daughter up after class was the least she could do for her only child.

It was the second Friday in October, Jill's thirteenth birthday. It was also the opening day of hunting season, and Otis had gone off with the boys. They had had a cake for Jill Thursday night, after which Otis rolled in a shiny new Schwinn bicycle.

Jill was ecstatic, and Sally was pleased to see her daughter so joyful. Earlier, she'd been depressed because Father would be off hunting on her real birthday, but this surprise made everything all right.

She wanted desperately to ride the bike to school, but Mother said, "Absolutely not. It's not safe."

"But Mama, all the kids ride to school."

"I don't care what all the kids do. I won't sit home and fret about my daughter getting run down by a truck or grabbed by some maniac."

So Mother was out front of Jefferson to pick her up as usual, when she saw Jill walking out of the drab green double doors with Ned Gregory. He was tall and rugged and handsome for a 15-year-old. Just before Jill saw Mother, Ned leaned close and kissed her. Jill smiled, then scampered away from him.

She slowed to a halting trot when she saw Mother's car. For a second she pretended she didn't see Mother, but then she saw Mother looking at her through the rolled down window.

As they pulled away from the curb, Mother said, "I don't want you to see him again."

"See who?" she tried.

"You know who, Jill. That boy. That Ned Gregory."

"Mama, he only—"

"He kissed you," she spat. "I saw him so don't try to say he didn't."

"It was a birthday kiss. He just—"

The slap cut off her words. Mother had used the back of her hand to silence her, and though it wasn't a hard blow it was enough to startle her.

Jill didn't cry like a baby anymore. She wasn't a baby, and besides, years of harsh treatment had toughened her. She stared straight ahead.

So did Mother.

Mother missed Jill's crying and whimpering and helplessness. Her daughter was growing, getting stronger and away from her control. Something had to be done, she thought, stealing a glance at the girl. When her eyes dropped to Jill's skirt she stopped worrying about losing control of her daughter. There was no room in her brain for anything else except a consuming fury.

Mother slammed on the brakes, the tires squealing, and stopped the car in the middle of Victory Road. Jill lurched forward against the dashboard and then flew back against the seat. "What is it?" she cried, looking around.

"Your skirt," Mother snarled. "Your skirt is open, girl."

Her heart beginning to race, Jill looked to her lap. The navy blue skirt buttoned up the front, and her eyes locked on the one button that was open—the fourth button from the bottom, not far from her panties.

Frantically, she reached for the button.

"It was him!"

The button wasn't there. Where the hell was it? Where in the fucking hell was it?

"That Ned Gregory. The two of you!"

"It fell off," Jill cried. "That's all. The button isn't there."

"The two of you, during lunch." Mother's eyes widened, growing black with the madness that smoldered behind them. "Now I know. Now I understand."

84

"Mama, I—"

Mother began to pelt her with closed fists. She aimed for her breasts, trying to do damage to those offending mounds that had begun to blossom.

Jill screamed in the close quarters of the car, but it didn't do any good. The beating went on. Then long before Jill thought it would stop, Mother *did* stop. They were driving again and that worried Jill even more than being hit. Something was on her mind.

As they pulled up to the house, Jill thought about running from the car, but it was too late. Mother grabbed a handful of her hair and pulled her from the car as soon as they came to a stop.

"You're hurting my hair!" Jill screamed as mother dragged her along.

But there was no answer.

Upstairs, in Jill's bedroom, Mother finally let go of her. She pushed her onto the bed, went to her closet and got a pair of blue jeans. She threw them at Jill and said, "Put them on."

"I don't under—"

"Just put them on."

When she did, Mother seemed to calm down. For awhile Jill thought just getting the offending skirt off was all that was needed. It was possible Mother blamed the skirt for what she imagined had happened. Anything was possible with her lately.

After a silent dinner, it began. Jill walked

through the living room toward the bathroom.

"Don't go in there."

"Why not?"

"You're not going in there."

"But I have to go to the bathroom, Mama."

Mother stood and walked to her. She looked Jill in the eyes and calmly slammed her fist deep into her daughter's belly. Jill doubled with pain. She felt Mother push her down to the floor. Then she felt something being slipped around her.

When the pain cleared she felt the length of rope cutting into her arms. Mother got her to her feet and pushed her to the couch. For the first time Jill saw that newspapers had been spread over the couch.

It lasted 49 hours. During all that time Jill remained tied and sitting on the couch. In the end, her eyes rimmed red, her lungs raw from screaming, her mind worked off into a frenzy of degradation and horror, Jill had completely emptied her bowels and her bladder.

Putrescence filled the room, and Jill could cry no more. She had sunk low into a pit of shame, the sickly soft ooze of feces sliding back and forth in the crevice of her rectum. The front and legs of her jeans were stained yellow with urine, and when she wheezed dry heaves for the last time on Sunday night, Mother untied her.

"Before you wash, you clean the floor and throw away the newspapers. And then you're going to pray that the filth you've been in has washed away the filth of that boy."

The next morning, in the confessional, Jill told Father Thyssen everything. It came out in torrents. The line waiting to give confession stretched out and down the aisle as Jill stayed in the booth for almost an hour.

When she came out her eyes were red from crying, but there was a smile on her lips. She had made peace with herself, and someone believed her at last. There was no smile on Father Thyssen's lips. There was no smile as he conferred with Sally, as he announced to those waiting that he would be delayed for an hour, as he escorted Sally back to the rectory where they could speak in private.

Jill had no idea what he said to her that day. Nor did she know the details of the conversations that took place between Otis and Sally and the priest in the weeks that followed.

The details didn't matter.

All that mattered was that this Prince of the Church had rescued her. Maybe Father Thyssen was even more than a prince—maybe a knight in shining armor on a white charger. Maybe they really did exist.

She had felt shame when she first began to tell him the details of her ordeal. The heat in the darkened confessional was suffocating, and she almost decided against it, almost wrenched the door open and ran from the church.

But in the end she told him everything, and years later she would remember it as a day of salvation. There was a strange thrill that ran through her body as she sat in the confessional that day and told of the unspeakable things Mother had subjected her to. Even more than her own father, this priest had earned her love and respect. He had saved her life.

After that Mother left her alone. She was a changed woman after that Sunday. Mother didn't speak much in the time that followed. Mostly she sat in the living room and read from the Bible, muttering softly to herself. She didn't cook at all, and she ate very little and then only broth and soft foods. She lost weight quickly and shriveled into a skeleton before Jill's eyes.

A year later she contracted pneumonia, and after lingering for nearly three months she quietly died in her sleep. The only thing Jill regretted was that she hadn't suffered.

Father still loved Jill, but he was quieter, too. He was sad, and a cloak of melancholy drew between them, changing him forever. The land seemed to respond in kind. His crops failed twice in the early sixties, and in '64 he sold the farm and moved to Texas where his brother owned a small dry goods store. Jill never heard from him again. It didn't matter to her.

By that time she was already married to Ned Gregory.

Evan scurried out of the pew ahead of Jill.

He had things to do and places to go. She knew he didn't care much for church, but that would change. She was sure of it. It would have to change.

As the exiting crowd filed past Father Hines, her turn finally came. She shook his hand and said, "It was a lovely sermon, Father."

"Thank you, Jill. I'm glad you could come."

"I never miss church. Not like a lot of others here."

"We'll see if we can make them into regulars, too."

"Anything I can do to help, you just let me know."

John smiled warmly and said, "That goes both ways."

"Thank you, Father. It's a comfort to know that."

John looked down, conscious that she was still holding his hand. When he looked up again, Jill let go of his hand. She wasn't looking at him any longer. She was looking out into the anteroom where Evan was standing in a corner talking with George Hayward, the richest man in town.

CHAPTER 4

"**W**hat do you want to work on today?" George Hayward asked Evan.

"The ship. All I need is a couple more Sundays at your house and I'll have it finished."

"You'll still have to paint it."

"I know, but that won't take so long. I've got until spring. It's really going to be great."

Jill walked through the crowded anteroom outside the church and stood before the pair. "Hello, George."

"Hi, Jill. What do you you think of our new spiritual leader?"

She glanced back toward Father Hines, who was still saying good-bye to the people moving past him. When she returned to George she said, "He delivers a good sermon."

George nodded silently.

"We met him already," Evan said. "Mom brought him a coffee cake yesterday."

"That was nice." George put his arm around the boy's shoulder and said, "We should get going, don't you think, Evan?"

Evan nodded.

"You'll have him back before dark."

George smiled. "You ask me that every Sunday, Jill, and every Sunday I have him back before dark."

"Jees, Mom, what if I didn't get back before dark? It's not like I'd turn into a pumpkin or something."

"Go on with Mr. Hayward. And mind your manners." She watched as the two walked out the door and into the parking lot where George Hayward's big burgundy Cadillac was parked.

The same uneasy feeling that always came when she watched them leave began to surface. George had taken to the boy over a year ago when Evan took a sudden interest in model building. He became a regular customer at Hayward's Woodcraft Shop in town, and Jill supposed it was good for Evan to have a hobby. He worked well with the kits he brought home.

George started working with him more closely when he saw how serious he was about model building. One day he called Jill and asked if it would be all right to show Evan his workshop at home. She agreed, and after that it became a regular thing. On Sundays after church Evan would spend a couple of hours at George's house.

What appealed most to Jill was that he'd be around a man. That was important. A boy needed to be around men. She didn't want him to grow up sissified.

The basement in George's house was a dream come true for any boy. It had been converted into a workshop and all the necessary tools and machinery were right there. Rows of hammers, different-sized screw drivers, pliers, wrenches and woodworking tools like rasps and planes and chisels were fastened to pegboard on the wall above the long workbenches. In the middle of the floor there was a big standing saw. It was a professional contractor's saw by Toolkraft with every feature you could imagine.

On the far side of the workshop there were rows of shelves that held everything from balsa wood and plywood to two by fours.

Evan's model ship, a brigantine, sat on the eight foot long workbench George had told him was his. It was a damned good job, Evan thought as he ran the silver X-acto knife along another piece of balsa. He liked the feel of the knife's blade as it bit through the soft wood. He liked being able to build something with his hands.

He'd been putting the model together with

an elaborate set of plans that came with the kit, and he reckoned he was about three-quarters through.

George was putting the final touches on a side table at a nearby bench. He'd been working on it for three weeks, and the wood had already been stained. The table would be finished today, and tomorrow George would set it in place in the family room upstairs.

Over his shoulder, George asked, "So what did you think of Father Hines?"

"He's an asshole," Evan answered.

George laughed, wiping the sweat from his palm on the front of his green workshirt. He never felt quite as good as he did down here in his workshop where the smell of sawdust and paint and varnish filled the air. Even screwing some slut didn't hold a candle to what he felt down here. Oh, maybe he felt good for the moment when he was in the sack, but woodworking was a more prolonged and satisfying pleasure.

"Your mom doesn't seem to share your low opinion of him."

"She's taken in."

"But not you, huh?"

"Not me."

He looked sidelong at the boy. "How come he could fool her?"

" 'Cause she's a sucker for religion. All a guy has to do is put on a black robe, bend his head and whisper some mumbo jumbo and she gets all impressed."

"She's kind of soft for that stuff, huh?"

"Yeah." Evan traced a line of glue along the edge of the balsa he'd cut. Then he pressed it into place next to the bulkhead on the ship. While he held the piece in place he thought about George. He was a good guy. No bullshit about him. He was what he was, and he didn't treat you like you were some little kid. He didn't go nuts if you swore once in awhile. Evan liked to swear. It made him feel grown-up and important.

George brushed varnish on the leg of the side table, the smell pungent and pleasing in his nostrils. He turned away from it for a second as the fumes misted his eyes. He blinked and looked at Evan toiling over his model ship. The kid was a bridge to Jill Gregory. George wanted her badly, but she wasn't your garden variety bimbo. You had to be careful with a broad like her. You had to learn about her and go slow. Evan would teach him what he needed to know about her.

There was a vulnerable quality about her that appealed to George, and he could easily envision himself piling her for hours on end until she bled, until she begged for him to stop and begged for more at the same time.

Alan Landano stacked the last of the hymnals in the closet, closed the door and locked it. John was still at the altar, knelt in prayer. He was saying prayers of thanks that the day had gone so well when he felt a presence.

He opened his eyes, turned around and saw Alan standing in the aisle, small and waiting. John looked back to the altar, crossed himself and rose.

"All finished, Alan?"

"Yes, Father. What were you praying about?"

John smiled. "I was offering a prayer of thanks."

"What else?" the altar boy asked, as if he knew there was something else.

John thought about it. He hadn't been conscious of praying for anything else. But sometimes thoughts could enter his prayers almost without him knowing about it, and later he would only vaguely remember having made the prayers.

"What else?"

"Yes, Father. That wasn't all you were praying about, was it?"

"Why do you ask?"

Alan shrugged. "Because you've been praying for so long, I guess, and it doesn't take that long to say thanks."

John walked down the steps from the altar and sat on the front pew. "I was asking for guidance."

"About how to run the church?"

"About how to fit into the community."

"Do you worry about that?"

"Of course I do."

"That you'll be accepted?"

John arched an eyebrow in surprise. "Yes. Everyone wants to be accepted."

"Me, too."

John touched his shoulder. "You don't have to worry about that. You already live here and—"

"But I wasn't born here, Father."

John nodded. The boy was watching him. Children could tell if you were trying to con them, he thought. "I know you're adopted, Alan. Does that bother you?"

"Sometimes, yeah. I wish I knew where I came from, you know."

"I know. But what's important is that you're here and you've got parents who love you and friends at school. What's important is now. I'm learning that myself." He smiled and said, "I guess we're alike in some ways."

Alan smiled back, happy with that. Then he turned serious and said, "I wish Father Dreiband didn't have to die. I liked him, Father Hines. Why'd he have to go and do something like that?"

John shook his head. "It's hard to understand, Alan, even for me. But it's in the past and you've got to put it out of your mind. We have to worry about the future. At least you knew him for a time and you've got good memories about him."

"No, I don't."

"You don't what?"

"Have good memories about him."

"But I thought you were friends."

"We were. That's why I don't have good memories about him."

"I don't understand."

"You don't like to think about your friend being so unhappy and scared."

"Father Dreiband was scared?"

"Yeah. He was really scared."

"Of what, Alan?"

"I don't know. He never said." Alan paused, too deep in thought for a young boy. Then he looked at John and said, "But it was a bad kind of scared, the worst kind of scared there could be."

Right after church, Russell Patterson raced back to his home on the outskirts of Nettleton, changed into jeans and a flannel shirt, tossed his Remington into the backseat of his pickup and headed over for Doc Brannigan's.

It was a short drive, and he raised billows of snow as he skidded the four-wheel Toyota to a stop in front of the physician's ranch house. Russell got out of the truck and pulled on his camouflage vest.

"Hey, Doc," he called, starting up the walk. One thing about Doc, you always had to light a fire under his butt to get him to do anything.

They had little enough time as it was. Russell had wanted to leave on Saturday, but his mother wouldn't hear of it. Not that he was tied to his mother. She lived clear on the other side of town, eight miles from Russell's small home. But he loved her and she'd raised him well and put him through college. She made few enough demands on him and was as proud as the mother of a peace officer could be.

The church was the center of her life after Clifford passed on. Russell had gone to church all his life, and he reckoned he would continue going every Sunday until his mother went to join his father. Then he'd slack off. He'd still go once in awhile because it was a good habit to be in, particularly for a police officer, but he didn't find it as necessary as his mother.

For the present, he picked her up every Sunday at eight and drove her to Sacred Heart in the patrol car. She liked that—being in the Bronco. "You let them see that a law officer is a churchgoing man and they'll remember come election time. You're going to be Sheriff of Nettleton one day, maybe even Mayor."

Sheriff, maybe. Mayor? Who knew. But she was right about how important it was to let people know you went to church. Folks in Nettleton still placed a lot of stock in that.

What hurt was how it cut into deer hunting. That was one thing Sheriff Koester could understand. Koester figured there was hope if the kid liked to hunt deer and ducks. It was a common bond. So he made allowances and let his deputy have off an occasional Monday during the season so he could go hunting with Doc Brannigan.

"For God's sake," Russell said, pounding on the white door, "will ya hurry up, Doc?"

Doc threw open the door, the permanent scowl on his leathery face etched even deeper. You couldn't see exactly what was on his chin through the salt-and-pepper whiskers, but you just knew the scowl was there somewhere.

"You don't have to knock the whole house down, Russell."

"Do you know what time it is?"

"I know exactly what time it is. Come on in."

"No way. I come inside and we'll end up screwing around for another hour. Come on, Doc."

"Oh, all right. Give me a second." He disappeared from the doorway for a minute. When he returned he had the tooled brown leather gun case he'd bought down in Mexico under his arm. "The way you rush around I'll be visiting you in a coronary care unit before you're fifty."

They walked down the path toward the car together. "I just want to get in the woods before it's too dark."

"You aren't going to bag anything anyway. Never do."

Russell opened the door of the pickup and climbed in. "Now that's a damned lie. You remember that ten point buck—"

"—that I hit first?"

"Let's not start that again." He gunned the engine and roared out of the driveway, kicking up an avalanche of gravel.

Doc looked out the rear window of the truck

at the bare tracks the tires had left in his driveway. "You're gonna put those rocks back when we come home tomorrow night."

"Like hell. It's your fault I'm in such a hurry."

"You're a young man, Russell, with a long life ahead of you." Doc sighed, then leaned back in the seat. "You'd better pray you never get sick in Nettleton."

Russell glanced sidelong at Doc, watching as the old man pulled his hunting cap down over his head. He smiled to himself and went back to driving.

Lying on the couch in his living room, his feet propped up on one end, a fire crackling in the fireplace, John thought about Alan Landano. There was something puzzling about the boy. He seemed withdrawn and tentative at times. Yet at other times he could be quite blunt.

His father, Henry, was probably part of the explanation. When he'd come to pick up Alan on Saturday, John met a man who barely spoke above a whisper. There was an odd quality to the man's behavior, somewhat like a frightened rabbit.

Alan's personality was not so limited. He seemed sensitive, but willing to talk about his feelings. There could be no doubt Father Dreiband's death had had its effect on him, as it had on the whole community, but Alan didn't seem to take the loss personally.

Rather, he was sad for Father Dreiband himself.

John drifted off to sleep, the fire warming him and making him drowsy. His last thought was of Jill Gregory and the way she had touched his hand.

"Damn, it's cold out here," Doc moaned as they trudged through the thick maple and birch.

"Keep your voice down, will ya, Doc. You're gonna scare off whatever's here."

"Yeah. Don't want those rabbits scared off, do we?"

Russell frowned, but had to admit Doc had a point. Hunting was getting piss poor lately. He had the dismaying feeling the area was getting hunted out. It happened once in awhile. He knew there were lots of hunters in past years who'd taken way over their limit. Then, a couple of years ago, there'd been a winter kill. That kind of combination could ruin a forest.

After Russell had parked the Toyota in a clearing back about a mile, they'd circled a half-mile area looking for deer tracks. For the past two hours all they'd seen were a few rabbit tracks. He looked up and saw gray clouds turning to charcoal. They didn't have much longer.

Four miles back down the road there was a cabin Willie Pollack owned and rented out. Russell had already paid him 20 bucks for the night, but he didn't want to call it quits yet. He wanted at least a shot at something before they packed it in. Hell, he wanted at least to see some tracks.

And then he stopped walking. Doc came up alongside him, but Russell threw his arm across his chest to stop him. Silently, he pointed to the ground about 25 feet in front of them. Three, four, maybe half a dozen sets of tracks were printed in the snow—and they were fresh. It was a deer path, and Russell felt his hands tightened around his Remington in response.

"Now there's something," he whispered.

Damn, Doc thought, sure is. He liked hunting, when it wasn't so cold. And he liked Russell Patterson's company. But it *was* cold, and he would just as soon be at the cabin. Another 15 minutes and he would have suggested as much. But now Russell had spotted the tracks and Doc knew what that meant.

"Told you," Russell said soft and low.

Doc nodded, watching as Russell bent low and scouted the area. It was hard to see anything at all, with the surrounding trees everywhere. But after a minute or so Russell was able to make out the path through which the deer had come. It stretched and wound southwest and down a small slope. Up, off to the right, the path followed a small ridge and disappeared over a rise.

They'd come back again, Russell thought,

looking around for a place to sit. Doc had already found a tree stump, and Russell wondered if he had already figured out the spread of the path or he was just tired.

Russell stepped gingerly in the snow, keeping one eye back on the path. You never knew when they'd come. It was like a royal flush. You could be sitting there one second drawing three cards with an ace, king of hearts, and the next damned second a 12 point buck would just trot right on by you. So he kept glancing back to the path as he hunted for a perch.

Finally, he found what he was looking for. It was a low boulder covered by snow. Perfect. Too big a rock and he'd be easy to spot. But this was low to the ground, offering him both comfort and cover. As Russell bent and brushed snow off the boulder, he stopped and looked at it.

Something was wrong.

He stared at the rock.

Something was real wrong.

When he brushed at it again, it moved. Rocks this size don't move that easily, he thought. It was too big to move that easily.

He pulled his padded gloves off and put his hand to it, brushing off more snow.

It didn't feel right.

It wasn't rough like a rock should be.

It was smooth and yielding.

Russell's eyes focused on it as his hands kept brushing more powder off the thing.

Eyes—wide open and staring straight up at him.

And hair.

He jumped back from the head, feeling the jolt from the massive dump of adrenaline into his system. His lips were already numb from the cold by now. With huge amounts of blood suddenly draining from his extremities, they felt as if they were frostbitten. He'd lost control of the muscles around his mouth and was unable to speak.

He tore his eyes away from the ground and forced his body to turn around and look at Doc. Doc was still sitting on that tree stump, still peaceful, still unaware of the thing Russell had stumbled over, the thing that was about to change everything and fuck up his hunting trip. That was when he shouted, "Dooooooooc!"

Harry Brannigan whirled on the tree stump, Russell's cry being about the last thing in the world he'd expected to hear. It was long and shrill, splitting the silence in the forest and scattering whatever deer there might have been in the area.

Doc forgot about the deer at once as he saw the abject horror on Russell's face. The rifle looked useless in his hands, and the physician wondered what it was that could throw such fear into the heart of a professional law officer who was carrying a Remington rifle.

All these thoughts took only a fraction of a second to sear through Dr. Harry Brannigan's mind, barely aware that they had been occurred. He was up from the tree stump and running in Russell's direction before he had time to contemplate what was happening and what had set his friend off.

"What the hell is it, Russell? Wha—"

Russell's conscious mind took over now and forced back some of the instinctual fear. The police officer in him was beginning to take control again, and he had most of his motor reflexes back. Speech was still slow in coming, though; the shock of discovery had been so great. So he took his rifle and pointed it down at the thing in the snow.

Doc followed the pointer and looked at the face. "Jesus God!"

Doc stayed with the head while Russell ran back to the pickup to get his collapsible shovel. That was the way it should be, he thought while running back. Doc was the physician and Russell was the young man. He could run farther and Doc could . . . could look at it and try to figure it out.

He pulled the shovel out of the back of the truck, his breath coming in frosted bursts like dragon's breath. Russell was about to run back into the woods when he stopped and remembered the radio in the truck.

He pulled the door open and got on the police radio. After a second, Koester came on.

"Yeah, Russell?"

"Doug, I think you better get out here."

Russell could envision the sheriff's knotted

eyebrows when the man said, "How come?"

"Police business."

"What kind of police business?"

Russell looked down at the mike, knowing that Howie Chambers and Mel Stratherton and probably half a dozen other old codgers were probably monitoring their Bearcat Scanners at that second. There was no need to let the whole town know what was going on until he and Koester had a handle on it.

"Damnit, Doug, just get out here, will you?"

In his office, Koester kicked his legs down from the desk they'd been propped up on. It was serious. He knew Russell well enough to know his deputy wouldn't talk like that unless he was shook, and there weren't many things that could shake him; he'd give Russell that much.

Koester depressed the button on his mike and asked, "Doc okay? You fellas haven't gone and shot off a foot or something, have you?"

Russell pulled himself together. "No, nothing like that."

Satisfied Russell didn't need medical assistance, Koester said, "All right, then give me directions."

It was more than a head. That was why Russell had run back to the truck for a shovel. They could see that now as the deputy dug. It was gruesome work, hard work because the ground was frozen solid and Doc kept scolding him to be careful the way he was digging.

"You don't want to mess it up none. Could be important later."

"I'm doing the best I can, Doc. Maybe you'd like to take over?"

Doc looked at the sweating deputy and shook his head. "Just keep going. It's getting dark."

Russell was about a foot down and now could see the corpse's shoulders. It was a boy, wearing a down jacket and a green flannel shirt underneath. Russell recalled seeing a travel program about Easter Island once, about the statues that were all over the place. That was what this looked like with just the shoulder and head exposed.

It's just a statue. That's all it is. We can leave it where it is because it's just a fuckin' statue.

Only it wasn't a statue.

It was dark by the time Koester pulled his patrol car to a stop alongside Russell's Toyota. He got out and stiffened against the cold north wind, thinking that this had better be damned good.

He began to trudge through the snow. Russell had told him east and that was good because the wind was only hitting him from the back and side. The further he got into the forest, the quieter it grew. It began to grate on him. He regretted not having gotten more information from Russell. Could be anything. What if some nut escaped from someplace?

What if it was some criminal and he was holding Russell and Doc and had forced them to call him so the could lure him out into the woods and . . .

"Doug? That you?"

Koester pushed the snap back down on his service revolver strap at the sound of Russell's voice. "Yeah, it's me. Frozen-ass me."

"Over here," the voice called.

"I got ears."

And eyes, he thought, walking toward the light. As he got closer he saw that they'd rigged up a couple of torches that were blazing. They were standing around something that Koester couldn't quite make out until he got closer. When he did he saw it was a hole, only that wasn't what they were looking at. They were looking at something next to the hole. It was long and low to the ground.

As he stood next to Russell, the light flickering on it, Koester felt himself go limp. "It's Frank Conforte."

Warren Conforte listened with rapt attention as Ted Koppel finished his explanation of the again increasing tensions in Iran. How long had it been going on? How long had Americans been subjected to hearing about the bickering and bloodshed that went on halfway around the world?

He hated the Iranians and the Iraqis and their damned wars. He hated them because he didn't want to care about them, but he had to care about them. The threat was oil, and he was certain it was the only thing that could destroy the American economy. The damned fool foreigners and their so-called religious battle could throw a monkey wrench into the whole works.

Conforte Construction had nearly gone belly-up not so long ago. The double whammy of the oil embargo followed by a crippling recession had nearly brought him down. Construction had dropped to nothing, and there were weeks, even months when his crews sat around and did nothing. Still he had to pay them or lose them.

Reagan had brought them out of it. He was sure of that. And that was no easy task after that peanut farmer had screwed things up so badly. Things were getting better, and he was just starting to get hopeful.

And here was Ted Koppel telling him that Iran was accusing the CIA of infiltrating Iraq and sending in advisors and trying to help them topple the Iranian government.

Maybe they were right. If they were, Warren sure felt no animosity toward Washington. The Iranians deserved to be toppled, he thought. Well, maybe not the Iranian people, but the government anyway. From the way he heard it, the Iranian people themselves would just as soon junk their own government and start from scratch.

But if it meant another oil embargo, if it

meant pump prices would start skyrocketing and interest rates would shoot up and the economy would be crippled again, then he wondered if it was really all worth it. Maybe it was just best to let them blow each other's brains out and try to stay out of the crossfire.

He was wondering how you could stay out of things the way the world was today when the phone rang. Warren picked it up on the third ring.

"Yes?"

"Warren," the voice said, "this is Doug Koester."

"Hello, Doug."

"I've got some bad news." The sheriff paused, then said, "We just found Frank."

Molly pushed through the door from the kitchen, looked at her husband on the phone and said, "Dinner's ready, honey."

CHAPTER 5

"I just want to kill someone," Warren said through the screen in the confessional. "I want to go out and wrap my hands around someone's neck and throttle them until their eyes bulge out and they die."

"Easy, easy," John said, feeling the man's hatred seething and pulsing in the tight quarters of the booth. He knew it was Warren Conforte. It was Wednesday, an hour before he was to say Mass. He didn't expect many people for the Mass and certainly didn't expect to hear confessions.

Then Warren showed up. John learned about Frank earlier in the week from Lucas Brenner, who owned Brenner's Grill. Along with Russell Patterson, Brenner was a councilman of the church and he had taken it upon himself to telephone John with the news.

"Just heard about it myself," Brenner said solemnly. "Between you and me I'd have preferred they never found Frank at all. Sure would have been easier on the whole family."

John reached for some way to minimize the grief. "At least the boy will have a Christian burial."

"The dead are dead, Father. I'm worried about the living. Warren Conforte's my friend. Molly's a good woman, and Tom's a fine boy."

"I know he is," John said, thinking about how Tom had driven through a blizzard to pick him up when he'd landed at O'Hare. "I'll talk with him, Mr. Brenner."

Now he was sitting in the confessional, listening to a parent who had to grieve anew for a son he'd counted as dead months ago. John let him tell the story he already knew. When he had spoken with Warren briefly on Monday the man was too shaken to talk coherently. Now it was flowing out of him.

"I thought it was all over. It's not an easy thing to put behind you—your son's death. But Molly and I were doing that. We were on the way. Not Tom, so much. I think he still half-believed Frank would just walk in the front door some day."

"Did you talk with him about it?"

"Not much. Not after it happened. Tom wouldn't hear anything about his brother, kept insisting he wasn't dead. I think this hit the boy harder than even me and Molly, if that's possible."

John was silent, waiting for him to go on.

"I know it's wrong, Father Hines, but I'm filled with such hate. All I want to do is lash out. That's a sin, isn't it?"

"You can't let it overpower you. It's not good for body or soul."

"I don't care about my body or soul. I want the person who did this to my boy."

"If you didn't care about your soul you wouldn't be going to confession."

"I'm going to confession because I'm afraid."

That was as good a reason as any for going to confession, John thought.

"Afraid for yourself?"

"No," Warren said. "Of what I'll do to someone. The way I feel now I could go into a restaurant and stick a knife in someone's gut. If someone said just the wrong word to me . . ."

The feeling began deep down in John's stomach. At first he thought it was something he'd eaten. He thought about his meal the night before—white fish.

His stomach twisted and gurgled, and he shifted positions in the booth, trying to dispel it. But it would not go away. It grew and stretched out in different directions and finally reached his head. He was dizzy from the impact of it, from the pain that made him close his eyes.

John could vividly picture Frank Conforte

lying dead on the ground. He knew none of the details, but he could imagine the way the body looked in death, a final expression of fear frozen forever on his lips.

An impulse to vomit lanced through him, but it passed surprisingly quickly. In its place was a strong empathy with the man sitting on the other side of the screen. How many times had he heard confessions? Uncountable times. Sad stories. Angry stories. Stories filled with guilt. Grist for the soap operas. Bad sins. Small transgressions. Imagined sins. Contrition.

For Warren Conforte the confessional was a refuge against the desire to sin that surged within him, and in one piercing moment John shared that rage and felt that it was his own. He *was* Warren, and *his* son had been killed. White hot hatred wrapped around him, possessing him completely. In that moment he felt his hands tighten, and they were tightening around a neck, any neck. To kill was all that mattered. To strike out at anyone. To return the hurt that had been done to him.

Kill!

Then it was gone, and he looked down at his hands, still held in a circle, still clutching for an anonymous neck. And he began to shake. Tears of shame and self-loathing at the thought of actually taking a human life began to flow down his cheeks.

"Father Hines?"

He wiped quickly at the tears and drew

himself together. "Yes, yes. I'm still here."

Does he know I'm crying? Why am I crying? What's wrong with me? I'm supposed to be comforting this man and he's worried about me.

"Go on, my son."

"I don't know what else to say. Mostly I'm sorry."

"For your son?"

"Yes. But I'm sorry for the way I feel, too. I know it's not right to feel that way. I don't want to hurt anyone. I know that can't bring Frank back."

"No, it can't."

Warren's voice sounded better now. "I don't like to burden you with—"

"I want to help you."

"You have," he said. "I feel better now, Father. Just talking with you has made me feel better. I think I'll be able to get through it now." He paused, then said, "I think I'll go now. I don't want to leave Molly and Tom alone for too long."

"If you need me again . . ."

"Yes. Thank you, Father Hines."

"I don't know why you need me down here, Doc." Doug Koester followed Doc Brannigan down the basement corridor, uneasiness settling about him as he walked. On the two floors above them were 26 patients in Nettleton Community Hospital. They ranged from tonsillitis cases to Myra Fletcher, who was three hours into labor. She'd give birth to a boy who would be elected mayor of Nettleton 46 years later, ten years after she died.

Doc was in good shape for an old man, Koester thought. There wasn't any fat on him, and he took long, sure strides as they walked down the hallway. But he looked out of place in surgical greens. It wasn't the image most people in town had of the physician. For the last 15 years he'd been in private practice— semiretired, actually—but he was still the official coroner.

The job didn't require much of him. There were not too many mysterious deaths in a town like Nettleton, but now there was this business.

"Wanted you to see this firsthand, Doug."

"Don't see why you couldn't just tell me about it over the phone."

Doc pushed through the swinging doors that opened onto the small morgue. "Because you're a policeman who might see something I didn't."

Koester grunted as he walked into the sterile white room, the thick medicinal smell drawing a frown. There was a single stainless steel slab. Frank Conforte's body lay on it under a white sheet.

Doc stopped on one side of the body, Koester on the other. It wasn't the first time the sheriff had been around a dead body. There'd been enough traffic accidents over the years, kids who'd had one too many beers on Labor Day and gotten themselves killed.

He'd have preferred a traffic accident to this, though. Something about being in the morgue set him on edge. It was too clean, and his stomach started to turn.

Doc hesitated, his hand on the sheet. "It's not pretty, Doug."

"Didn't expect it would be. Go on."

It was worse than he'd thought it would be. Frank Conforte was naked when Doc pulled off the sheet. He barely looked human. Back in the woods it had looked like the boy was just sleeping. Here it was different. His body was all white and strangely limp, as if someone had sucked his muscles and bones out. Koester had expected the stiffness of rigor mortis, but the child was almost formless, like an earthworm.

Koester turned away from him for a second, swallowing hard. He asked Doc, "How come he looks like that?"

"Like what?"

"All collapsed, like he doesn't have any skeleton inside."

"Blood's been drained from him."

"By you?"

"No. He was that way when we found him. Didn't notice it then because he was frozen." Doc picked up Frank's right hand, turned it over and said, "See here?"

Koester looked at the corpse's wrist. There was a thin slice on it. "You aren't going to tell me the boy killed himself, then dug a hole and jumped in."

"No. Looks to me like someone cut his wrists, tied him up and buried him up to his neck."

"Jesus."

"Yeah."

The sheriff kept his eyes on Doc, not wanting to look at the boy. "You think he was dead when they buried him, Doc?"

"Nope."

"Why not?"

"His throat."

"What about it?"

"It's raw, Doug, raw from screaming. You can also see bruises on his legs from struggling to get free from the earth he was buried in. And there was gauze taped loosely around his wrists."

"Gauze?"

Doc nodded. "Like someone was trying to slow the bleeding so it would take a long time for him to go. Torture is what I'm talking about, Doug. They let this boy bleed to death slowly, buried up to his neck."

"Who the hell would do a thing like that?"

Doc pulled the sheet back over him. "That's for you to find out."

The funeral was held on Saturday. It was a three-quarter size casket, black with polished brass handles. Naturally, it was closed in the church. The autopsy had necessitated that.

As Sheriff Koester stood, his hands folded in front of him, he looked around the circle of mourners at the gravesite. Warren Conforte and his son stared at the ground during the entire ceremony. Koester had expected something more, some moan of grief. Molly had come the closest to that, weeping softly as Father Hines spoke. Koester remembered her as being thin but pretty. Now she looked old, her skin drawn and her auburn hair the texture of straw as it peeked out from under a black hat.

Shock, Koester thought. It still hadn't hit them.

But he was wrong. It had hit them a long time ago—this business just dredged it up again—but Warren and Tom had used up all their grief. All they felt now was anger and hatred. If Koester could have read their thoughts he probably would have placed them both under protective custody. They were in a bad state.

If there was a suspect, Koester might have been more concerned, but there was no one. He'd gone over it in his mind countless times since the night he'd stood in the forest with Russell and Doc, and he was still no closer to a name.

The Confortes were just average people. They didn't have any enemies to speak of and they had more friends than you could count. Why someone would slit young Frank Conforte's wrists, tie him up, bury him and leave him to bleed to death in the middle of nowhere was a monumental puzzle to Doug Koester.

Koester had already spoken with Elmer Fortmann, going to the school and talking with the principal in his office. It was a wasted trip. Frank got good grades, was popular in school and didn't have a record of fighting or troublemaking. He was in the scouts, played football like his older brother and even served as altar boy at Sacred Heart. It was an unremarkable picture of a normal kid from a normal family. Everything about him was normal, except for the fact that someone had taken it into their head to torture and murder him.

As he helped lower the casket into the grave, Koester thought it wasn't Frank's problem anymore. Frank didn't have any problems. It was his problem now—a serious problem. It was one thing for a priest to crack up and commit suicide but quite another for one of the townspeople to be murdered. Folks were stunned by it right now. But before too long they'd want an answer. They'd want to know who did it, and Koester would be the one they'd turn to for an answer.

He was confident he could provide it. He just hoped it would turn out to be some out-of-towner. As he walked from the gravesite, he stopped by the Confortes.

His voice subdued, Koester said, "Folks, I want you to know how sorry I am about this."

Molly started to thank him, but the words wouldn't come. Instead, she began to weep again. Her sister, Aggie, took her away, leaving him alone with Tom and Warren.

"I'm going to do everything I can to find out who did this to Frank."

His eyes still red from tears shed in the church, Tom said, "You'd better find him before I do, Sheriff. If I get him first there isn't going to be much left."

Koester watched as the boy walked away from his mother. Then he turned to Warren. "I hope you keep him in line, Warren. This is a police matter and—"

"Then the police had better tend to it quickly."

"I told you I'd do . . ."

But Warren had already gone, hurrying to catch up with his family.

"I just can't imagine anything more awful," Jill said as she walked back to her car with John. "Evan was so upset he couldn't even come to the funeral."

John asked, "Did he know Frank well?"

"Of course he did. They went to Jefferson together. They'd known each other for years."

"In the same class?"

"No. Frank was a year ahead of him, but they were good friends. Frank was very popular." She shook her head. "The pain that family has had to go through."

"Twice."

"Yes."

"I didn't know Frank was an altar boy."

"Yes. For Father Dreiband. Father Dreiband was broken up over his disappearance. For a long time everyone thought he'd run off. There was a big search, but he never turned up."

"And Alan Landano took over after that?"

"As altar boy?" She nodded.

"He's a bit shy."

"You know he's adopted."

"Yes. Is he friends with Evan?"

"They're in the same class at school. Do you think Sheriff Koester will find out who killed Frank?"

"I don't know. There's not much for him to go on." They stopped in front of Jill's Pacer. John looked up at the threatening sky. "I think it's going to snow again." By now he'd forgotten what the sun looked like.

"Do you think you could speak with Evan, Father?"

"About what?"

"About Frank. He's been having nightmares. This business is hard on a young boy—death, I mean." She shook her head. "I don't know what he's thinking half the time. I know he's been brooding a lot. It's not good."

"I'll talk with him. Where is he now?"

"Over at George Hayward's house. He wanted to work on his model ship. George has a workshop in his basement."

* * *

The ship was just about finished. Evan picked it up and held it out at arm's length. He'd done a good job—a professional job, George had told him. And George knew what a professional job was. He'd paint it soon, and when spring came he'd sail it on Morgan's Lake.

Evan turned as he heard the sound of the table saw whirl to life. George was standing over it, feeding a piece of plywood into the circular saw. He'd finished working on the side table and now was beginning another project.

Evan set the ship back on the workbench and walked over.

"What's it gonna be?"

"Stereo cabinet," George explained, keeping his eyes on the silver disk that bit smoothly into the wood he fed.

"Who's it for, George?"

"Russell Patterson."

"How much is he paying you?"

George grinned. "Enough."

"Too much, probably."

"Fuck you," George laughed.

"Fuck you back."

The wood separated into two pieces as the saw completed its work. George pushed the power switch off with his knee and set the two pieces safely to the side.

He looked down at Evan. "You got a big mouth on you, boy."

"Look who's talking."

"When you get to be my age you can—"

"I don't want to hear that crap. You sound like my mother."

George walked to the storage rack and pulled another long sheet of plywood from it. He laid it on the workbench, set a combination square on it and began making pencil marks for his next cut.

"I'd think your mouth would be a little more respectful, what with Frank and all."

"Why? Is that gonna bring him back?"

"No, but—"

"Besides, he's been dead for a long time."

"You could have some respect for the dead."

"Frank was an asshole."

George glanced at him. "That's a helluva thing to say."

"It's true. Anyway, what am I supposed to do? Fall down on my knees and start crying because somebody offed him?"

"You're a cold-hearted little bastard."

Evan smiled. "That's why you like me, George. I remind you of you."

George set down the pencil and said, "Sometimes you're too smart for your own good."

"Altar boy," Evan huffed. "Like that was some kind of big shit."

"Like Alan Landano."

"Yeah," Evan agreed. "Another asshole of the first order."

"Your Ma says you been having trouble sleeping since they found Frank."

"She told you that?"

He nodded.

"When?"

"I ran into her in Dave's Grocery." George thought he read a hint of concern in the boy's question, so he pursued the point. "Maybe you been lying in bed trying to figure out who killed little Frank Conforte. Maybe you're afraid whoever did it is still in town."

"Why would I be afraid of that?"

"Because they could come after you next."

Evan spit into the sawdust. "Why would someone come after me?"

"Why would someone come after Frank?"

"Because he's an asshole. Why else?"

"Because he's young. There are people like that, you know, people who get a kick out of going after little boys and tying them up and playing with their cocks."

"You're fuckin' sick, George."

"Maybe I did it to him," he teased, turning the plywood around on the table.

Evan closed his eyes, gales of laughter rocking him so hard he had to grab hold of the workbench to steady himself.

George straightened up and looked down at the boy. "You think that's funny, huh?"

He nodded, trying to stop laughing, but the thought struck him so funny that he burst out laughing again. Evan was having trouble catching his breath now and held his sides.

"Maybe I tied him up," George pressed, "and cut his wrists like Doc Brannigan said. And maybe I went out in the forest and dug a deep hole and tossed him in."

Evan wiped at the tears flowing from the corners of his eyes. Between chuckles he said, "You forgot the part about playing with his cock."

George shooed him off with his hand. "Oh, that was just bullshit. I don't have a thing for boys. You know me; I'm into pussy."

"So you killed him, huh?"

"Maybe," George said, slashing the pencil across the grained wood. "Could be me. Hell, Evan, it could be me, and here you are alone with me now."

Evan took one end of the plywood, helping George carry it to the saw. "Man, you got me shaking in my goddamned boots, George."

"Yeah. You're a brave little fucker, ain't cha? I'll bet Frank Conforte was a brave little fucker, too."

"You'd lose that bet."

"How do you know?"

" 'Cause I went to school with him. I saw Mike Kopernik whip the shit out of him in the playground, and Mikey must weigh fifteen pounds less than Frank. He gave him a bloody nose, and the second Frank saw he was bleeding he started crying and ran to old man Fortmann."

"You'd probably start crying, too."

"Hah!"

As he laid the wood on the saw table, George said, "So you think you're pretty safe here, huh?"

"Hell, yes."

George hit the power switch with his knee, watching as the toothed edge of the blade disappeared in a whirling flash, the engine bleating to life. "Maybe you got balls after all. Help me feed this piece in, Evan."

Evan stayed at the far end of the four foot long piece of plywood, while George focused his attention on the pencil marks. Evan was right, he thought. He *was* getting a little more for the stereo cabinet than he should. Russell could afford it, though, and he'd do a great job on it. He could have charged him a fair price, but there was a kick in knowing you could juice people, squeeze just a bit more out of them than you deserved, screw them just because you were the one—

The hand on his wrist broke his thoughts. It was a small hand, and the first thing that occurred to him was how strong Evan's hand was for its size. He tried to pull free from it on instinct alone, but he couldn't break the grip. Somewhere he'd heard that if you applied pressure against the thumb/forefinger point you could break your hand free from just about anyone's grasp. That memory flooded back to him, and he pushed against that point on the small hand.

The small hand remained wrapped around his big wrist.

Now it was pushing his hand in a direction it definitely didn't want to go. George let go of the plywood, suddenly unconcerned about Russell Patterson's stereo cabinet. He heard the wood begin to splinter as it went through the saw offline, and a part of his mercantile mind was pissed because it was a $16 piece of plywood he'd just ruined.

He swung his head around and looked at Evan standing right behind him, pressing his body against his leg and waist. The kid looked small, just like his hand, but there was something about him that wasn't a kid anymore. There was something awful about him that George had never seen.

Evan wasn't looking at George. He was looking at his wrist and the grip he had on it.

"Hey, let go," George said, knowing that it was a stupid thing to say, a waste of breath, because Evan had no intention of letting go.

"Evan, let go of my fuckin' hand!"

He tried to pull free again, but it didn't work. He couldn't even budge his hand. Evan was still pushing him forward—toward the saw.

And George realized what was happening, realized that it wasn't Evan who had to be afraid of being with him, but *he* who should have been afraid of being with *Evan*.

"You want to screw my mother," Evan said softly.

"To hell with your mother," George gasped, pushing his body back against the boy. It didn't make sense. The kid was so small, and George was so big. What was he, two or three times heavier than the boy? Why the hell couldn't he push him back?

He shoved harder, using all his weight, but it was like pushing against a solid wall. "What the hell are you doing?"

"You did a nice job on the confessional," Evan whispered, and the whisper shot a fresh shaft of terror through the one that was already sapping George's strength.

"The confessional? What does that have to do . . ." He spun around and looked at the blade. His hand was six inches from it now, and though he couldn't see the individual teeth he knew the pain the steel held and shut his eyes tightly.

His hand inched toward the blade.

The switch!

He moved his knee beneath the bench, feeling for the off switch, but Evan's leg blocked him. George battered his meaty thigh against Evan's thin leg, but it was no use. Things had ceased to make any sense. He should have been able to knock him over with his leg, but nothing was happening.

"You've done your job," Evan continued.

"The confessional!" George shrieked in a moment of stunning clarity.

"Done your job and now it's over."

"Why are you doing this?"

"They found Frank. That's not good."

"You killed him."

Evan began to laugh, but it came out of an unsmiling face. "You're so stupid. You don't know anything."

"Let's talk."

"Too late for talk. You talk too much, George. They found Frank and they could come to you and you'd joke about it or say something stupid and maybe get someone thinking."

"No. I won't!"

"You did a nice job, though," Evan said. And then he pushed forward and George knew that up until then it hadn't even been a fight. Evan could have overpowered him at any moment and pushed his wrist through the blade at any second. He was giving him as much of a fight as a piece of balsa wood gave George. The boy had been playing with him; that was all. He just wanted to see him sweat, and he *was* sweating. It was pouring off him, leaving huge rings under his arms.

In that last moment, before the agony, George hated the boy because of the game.

George's wrist offered no resistance to the blade at first. The silver edge turned scarlet as skin sliced away. The first time Evan's efforts were slowed was when the saw's blade met George's wrist bone. For one split second Evan felt the resistance. He pushed a little harder and felt the blade begin to eat into the bone.

George's scream was louder than the saw's engine.

The muscles in his throat tightened and stretched and collapsed, trying to adjust to the incredible strain his screams were placing on them. It didn't matter to George. The pain there was nothing in comparison to what was happening to his hand.

Nothing could hurt this badly.

It wasn't possible.

His eyes were snake eyes—wide and unblinking, without any lids. They were frozen open and, as with a hideous traffic accident, he was unable to tear them away from the scene of revulsion unfolding in front of him.

The blood was splattering through the air now, landing in splotches on his green work clothes. There was a different feel to the blade cutting into bone than there was when it cut only skin. His entire body shook, like when you were a kid and you had a baseball bat and you hit a stone with it. It was the same kind of thing. It went to his core at the same time that a different set of communication lines sent a desperate message to his brain.

Get away!

Even the sound of the blade was different now. It wasn't a blade anymore. It was a dentist's drill, and it was having a damned hard time getting that stubborn cavity loose. It was getting stuck, and that meant it had to grind harder.

George felt the copper taste and knew it was the taste of his blood. He could feel it as it spit all over his face and into his open, screaming mouth.

Everything went white from the pain.

And suddenly there was a release.

He didn't know it, but he had pushed hard, harder than his conscious physical body was capable. The limits of logic and reality were removed from him by the pain and that had released his total inner strength. It was enough to break Evan's hold on him. Maybe it wouldn't have been if he had pushed back, in the direction Evan had been anticipating, but he had pulled forward toward the blade because he hadn't been thinking clearly. And that was something Evan hadn't been prepared for.

He was rolling on the floor, the coppery taste mixing with newly hewn wood shavings to form a ghastly paste. He could feel pain in his shoulder and was so grateful for that that some of his fear receded. Anything that could take away from what had happened to his hand was welcome.

Evan had been caught off guard and was angry with himself for that. He watched as fat George rolled on the floor like a giant medicine ball. Only he was a bleeding medicine ball. He was more like a balloon that you let go of and the air spurted out of it all at once, except it wasn't air coming from George.

It was blood.

It was all over George, and when he got to his knees Evan saw that the sawdust was sticking to his face and arms because of the blood and that looked kind of funny, so he laughed.

"What are you laughing about?" George roared. He looked away from Evan, trying to get his bearings, and he saw his hand lying on the floor, just under the edge of the table. Sadness filled him as he looked at the hand. It was still bleeding, but after it finished doing that it would never do anything again.

He looked down at his wrist and saw blood pumping from the vessels hanging out the end of his arm.

He clamped his hand around the stump to stop the bleeding and was surprised to find there was very little pain. For a second he wondered why there was so little pain, but then anger and rage at the monster who had cut off his hand flooded over him.

From his kneeling position he lunged toward Evan. For the second time he'd caught the boy off guard. Old George had more guts than he'd thought. Evan tried to jump out of his way, but only half-succeeded. George managed to catch part of the boy's leg and wrapped his arm around it.

Evan was laughing again, half-dragging George across the floor like a lover who wouldn't let go.

". . . kill you, you bastard. I'll kill you for this!"

George wasn't going to kill anyone. He knew that in a flash. He saw the blood spewing out on the ground below him.

When he'd grabbed for Evan he had to let go of his severed wrist, and the blood had begun pumping freely again. Dizzy from its loss, a sheet of nausea stunned him with it's power.

To hell with the boy. Save yourself!

He let go of Evan's leg and fell to the ground. Again he grasped his wrist, and though the blood bathed his hand, it slowed. He was amazed to feel his strength grow in direct response to the slowed tide of bleeding.

He had to stop it for good.

He let go of the wrist for a second, trying to get his belt undone. But then the bleeding started, and he went back to squeezing his wrist, then back to the belt, then back to his wrist like Mack Sennett in some long ago silent comedy.

The two by four cut into George's performance. Evan's aim was a little low. If it hadn't been it would have been over right then. George would have been knocked out and just would have bled to death.

But he had missed George's head when he swung the board and had hit him about an inch or two below his neck. As it was, it sent him sprawling on the floor again. George rolled away from him, knowing that if he was going to live he'd have to get away from the boy long enough to take care of his arm.

He scrambled to his feet, dizziness clutching at him again, and forced one foot in front of the other until he was half-running, half-stumbling across the basement floor.

Evan swung at the lurching target and missed. The board was too short, making him reach up to hit anywhere that would do any damage. Besides, he was a little tired now. It had taken a lot of effort to push George's hand through the saw, more than George knew. Evan had only been half-conscious when he was doing it, letting some infernal internal mechanism take over, like a person who lifts a car off their son or daughter in the heat of the moment and then later realizes they've pulled every muscle in their body.

He watched as George staggered up the stairs. That was okay, because George wasn't going to get anywhere. There was time. He wanted to catch his breath.

The two by four had hurt George. He could feel a dull throb in the back of his neck. To hell with his neck, George thought. His arm was the problem.

He leaned against a wall in the foyer, the same foyer in which Cindy Breslauer, that little slut, had shouted "Fuck you, you bastard." She'd surprised the hell out of George by actually quitting. He'd thought about driving out to Millburg, where he'd first picked her up, find her and beat her ass. But it wasn't worth the trouble.

Now he was standing in the foyer, bleeding to death. George got the belt loose with a final tug, wrapped it around his wrist and pulled tight just as he heard the thudding.

It was coming from beyond the foyer, and he knew it was Evan. He also knew it was the sound of a two by four being tapped rhythmically on the slate floor. George thought about it, but not for too long. His stomach was fluttering and he knew it was from loss of blood.

Any other time he would have gone against the kid, but not now. He was too weak. He needed help. There'd be time to get revenge later. George looked at the door, but it was all the way across the foyer and he didn't think he'd be able to make it before Evan got him.

Even if he could make it, so what? He couldn't run all the way to town. The Cadillac was parked in the garage, and Evan would be all over him with the two by four before he could get to the car. The kid was nuts. He'd hack him to pieces before he'd let him get away.

George bolted for the stairs. There was a chance, his brain told him, if he could get to the phone and call for help. All the way down the hallway on the second floor he was leaking blood on the carpet. It'd be a helluva mess to clean up.

"I'm gonna get you, George," a voice sing-songed from below. "I'm gonna stomp your fat ass."

George pushed into his bedroom, closed the door after himself and locked it.

Screw you, kid!

For a moment everything went dark, and he was sure he was about to die. This was it. It was over. He'd bled to death. Then he was conscious of his crotch and the fact that it was wet and that he'd pissed on himself. It was the most blessed feeling in the world because it meant he was still alive.

The room came into focus again. If he wasn't dead, he knew he would die soon if he didn't get help.

George sat on the edge of his unmade bed and pulled the phone from its hook. He set the receiver on the nightstand and dialed the number for the police. Koester would pick it up on the second or third ring. He'd come running himself and arrest the little bastard.

His leg was wet, and George felt an absurd wave of shame at having pissed in his pants. But then he looked down and saw that it wasn't urine at all. It was blood that was soaking through his pant leg.

"Idiot!" he screamed as he grabbed the loosened belt loop, tightening it again. The blood from his wrist slowed to a trickle. He lifted the receiver to his ear.

"Nettleton Sheriff's office."

"Doug? Doug, that you?"

"This is Sheriff Koester. Who's this?"

He began to cry, laughing crazily. "This is George Hayward."

"Hi, George. What's—"

"Just shut up and listen to me. You got to

get out here right away, Doug. Fuckin' Evan Gregory's cut my damned hand off. The kid's gone crazy. He's trying to kill me."

"Slow down. You drunk or something?"

"Nooooo!" he screamed. "I'm not drunk. I just told you. Christ, I'm sitting in my bedroom bleeding to death. Doug, get your ass out here. If you—"

"Don't think I can do that, George."

"What?! Didn't you—"

"Nope. Don't think I can do that at all." Then the singsong voice on the extension hummed, "I'm gonna get you, George. I'm gonna stomp your fat ass."

George threw the phone across the room, the cradle tumbling from the nightstand as he did. He leaned back and lay on the bed. He was in worse shape than he'd thought. If he couldn't tell the difference between Evan's voice and Koester's then he was in big trouble. He'd wanted it to be Koester's voice, he told himself. That was what it was.

For a long time he lay there, trying to calm himself. He lost consciousness once. Maybe he fell asleep. He wasn't sure which it was. Either was just as bad as the other because it meant he'd let go of the belt and the bleeding would start again.

Now the pain returned. He was almost glad for it because it forced him to stay awake. The sonofabitch had cut his hand off. He'd never be able to work with wood again. It was enough to make him sit up, even stand up.

"No goddamned little punk kid is going to scare the shit out of me." George tried walking from the bed to the door.

But the walk left him weak. He needed help. He'd have to get away from the house, get into town where Doc Brannigan could patch him up. It meant going downstairs and out to the garage. He had to get away.

It was no good waiting around like this. The longer he waited the weaker he'd be. It had to be now.

George leaned against the door, listening for anything. But there was nothing. Maybe the kid was crouched outside the door, with the two by four wound up like a baseball bat, just waiting for him to open the door. George looked around the room. He needed something to even the odds, but there wasn't much he could use in the bedroom. There was hardly anything, George thought.

Then he looked at the fireplace and the fireplace tools and the fireplace poker.

He hefted the solid brass poker. It felt good and solid. He even managed to smile. A new strength surged into him. To hell with Koester and the police. He'd take care of this little mother himself. Let the cops come out and mop up afterwards. What fucking jury would hang him when they looked at the stump at the end of his arm?

He'd have to be able to use his left hand, though. So George took a second and wrapped the rest of the belt around his mangled arm.

The belt had been black when he'd taken it off. It was maroon now and slick. He twisted it around and around and then he tucked the excess into the coil.

George flexed his right arm, making sure the belt would stay in place. It did. A few drops of blood oozed past the tourniquet now and then, but it didn't matter. Nothing mattered except Evan Gregory's ass on a silver platter.

The poker in his left hand, George walked to the door. He set the weapon down, unlocked and opened the door, picked up the poker and walked out into the hallway. He kept low, just in case Evan was out there with the two by four.

But he wasn't.

George walked down the darkened corridor. Evan had shut the lights off. George's breath came in strangled rasps.

"All right," he growled. "All right you motherfucker. You want to play hardball, we'll play hardball. Your little ass is mine."

The poker out in front of him, George passed by the doorways on either side of the hall. Evan wasn't in the guest rooms. Something told George he wasn't, and the something was right.

George wasn't all that sure the kid was even still in the house. He might have gotten spooked and run off. If he had it would be his ass—the cops would take care of him—and if he was still here it would be his ass. Either way, it didn't matter to George.

Then he thought about how the kid was a minor. He was a slick little sucker. Maybe he'd tell the cops George had gone weird on him and tried to grope him. Maybe he'd tell the cops old George had tried to get him to blow him and that what he'd done was in self-defense.

"Doesn't matter," George said aloud as he walked toward the second floor landing. "Even if you get off, even if they send you home with a slap on your wrist, the day's gonna come when it's just you and me, boy, and I'm gonna cut your goddamned prick off and stuff it down your throat."

George stopped at the top of the stairs and looked down. There were 16 wooden steps leading from the second floor. They emptied onto the foyer. The boy hadn't left the house. He was somewhere down there, waiting to finish the job.

Fine!

George thudded the poker hard against the wall, cracking the plaster, white dust puffing out as he did. He wanted Evan to know he had a weapon. He wanted him to be scared for a change.

"So you're gonna stomp my ass," George said, walking down the first step. "You're gonna stomp my fat ass, huh?"

The foyer was dark, too, and George liked it that way. Kids were afraid of the dark, not men.

"We'll see who's gonna get whose ass, you cocksucker." He took the next step down and spat, "You're talking to a former goddamned Marine. I was killing Japs before you were a twinkle in that slut mother of yours' eye."

As he walked down the third step he said, "I'm gonna—"

But that was all he said.

It was a cat's eye, a big one, yellow and black.

There were others on the stair, too—an agate, a couple of steelies, a mig and three taws.

But George's heel had stepped on the cat's eye.

He stumbled on the step, trying to catch his balance, but it was impossible. George brought his other foot down and stepped on one of the steelies. He was doing a crazy Three Stooges dance on the marbles, and it ended with a pratfull down the stairs.

Only, after the Stooges did it the director would call "cut" and Moe and Larry and Curly would break for lunch. In George's case it was his back that broke. His left arm fractured when he hit the fifth step down, but by then it didn't matter. The real damage was done when they first impacted on the hardwood stairs. He'd landed on his tailbone and his great weight had been too much. The bone was pulverized, searing pain engulfing him and following him down the long pinwheel fall that ended in the foyer of the biggest house in Nettleton.

That was when all the lights suddenly came on.

No one shouted "Surprise." There were no balloons. There was no cake or ice cream.

There was only Evan Gregory—and the hammer he held in his hand.

CHAPTER 6

It was snowing, but it was only a flurry, so light that it wasn't even necessary for John to turn the wipers on. The heating system worked well, and the interior of the Sentra was almost balmy. Although the car was light, snow tires and sand bags in the trunk helped it hold the country road.

He didn't know exactly where he was driving—out of Nettleton, that much he knew for sure. It was dangerous to be in Nettleton with the alleyways his mind had been creeping through for the past hours.

He had had bad thoughts all Sunday long, even through Mass. He'd long ago accepted his own mortality and the fact that temptation would sometimes creep into him. It couldn't be avoided. Years ago he'd gone to Bishop O'Donnell about the problem of incorrect thoughts. O'Donnell had told him certain thoughts could not always be evaded. To think they could, that the brain could be made to harbor only good thoughts all the time, was to set yourself up as a deity. So it was nothing to be ashamed of.

In the past the thoughts had always been fleeting—a curse here, a wish of ill fortune for someone there. John had always been able to banish them by raising them to a conscious level and then expunging them.

That was not the case today, and when they persisted for hours on end, like a bad headache, he finally decided a drive might do him good. But on another level he knew he was telling himself to get some distance between himself and his church because what was going on in his head would shame his church if anyone found out about it.

In the morning he awakened short of breath. He'd been dreaming that he was running, and he realized he had actually been running ever since he got to Nettleton. It was one thing after another—coming in with Father Dreiband's death to deal with, the big change from what he had been used to down in Miami, Frank Conforte's body being discovered. He wasn't being given any time to settle in.

John sought solace in the routine of preparing for the daily service. Alan arrived at 7:00 o'clock and had a calming effect on him. For awhile John watched the small child readying the church and drew comfort from it. He wanted to know Alan better but knew it was best not to rush into things. Besides, he seemed a withdrawn, sensitive child at times.

At 7:30 Alan surprised him by asking, "Do you enjoy hearing confession, Father Hines?"

They were standing in front of the confessional, Alan polishing the woodwork.

"That's an odd thing to ask."

"Not when you're polishing the confessional, it isn't."

John smiled. "You're doing a nice job."

"Do you, Father?"

"It gives me pleasure to know I'm easing people's burdens."

"Is that what confession does?"

"Of course." Then it occurred to him that a priest's attitude toward hearing confession could be a mystery to one so young. "It purges people of sin."

"So they can go out and sin again."

"Alan," he snapped.

The boy worked on one of the carved saints with a rag. "It's true, isn't it?"

"It is in man's nature to sin."

"I don't see how confession makes it any better."

"Penance makes it better."

"But if they just go out and commit the same sins over and over . . ."

"The idea is to learn from one's mistakes."

"Oh, I see." Then he looked up at John and asked, "Do they?"

"Not often enough."

When confession began, John listened to a long procession of admissions. Lying seemed to be number one on the Nettleton hit parade. Covetousness wasn't far behind. It seemed no one in Nettleton was happily married. This one wanted that one's wife and that one wanted this one's wife and a lot of time the want list matched up nicely. He could easily start the Sacred Heart Dating Service.

Frank Conforte's death—or at least the discovery of his body—was on many minds. More than a few of his flock confessed feelings of hatred and mayhem toward whoever had done the deed. Part of the comfort he had told Alan Landano about came from being able to soothe the rage of the people who wanted to strike out blindly in their anger about a crime done against their town.

But he had to walk a tightrope. He couldn't simply tell them to forget about the Conforte boy's death. So he had to be extra careful to sympathize with them, and when he did he felt the same feelings of anger begin to surface as when Warren Conforte had confessed his own murderous thoughts earlier in the week.

There were only 15 minutes left before he had to begin Mass. That was when the door on the other side of the screen opened and a girl came in. He could tell that from her cologne, which was flowery and strong. A young woman, he guessed correctly.

He didn't know the townspeople well enough to guess exactly who it was going to confession all the time, but already he could match a few of the voices with faces—Deputy Patterson, Elmer Fortmann, a few others.

This voice he couldn't place, but he guessed she was around 16 or 17.

"Bless me, Father, for I have sinned."

"When did you last go to confession, my child?"

"Last month."

"How have you sinned?"

She was silent for a moment, the confession coming, as it often did, with some difficulty. After a second, John asked, "Are you there?"

"Yes, Father."

"Don't be afraid, my child. How have you sinned?"

"I . . . I haven't really sinned, Father. Well," she corrected, "I don't know if it's a sin yet, but what I've been thinking about is a sin. Maybe what I've done already is a sin, too."

"Tell me about it," John said in his most avuncular voice.

"It's hard to talk about it, Father."

"You're doing the right thing. Now go on."

"I've got a boyfriend, Father. I know he loves me and I love him. We want to get married when he graduates high school."

"Go on."

"Last week we were out on a date and . . ."

Again she hesitated and John thought he would have to prompt her once more, but she continued. "I let him touch me, Father." Quickly, she blurted out, "I know I shouldn't have, but I couldn't help myself."

"Why couldn't you help yourself?"

"Because I wanted him to. These feelings in me have been growing stronger each month, each week, and I wanted him to touch me so badly."

"Did he do anything more than that?"

"Oh, no, Father! I swear he didn't."

"You're certain?"

"Yes, Father. But I think I wanted him to. I know I did. It felt so good. But at the same time it felt bad, if you know what I mean."

"Tell me how you felt."

"I . . . I felt like I was burning up, but it was a delicious fire. My breasts were all tingly, and I could feel myself shaking and getting all warm."

"How did he touch you?"

"Through my clothes, at first. And I tried to stop him. But I couldn't hold back any longer. He unbuttoned my blouse and touched my breasts through my bra, and when he saw I wasn't going to stop him he slid his hand under my bra and touched my bare breast."

"For how long?"

"I don't know. I lost track of time. Time didn't matter anymore. He kept feeling me and I felt myself responding to him. Then I felt his hand on my bare leg and he was moving it higher and higher up my thigh."

John closed his eyes and leaned his head against his balled fist. "Did you stop him then?"

"Yes," the voice behind the screen said. "But it wasn't easy. I wanted him to touch me there, too. And he knew I wanted him to."

"And what about him? Did you touch this boy?"

Miserably, she confessed, "Yes, Father. But only through his jeans. I wouldn't . . . I couldn't do any more than that."

"And how did you feel about touching him?"

She didn't answer for a moment, thinking, then she decided to tell him the truth. "I felt good about it. I know that's terrible, but I felt good. I wanted to do more. What can I do, Father?"

"You must try to contain yourself," John said, opening his eyes. "Sex is a sacred communion between people who are blessed in marriage by God. You must control yourself. If your love is strong and true, then you will find that strength. Remember that. Your control or lack of it is a measure of the goodness of your love. When you feel temptation you must resist."

"Yes, Father."

"For your penance you will say fifty Hail Marys and twenty-five Our Fathers and think about what I have said as you do."

"Yes, Father." Her voice carried that tone of relief he often heard in penitents. "Thank you."

As she opened the door to leave, John looked toward the ceiling of the confessional. Again his fists were balled. Sweat had beaded on his forehead, and he felt it dripping beneath his robes. Also, he felt the intense erection hearing the confession had wrought.

Maleness was a problem all priests had to acknowledge. John reckoned that femaleness was nearly as great a problem for nuns—not nearly as great, though, because they could usually put it down to the Divine Spirit moving within them or a feeling of heavenly rapture flowing about them. Maybe it sometimes was that, but John guessed it was just as often the surfacing of repressed sexuality.

For a priest it was not so easy. An erection was an undeniable confirmation of his weakness. You couldn't say the quickening feeling was the Divine Spirit moving within you when you were hard. It just didn't work.

The dilemma stuck with him all through Mass. He felt hypocritical standing in front of the packed pews. John was certain they knew, even though it was absurd to think they did. What mattered was that he knew. He had shown weakness.

Weakness was a condition you reconciled

yourself to if you were a priest. What it came down to was a question of time. You accepted weakness if it was a temporary condition. If it lasted seconds or minutes it was something you could live with.

Usually that was the way it was.

This time it wasn't.

John couldn't chase the girl's confession from his mind. It stayed with him all day long, haunting him during the confession, during Mass, at Communion, after Mass, at lunch. In the afternoon it left for a short time, but then he was sitting in his living room, talking with Hal Buchanan about nothing in particular, when he felt his penis begin to swell.

He tried multiplication tables. Sometimes that worked. He was up to fives when he gave up, the erection full-blown by then.

John switched the windshield wipers on and glanced down at his lap.

No problem.

It was like a bad tooth that knew you were taking it to the dentist and suddenly the pain was gone.

Irrationally, he wanted the erection back. It had put him through too much trouble not to be here—changing into street clothes, driving away from the church, away from Nettleton. It all meant something, and it was a damned lot of work.

He tried to think about the girl who'd gone

to confession earlier. His mind drifted back to her words and tried to turn them into images, imagining her in the embrace of her young man. He could picture them together, their arms about each other, his hands exploring, opening her blouse, wrapping around her young breasts, bringing them closer to his open mouth and . . .

The blare of the horn brought him out of it, and he jerked the steering wheel hard to the right. It would have been all right if it was June, but it was February and the roads were icy and he went into a skid.

John spun the wheel back in the opposite direction, at the same time knowing it was useless. Nothing was going to help. The impact was hard and sudden, and he lurched forward against the steering wheel as the car was brought to a complete stop. Pain shot through his left arm as he groaned aloud.

He had the presence of mind to reach forward and shut off the ignition. Then he fell back against the seat.

"Goddamnit, what the fuck is wrong with—" The voice stopped, then. There was a knocking on the window, and John turned to see a black man peering through the glass. "Hey, you all right?"

He nodded and rolled down the window.

"You all right?" the man asked again.

"Yeah, I'm okay."

Anger returned to the man's voice. "Well what the hell's wrong with you? You drunk or something, man? You came clear across the fucking line."

"I must have drifted off."

"We could have drifted off to hell together. You almost hit me head on. Man, you must be crazy. You sure you ain't drunk?"

"I'm sure."

The black man looked at the car. "Gonna cost you plenty to get that fender fixed. And don't try to put this shit on me. You was the one who—"

"I know," John said, opening the door. "It was all my fault." He climbed out of the car and inspected the damage. The man was right. The Sentra's front left fender was crushed inward.

The man bent for a closer look. "I think it'll drive. Fender ain't pressing against the tire or nothin'. Lucky at that." He looked back up at John. "You can't be driving like that on these roads. You ought to know better than that."

"I'm new out here."

"I believe that. Don't see as how we have to call the cops. You missed me but not by much. This thing's your fault, so you gonna have to pay for it. Maybe you can tell your insurance company you got sideswiped or something. Fuck of a thing."

John frowned at the man's profanity.

"Forget it. I'll take care of it."

"You sure you're okay? Must be shaken up." He pointed in front of the car and said,

"Bridge abutment. That's what you hit."

John rubbed his shoulder. "I'll be all right."

"Let me give you a push back on the road, then."

"That won't be necessary."

"It is if you ever want to get outta here."

He looked around and saw that the front wheels were slightly down the embankment. He couldn't back out without a push. "I guess you're right. I feel bad after what I've put you through already."

The man waved him off. "Forget it. Ain't nothing compared to how bad you're gonna feel when you get the bill for that fender."

Cindy Breslauer was feeling weird. Something strange was in the air. She could tell about things like that. Certain things she was particularly tuned into. She could tell when the phone was going to ring half the time, and she could make Ginger, her cat, come into the bedroom by concentrating hard enough sometimes. Once in awhile, if something was very important, she could snatch it from the air. She knew the exact second her grandmother had died, even though it had happened 2300 miles away in California.

Yeah, she could tell there was something strange in the air.

"Another Lite, Benny."

The bartender glanced at her, a little

irritated that she was taking his attention away from the Bucks' game on the television over the bar. He drew the beer and set the new glass in front of Cindy.

"Gulping those things down tonight, aren't you?"

"They're only Lites."

"Yeah, that's what my old lady used to say." He lingered another second. "Something bothering you, kid?"

"Nothing."

"Something, I think."

"Ah, just something strange in the air."

He looked over his shoulder at the TV. The Lakers had called time out. "Strange how?"

"Nothing," she said, not feeling like talking.

"You sure the Bucks are gonna win?"

She nodded.

Benny fired up a Winston, feeling more confident that he'd win the $20 he'd bet earlier with Ram Kelly. Cindy was good at guessing basketball. That, in itself, was kind of strange, the bartender thought, since she didn't know shit about the game or the players. But he'd won a tidy sum betting the way she told him to bet, so he'd stayed with her choices.

"In a walk," she added.

Benny went back to the game. Cindy took a sip of beer. Benny's place was quiet tonight, and that was good because she didn't feel like conversation. Earlier, in the morning, she'd been horny. She'd woken up horny, in fact, and had made plans to score at Benny's. It had been awhile since she'd had any sex, and if George Hayward was good at nothing else he was good at sex. She admitted to herself that she missed that.

George knew how to get her hot, really hot. The punks in Millburg didn't know shit about getting a girl hot. Wham, bam, in and out. "How was I, babe?" She was sick of young boys grabbing at her and fumbling and shooting their wads before she could get off. That was why she'd gone home with George after he picked her up here in the first place. That and his Cadillac.

Well, it was over now. But she missed that part of it and that was why she was in Benny's. Only she was feeling weird now. It had started on Saturday morning. She woke up feeling out of sorts and for a time thought she might be coming down with the flu. But she knew that wasn't it.

She put it down to the change in her routine. She'd made good on her threat to quit working at George's shop in Nettleton. The drive was becoming a pain in the ass anyway. Being a free spirit had been fun the first couple of days. She went down to the unemployment office and filed for compensation. They told her it would come in a couple of weeks. It was damned near as much as George had been paying her, so it would be like a vacation. She could stay home and watch what was happening to Victoria Lord Buchanan and Tina and Beau and the rest of the gang on *One Life to Live*. The nice thing about the soaps was you could miss them for six or seven months and in a couple of days you were right back into them.

Then Saturday she had been right in the middle of watching an old Jerry Lewis movie on the tube when she began to shake. It was weird.

It passed, though. The rest of the day she was okay, but she stayed in Saturday night. Tonight she was up for some action, ready to hook up with someone and chugging down Lites when the feeling hit her again.

Somehow it was about George. She was pretty sure of that. It was more than just the fact that he'd been on her mind all week. There was something major happening to him, or maybe it had already happened.

She set her beer down and looked around the bar. Half a dozen scruffy-looking guys were putting the make on half a dozen tired-looking broads at half a dozen beer-stained tables. Two truck drivers were standing at either end of the bar, with her in the middle. One of them, Bill, had put the make on her about an hour ago. She'd turned him down politely, and he'd accepted it. Cindy figured the other guy was biding his time.

And then she was really worried about George because the feeling was hitting her hard. She got up and walked to the pay phone on the other side of the bar and began dialing his number.

It was stupid to give a damn about that bastard.

She hung up on the fifth ring and was surprised to find her uneasiness fading. That was when the guy walked into the bar.

It stunk, John thought. He wondered how long it had been since he'd been in a bar. Half his life. Enough time to forget how bad stale beer smelled. He looked down at the cheap wood planking. They'd never get the smell out.

Doesn't anyone else smell it?

Heads turned as he closed the door behind him, and he reminded himself that he was out of his element and dressed too well anyway. He was drawing enough attention to himself without commenting on the assault to his senses.

The place was dark—like the confessional.

He squinted and tried to make out his image in the mirror that ran the length of the wall behind the bar. It was a man he didn't know, and for a moment he thought about turning and running out of the bar and getting into the car and hightailing it back to Nettleton. Only they'd all laugh at him, and the thought of these people, who he didn't know or care about, laughing at him suddenly seemed important enough to make him stay.

He needed to fit in, to do something that would tell them all that he hadn't just dropped in from outer space. So he walked to the bar, nodded to the bartender and said, "A beer, please."

"You got a preference?"

"Lowenbrau."

"We don't have Lowenbrau."

"Bud, then."

Benny drew a draught and set the schooner in front of him. John lifted the glass and took a long drink. It was cold, the sting of carbonation feeling good down his throat. It was something to concentrate on.

When he turned around on the stool he saw everyone had forgotten about him.

"You're new," Benny offered.

"Just passing through."

John set his glass down. So this was it—his rash act after eight years as a priest. Sneaking off to have a beer in a roadhouse. His spirits lifted slightly. It wasn't so bad. Nothing to be sent to Purgatory for. You could do a lot worse. In fact, maybe it wasn't even a sin. Maybe it was just a bit unethical. Maybe it was—

"Hi."

John blinked and looked at the girl standing next to him. She was blonde and pretty and far too young, and this wasn't Sacred Heart.

"Hello."

"Mind if I join you?" Cindy asked, already

sitting on the stool.

"I . . ."

"Haven't seen you around here before."

"I'm not from—"

"Millburg. Yeah, I know. I'd know you if you were from Millburg. Where're you from?"

"Nettleton," he said, immediately cursing his stupidity.

She nodded. "I used to work over in Nettleton." She held out her hand and added, "My name's Cindy."

"John," he answered, taking her hand. It was soft and moist, the way a young woman's hand should be. Then he stopped thinking about her hand and started thinking about how quickly he'd told her where he was from and what his first name was.

Cindy tapped a Vantage from her pack on the bar, held it between her lips and asked, "Got a light?"

He stabbed for a book of matches resting in the empty ashtray in front of him. John fired the match and held it to her cigarette. She cupped her hand over his, holding it.

"Hey, you nervous or something?"

"No. Why?"

"Your hand's shaking. You aren't an alky or—"

"I had an accident in my car. That's why I stopped in here."

She blew out the match. "Yeah? A bad accident?"

"I went off the shoulder and hit a post."

"Christ! You okay?"

"I'm fine. Just a little shaken up. Anyway, I'm in better shape than the car."

"Messed it up, huh?"

He nodded. "The front fender's had it."

"You gotta be careful with the roads the way they are. You'd think they'd salt them more."

"Yes, you would." He took another sip of beer and asked, "You said you worked in Nettleton?"

"I used to. I quit my job."

"Jobs are scarce. You must have been very unhappy."

"That's a good observation."

"One of my strong suits," John said.

"Maybe you know the guy I used to work for—George Hayward."

"I know him."

"He's an A-number one bastard."

"I don't know him that well."

"If you're smart you never will." She put her cigarette in the ashtray on the bar, eased closer and asked, "Want to buy me a drink?"

John looked at the lick of smoke drift up from her cigarette. He nodded and said, "Sure."

It was rare that Cindy picked up a stranger. That was dangerous, even in a small town like Millburg. Hadn't they just found that kid buried up to his neck out in the woods around Nettleton last week? You just couldn't be too careful.

So she usually stuck with the townies. Of course, George had taken her out of that action for some time. She was anxious to get back into it, and that was one of the reasons she decided to invite John back to her apartment. Something told her he was all right. At least she had been sure all the while he followed behind her car.

Once they were in her apartment, she wasn't so sure. He was on edge and nervous, not in a mean sort of way, but it made her uneasy all the same. She started to wonder about him. Cindy locked her cat in the kitchen.

The living room was about the size of John's bedroom. There was nothing wrong in that. It wasn't the girl's fault she couldn't afford anything larger. But the open cans of Pepsi on the coffee table, the brimming ashtrays, the worn sofa seat cushions that hadn't been plumped in weeks were her fault.

John watched her hurrying around the living room, cleaning up.

She'd chosen white sofas, going for a contemporary look. The coffee table was chrome and glass, only it wasn't real chrome. John saw some of the gleam peeling off the plastic legs of the table. An arc lamp that looked like it had seen better days provided illumination.

Surprisingly, she had selected a couple of very nice posters for the wall behind the sofa. One showed a pair of legs belonging to a ballerina, the ballet slippers on her feet in tatters from use. The second was a Klee print of a trio of elephants. Both were framed in real chrome, non-glare glass covering the posters.

". . . or would you like some wine?"

"Yes," John said, turning from the posters, "wine would be fine, if you've got a bottle already uncorked."

"Unscrewed, you mean."

"Hmm? Oh." He laughed. "Wine would be good."

She gave him an odd look, then disappeared into the kitchen. She was worried about him. That was smart, John thought. He was acting rather out of the ordinary. She didn't have any idea why, though. He simply wasn't used to this. He didn't know the ground rules.

He wanted to learn the rules, because he wanted the girl badly. It came in a surge that was overwhelming, as though he were caught in an undertow. She was even more desirable here in the apartment. Even the disarray of the apartment seemed fitting now.

When she came out of the kitchen with the green liter bottle of Gallo in one hand and two glasses in the other, John had to fight the urge to leap from his seat, grab her and make love to her. No woman could look more sensuous than she, he thought. Her jeans were cut as

173

tightly as they could be, and John saw the distinct outline of her lush vaginal lips as she walked toward him.

Above, the nearly transparent beige blouse she wore revealed breasts that caused that swelling in his crotch to erupt anew.

Cindy smiled as she set the wine bottle on the table. As she bent, her blouse flared out slightly.

She poured wine into both glasses, came around the table and sat down next to him. Perfume snaked across the small space separating them and John felt his legs disappear. How much longer could he hold back?

And then she was in his arms and their mouths met and their tongues danced. His head swirled at the press of her full breasts against his chest and her fingernails grazing his neck. She smelled so damned good.

She felt small in his hands, as he caressed her shoulders. Cindy drew closer and pushed her pelvis against his legs so he could feel the warmth there. She looped her leg over his and he heard her coo. It was deep in her throat, the sound a cat makes when it's lying on a bed and a sunbeam hits it.

The cooing sound was in his ear now, and he opened his eyes to discover she'd moved her lips from his mouth. He looked down to see his hands moving from her shoulders, down toward her full breasts. Only a single button blocked him from those nipples that waited for his lips.

Only a single button. He closed his eyes again, the exquisite liquid ecstasy of her tongue delicately bathing his ear and bringing him a pleasure that was ever-increasing. Her hands teased at his shirt, unbuttoning it. He felt her fingertips dance inside and reach beneath his armpit and jolt him with a passion he didn't know that part of his body was capable of.

Cindy's tongue swirled deep inside his ear, his moaning strengthening the rigid manhood that raged to be free. Her fingers moved from his armpit to his nipple and toyed with it as she said, "I want you to touch me, now. Touch my tits, okay?"

And John's hand moved to the single button guarding that goal. His fingers closed on the button and as he began to undo it he opened his eyes.

It was as if he were removed from the scene, merely an observer on the outside. He was watching an event that had nothing at all to do with him. It was somebody else, these two people.

But it wasn't.

As his eyes took in Cindy's pouting, erect nipple, John turned away. His hands followed in retreat. Cindy half-opened her eyes.

"Wha . . ." She moved closer to him, reaching for his hands. "Don't stop. Hell, don't stop now."

He moved away from her on the sofa, the spell completely broken now.

Cindy glared at him, the heat still pulsing through her. "What the hell is this?"

"Nothing. I . . ."

"You just out of prison or what?"

"What do you mean?"

She buttoned her blouse, realizing the game was at an end. "That's the only other guy I ever met like you. He was just out of prison and couldn't get it on with a chick."

"It's not you," John said.

She laughed. "Damn right it's not me. I didn't say it was." She got up from the couch and lit a cigarette. "It's definitely you. I'd just like to know why?"

"It doesn't matter."

"It matters to me, Mister. You pick me up in a bar, come home, have a drink with me, get me all worked up and just quit?" She laughed again, but there was no humor in it. "I think I got a right to know why."

It was a mistake. The whole thing was a horrible mistake. He just wanted to get out of here, back to Nettleton, back to Sacred Heart.

He stood, but his legs were weak from the passion and he wobbled. "I made a mistake. That's all."

She watched him as he went for his coat. One part of her wanted to rage at the guy and call him a fucking freak, but something told her to hold her temper. What if he was a freak for real? Better to let him split. Mr. Goodbar comes to Millburg. You never knew.

John walked toward the door. He stopped and looked back at her, wanting to say something else. "Look, I'm sorry."

She nodded. "See ya around." After the door closed she added, "Fucking freak." But she said it under her breath. Then she walked to the door and locked it.

Now, driving into Nettleton with a dent in the front fender of the Sentra, John wondered what had possessed him to do what he had done. The accident had clearly been a sign for him to turn back, but he had disregarded it.

It didn't seem possible that he was capable of doing the things he'd done this evening. Actually going to a bar, picking up a woman and . . .

He corrected his thinking. Hadn't she actually picked him up? She had seduced him. She'd lured him back to her apartment. She was temptation and, in the end, he had resisted her—but barely.

It had been a test and in that light he had passed. He had resisted, and it had not been easy. Yes, that was how it was, but he shivered at the madness of it. Millburg wasn't that far from Nettleton. Someone from the town could easily have walked into the bar, the way he had, and seen him. And then what?

But they hadn't. He was safe, pulling into the driveway of his house. He was in the shadow of the church, a full moon breaking through as clouds passed by. He was safe.

The embers still glowed in the fireplace and John thought about throwing a fresh log on and starting a new fire, but it was too late for that. It was nearly time for bed and he'd had a long confusing day. There was a great deal he would have to meditate about concerning this day. It wasn't all clear to him yet.

He undressed and got into bed.

At about the time Cindy Breslauer had seen John walk into Benny's, Deputy Russell Patterson was pulling on his jacket. Koester, sitting at his desk, had just fired up a cigar after having a late dinner.

Russell thought he was leaving none too soon. The smell of the sheriff's cigars nauseated him this late at night.

He was anxious to get home, but something tugged at him, one last thing he had to tell Koester. He almost decided to put it off until morning, but procrastination wasn't part of his nature. He was too good a cop.

Squaring his hat, Russell asked, "You seen George Hayward around?"

Koester didn't bother looking up from the sports page of the *Chicago Tribune*. "Nope. Why?"

"Mary Kimble said he didn't come in to his shop on Saturday."

"Probably took the day off."

"It's not like George to take off on a

Saturday."

Koester turned all his attention back to the article he'd been reading. "No law against it."

"I suppose."

But when Russell turned for the door, Koester said, "It is kind of strange him taking off on a busy day like Saturday."

Russell hesitated by the door. "Yeah."

Koester said, "Maybe you want to take a run up to his house on your way in tomorrow afternoon."

"Right," Russell said. Then he opened the door and walked out into the night.

As it turned out, he would be at George Hayward's house long before noon.

John knew he was sleeping and knew he was dreaming. Sometimes he dreamed and didn't realize it was a dream, but not this time. He was on the road back from Millburg again and it was night. Everything was the same. He'd gone to Benny's, picked up Cindy Breslauer, gone to her apartment and made his escape.

Everything was the same except the way he felt, and the way he felt was good. He didn't have the same feeling of guilt and shame he had had earlier and that was how he knew it was a dream. There was something against which to compare and contrast the feelings he had now. He'd been here before.

He stopped at the traffic light just outside of Nettleton when he first was aware of the humming. It was soft but there, and John cocked his head. He revved the engine for a second, and when it went back down to idle he heard it again.

It was an engine noise, he thought. Nothing too serious, like a timing chain or the trans. Just an irritating hum that shouldn't have been there.

He drove along for awhile, trying to ignore it, but he couldn't. The hum was getting louder. He rolled down the window and cocked his head, trying to hear it more clearly, as if that would help him decide what was wrong with the engine.

The sound was so loud now that it didn't seem as if it could be coming from the engine.

It wasn't.

It was coming from the confessional—and that was when he woke up.

He lay in the bed for a full minute, flowing up the river toward consciousness. When he got there John realized the humming had followed him. He sat up in bed, listening to it. It was distant but definitely there, and he cocked his head, as he had done in the dream, trying to hear it better. What had he thought in the dream?

The confessional!

But that had been a dream. This was real and what did the confessional have to do with anything anyway?

The floor out in the living room was so cold that he almost turned around and went back to the bedroom for his slippers, but he didn't.

Out here the humming was louder, like an electrical generator. Maybe that was it. Maybe the wind had downed a power line.

He walked to the door that opened onto the narrow hallway leading to the church. It was when he opened the door that the smell assaulted him for the first time. He turned from it, physically feeling the stench. John rested a hand on the doorjamb, feeling a sudden urge to vomit. Vomit was what it smelled like, but it was more than that. It was decay, but even more than that—much more.

Every cell in his brain screamed at him to turn away and retreat to his house, but the humming had turned to a low buzz now. It was clear that it was coming from the church itself.

He was afraid, stupidly afraid, and he was embarrassed by his fear.

It might be a gas leak.

That worried him, and the worry brought feeling back to his legs again. He began walking down the black corridor, his hands stretched out in front of him like he was Patty Duke playing Helen Keller.

The confessional!

It was a numb fear that registered far back in his head right about at the spot where Gary Donovan had elbowed him—accidentally, of course—in a basketball game when he was 14.

Why the confessional?

Because of the confession you heard, he

thought. Because you've been thinking about it all day. That was why you ran away earlier. That was why you sprang a boner, my friend. And now you think the bloody thing's going to reach out and punish you because you let it down. Priests aren't supposed to get turned on in the confessional booth, you know.

He jumped back when his hand brushed against the door at the end of the corridor. On the other side of the door the buzz shifted to a different pitch, went back to the original tone, then shifted to a different pitch again.

John's eyes were drawn downward to the light. It was coming from under the door. It was blue and bright—and electrical.

He grasped the doorknob and pulled the door open.

The light was the first thing he saw and the sound was the first thing he heard. Both were intense, blinding and deafening. John closed his eyes tightly and threw his arms up on instinct. A documentary film flashed through his mind as he recalled people in the film reacting the same way he was, only they were responding to an A-bomb test.

His eyes closed, and he felt dizzy. He couldn't decide if what he'd heard was the sound itself or his brain percolating. It was the kind of sound you could feel, like a thunderclap. He was about to close the door against the pain in his ears, when the sound grew more bearable.

His eyes became slits now, more accustomed to the glow. He could make out things a bit more clearly. The inside of the church was brighter than he had ever seen it. Row after row of pews were visible, all the way to the back of the church. He looked up and could see the beams on the ceiling and the shadows they cast. His pupils turned to pinholes to admit the brilliance that made daylight pale by comparison.

John cupped his hands, trying to form a tunnel he could look through. Since that worked, he began to survey the church, looking for the source of the light. At the back of the church he could see the light switches. He took a step or two into the chancel, leaving the door open behind him.

There didn't seem to be any damage to the switches. He started to scan the rest of the church. Off to the right he gazed at the confessional, only it wasn't there.

He closed his eyes for a second. It had to be there. When he opened them again he saw the mass of swirling light, like a miniature tornado, that hovered around where the confessional should have been. It *was* there, John discovered as he walked toward it. As the light danced and vibrated he could catch glimpses of the wooden booth.

The confessional was the eye of the storm, and as he walked slowly toward it he discerned that both the light and the low sound were emanating from it. His mind raced down the pathways of possibilities. There were no electrical outlets by the confessional. There was no one in the church except him. Could it be fire?

That was a possibility.

It was the fear of fire that propelled him toward the booth. When he was 20 feet from it he stopped. This was no fire. The confessional *was* the sound and the light. It was the source. Arcs of blue and white sheeted out from the booth, rising up, then falling like eruptions on the face of the sun. As each shaft of light was born, rose and died, it was accompanied by the unearthly cacaphony of taunting, haunting sound.

John regarded it from behind a pew, not really knowing what to make of it. And then the light began to move outward, toward him, in ever-reaching circles. It was traveling toward him. It knew he was there and was coming for him.

When he began to back away from it, the sound shrieked with such intensity that he felt it shake his bones. He teetered against the pew, unable to move. The light rolled up the back of a pew, down across the seat, up over the back of the next pew, down over another seat, coming toward him, coming for him.

As it grew closer he could make out smaller flashes, like sparklers, that shot away from the main form and then died off. The body of light snaked toward him, still linked all the way back to the confessional.

And then it reached John. As it moved

around him, a new horror threatened his sanity. It wasn't just light and sound. It was something more. It was something evil.

The thing wrapped around him and spun him around, deciding what to do with him. John felt its presence, and the feeling it brought was nausea and panic.

He tried to turn, but he could not. It had him in its grasp.

"This can't be!" he screamed, and the light responded by pulling him. He felt his legs give as he stumbled in the direction it pulled. The light pulled again, and he stumbled three more feet toward the confessional. It was retracting, pulling him toward the booth.

John shook his head and opened his mouth to scream, but heard nothing come out. As his lungs flamed from the pent-up air, he prayed he wouldn't black out. Still the light pulled on him. Like a marionette on a string he lurched against his will.

Five feet from the confessional he ceased to see anything but the booth. The glow totally engulfed him. The booth was the only thing bearable to look at, the light around him being so intense.

And the confessional looked back at him.

The carved figures on the front of the booth stared at him through eyes that were alive, yet not of any living thing he knew of. The eyes were small and piercing and fierce, and they were terrible. The faces were contorted with evil laughter as the demons gleamed at the priest whose lust had betrayed him.

They seemed to know everything.

He recalled the girl's confession and how his passion had swollen, and he knew that the carved wooden figures on the confessional had witnessed his shame. They were able to get inside his head.

The light jerked again and he stumbled another foot, the muscles in his legs aching as he tried to resist. With mortal dread he watched as the door of the booth began to open, yellow liquid oozing out from the bottom. It was in there. The thing most to be feared was in the confessional, and it wanted him. In his blind terror he ripped open his pajama top, grasped his crucifix and screamed, "Dear Christ in Heaven, protect your servant!"

The void he fell into was like a yawning pit of blackness. It was like falling off a mountainside. All sound ceased. All light ceased.

He blinked his eyes and felt the hard press of wood against his back. He felt around his side with his hand and discovered he was lying on one of the pews. Cold was the first real sensation he was aware of and then the dampness of sweat on his torn pajama top. His other hand was still clenched around the crucifix, and he would not, could not, let go of it.

John sat up in the pew, his entire body shaking, almost convulsing. He looked toward the confessional. It no longer glowed or groaned. It was only wood now, and he could barely make it out in the faint light of the church.

He crawled along the pew, toward the center of the church, his hand still grasping the crucifix. He came out into the center nave, stumbling toward the altar, and genuflected. The floor was cold against his knees, but it didn't matter. He was already lost in prayer.

He continued praying long after the first shafts of dawn broke through the stained glass windows above.

CHAPTER 7

Jill Gregory knew Evan was a special child. She also knew that most mothers think their children are special. The difference was that it was true in Evan's case.

She stacked three Downyflake Waffles, Evan's favorite, on a plate and wondered if he was special or just different. There was no question that he was different from most children. He was his own best friend. He could sit up in his room and play with his *A-Team* soldiers for so many hours, that she often had to trudge up the stairs and literally drag him down to the kitchen for dinner.

Evan didn't get along well with other children at school. There were fights—most of which he usually won—and there were phone calls from Elmer Fortmann and complaints from other parents. He got along much better with adults, and that was why Jill felt he was special. He was smart beyond his years. Maybe he was bored by other children who didn't seem as bright and creative as he did to himself.

He was moody, too. Sometimes he'd seem to withdraw deep into some secret thought, and no amount of coddling or coaxing could get him to open up. That worried Jill. She wanted to have an open line of communication with Evan. She had gone through far too much to have her child not to be able to talk with him.

You couldn't press it, though. She'd seen enough TV talk shows and heard enough radio psychologists to know you had to go easy with kids nowadays. Look at all they had to deal with—the bomb, drugs, increasing competition in the workplace. You had to take it easy on them, but you had to remain a guiding parent at the same time. It wasn't a snap.

He'd gone into one of his moods Saturday when he got home from George's around 2:00. She supposed he was upset about Frank Conforte's funeral. Jill had asked him if he wanted to attend, but he'd said no and that was that. He had decided to spend the morning at George's house, and George had promised to drop him home on his way in to work.

Evan had his ski jacket zipped all the way

up to his neck when he got home and headed straight for the stairs.

"Something wrong, babe?" she called from the kitchen.

He shook his head.

Jill crossed the living room as he began up the stairs. "Where are you going?"

"To my room."

"Honey, are you okay?"

Evan nodded.

"You didn't have a fight with George, did you?"

"Everything's fine," he insisted.

Jill took the first two steps and turned Evan around to face her. He looked pale, and she placed a hand on his forehead. "You coming down with something, tiger?"

"I'm fine, Mom. Just a little tired."

His head felt cool, so Jill said, "Wash up and I'll make some lunch."

"I'm not hungry, Mom. I had a sandwich at George's."

"Eating junk food, huh?"

"Just a sandwich. I'm gonna take a nap, okay?"

Jill watched as her son turned and disappeared up the stairs. Something was on the boy's mind, taking a nap on a Saturday afternoon.

Sunday he begged off from church. He was quiet all day long, and by evening she was concerned he was coming down with the flu. Monday morning there had been a moment of panic when she tried to wake him for school and he didn't respond. Even when Jill shook him hard, he still didn't open his eyes. She bent and felt for a pulse. Finding it, she relaxed and said, "Evan, wake up."

He opened his eyes, but they were red.

Jill felt his head again. He was still cool, but there was definitely something wrong with him so she decided to keep him home from school.

Now, an hour later, as she carried the plate of waffles and bacon up the stairs, she banked on his favorite breakfast to snap him out of his mysterious gloom.

She opened the door of his room and said, "Here you go, babe. Your fav—" As the plate fell from Jill's hands, her scream came before it hit the ground. Evan was lying naked on the bed, the sheets about his feet. A leather belt was looped around his neck and he held one end in his left hand.

Evan's bellybutton lay hidden beneath a pool of semen.

It was 8:30 when John walked out to the Sentra parked in the backyard. He had shaven. It was a natural thing to do, but somehow it seemed very important today. The ordinariness of it brought him some small measure of calm. It gave him time to think.

Now, in the bright morning light, he wondered if what had happened the night before had really happened. And if it had happened, what exactly was it? It wasn't the kind of thing you could put into words, at least not without people calling the men in the white coats.

He frowned when he looked at the car. The dent on the fender was worse than he thought. It was more a crush than a dent. But the car was still drivable and that was good because he had to take a ride this morning.

As he drove down Bradley Avenue he worked things over in his mind. There were pieces that were beginning to fall together. They seemed random, but actually they weren't. Dreiband's suicide was somehow connected with himself getting aroused while hearing a girl's confession and whatever had happened last night. There was a common denominator, and it was the confessional. He should have seen it that second night he was in Nettleton, when he looked at the booth and thought he'd seen the carved figures moving. But he'd been tired then. It could have been a mistake.

Last night was no mistake.

There was something about the confessional that needed to be explained, and John decided to go to the one man who knew the most about the booth—the man who made it, George Hayward.

It was a big house, John thought as he pulled up to it, too large a house for one man alone even if he was the richest man in Nettleton. Hayward had impressed him as rich when he met him. *Nouveau riche*, to be more precise. The man was loud and animated and was accustomed to being in the center of things. That would work in John's favor. He would be a talkative sort and more than willing to fill him in on the details of how he'd built the booth. Maybe Hayward didn't know about it, about what it was capable of—what was it capable of?—but at least he could give him a clue.

After John banged the wolf's head brass knocker on the front door the second time, he began to grow apprehensive. Maybe it was a mistake.

Just before he turned to leave for the security of his wounded automobile, John reached out and tried the doorknob.

It turned.

He pushed and the door swung inward.

John stepped into the foyer and closed the door behind him. It was hard to see in the foyer, only one high window giving any light.

"Hello?"

There was no answer, but as his eyes adjusted to the room he saw that things were not as they should have been. There was a smell, too. It was putrid.

Oh, God!

He stepped backward, his back hitting the wall, and he felt for the light switch. Blindly, he clawed and the chandelier came on.

The lump that had been George Hayward lay near the stairs. John knew it was him from the clothes. That was the only way he could tell. He was in green workclothes. John recalled that the man had a woodshop in his basement and liked to brag about it.

He didn't want to go to the man, but there were a lot of things you didn't want to do but did, because you were a priest. The closer John got, the worse the stench was. It wasn't just the smell of death. He'd smelled that before at an auto accident he'd stumbled onto down in Florida. It was far worse than that.

As he drew closer John felt the skin on his arms begin to crawl and felt his breathing come in tight gasps. His gums grew numb, and the only sensation he had left was the taste of bile rising in his throat.

It was the odor of decay that made John realize the man was not freshly dead. He'd been lying there for some time, perhaps days. There was a great deal of blood around him, but most of it had dried on the floor, like someone had spilled wine awhile ago.

John crossed himself.

He wanted to pray, but could not. That took too much thought, and all of his mind was occupied with the horror he saw. The man had no face left. It had been beaten in. There were gaping holes in his forehead, in his cheeks, and gray bits of brain had oozed out. White strips of tissue, stained maroon, lay exposed beneath the skin that had once covered his skull. Bone had splintered around his jaws and trust up out of his face like so many toothpicks. The sockets where his eyes had been were filled with drying lakes of blood.

It was murder—again.

There was nothing he could do for the man. For one instant he thought about using the telephone, but it wasn't possible. He couldn't stay another moment in the house. He had to get away, right now, before the decaying creature on the floor came to life and reached up and latched his bony hand around his neck and pulled him down to wallow in the bath of blood.

That was when John felt the hand on his shoulder.

"I'm going to admit him to the hospital, Jill. I want to keep him under observation for a few days."

"Is he going to be all right, Doc?"

Doc Brannigan pulled a cigar from the desk drawer in the office he had in Community Hospital. Peeling the cellophane off, clipping the end and puffing it to life gave him something to do. He didn't feel like looking at Jill Gregory right now.

He'd delivered her baby, called on Evan when he had gotten pneumonia at age four and given him all his shots. Once a year he'd perform a gynecological on Jill. He'd tried to save her husband's life after his auto accident. He'd consoled Jill after his death. He knew the family as well as any doctor could know a family. He was more than just their physician.

He was their friend, and that made it much more difficult.

"He's out of any immediate danger."

Jill exhaled a great rush of air, certain it was the first time she'd breathed in an hour. She smiled weakly, the corner of her mouth trembling with relief, but it was short-lived. There were questions to be answered.

"What was it, Doc?"

Doc watched the smoke billowing. He couldn't stall any longer. He had to look at her now and when he did he saw a frightened woman. Hell, she had good reason to be frightened, Doc thought.

"He almost killed himself, Jill."

"Killed himself? Evan?" She looked to the window, as if hoping someone would be standing there to help her tell Brannigan he was nuts. "Evan's got no reason to kill him—"

"I didn't say he did it on purpose."

She wrapped her hands around the arms of her chair. "Then say what you mean."

"It's called auto-asphyxiation. A couple hundred kids in America die from it every year." Then he said something that made Jill sadly certain that he knew what he was talking about. "They're all about Evan's age."

She sat there, her knuckles very white. Because they ached, Jill straightened her hands which only made them ache more. "Auto . . ."

"Auto-asphyxiation. It's a form of masturbation where—"

Swiftly, Jill said, "Evan doesn't do that."

Doc frowned. Damn, she wasn't making this any easier. "Of course he does, Jill. All young boys ma—"

"Not Evan," she said more emphatically than Doc had expected.

He looked at her quizzically. No mother wants to consciously admit her kid plays with himself, he thought, but it was such general knowledge. It wasn't possible she actually thought . . . And he saw that something had taken place of fear in her eyes. It was anger.

He traced back Jill's family tree and found the spoiled fruit that had been Sally Crandall. There was a strange one. The woman had withered after something terrible had happened to her, and Doc knew it had something to do with the Church and her daughter. He strained for the memory. There was something about Father Thyssen, the priest before Nicoletti. No one ever knew exactly what it was, but the memory of Sally Crandall came into clearer focus now.

Yes, she'd been one of those religious fanatics. Anything was possible, then. Maybe Jill had inherited some of that fervor from her mother, but she couldn't possibly believe her son didn't . . .

He smiled. "Jill, it's prefectly normal for a boy Evan's age to experiment with his sexuality."

She clutched the chair again, this time to contain her rage. "You telling me what he did was perfectly normal?"

Doc's smile disappeared, but inside he felt a degree of relief. They were going to skirt the issue of ordinary masturbation being normal, which at least meant they could get on with the business at hand.

"No, I'm not going to tell you that. What Evan did was extremely dangerous, and he's fortunate to be alive."

Jill felt the anger pulse out of her nostrils and grew weak from it. It wasn't a good idea to take all of this out on Doc Brannigan. He was important. He was a way for her to find out what had happened to her son.

She drew a deep breath and said, "Tell me why he did it, Doc. Why'd he have that belt around his neck like that?"

"In auto-asphyxiation a boy ties either a rope or a belt around his neck in order to cut off the circulation of blood to the brain while he masturbates. As he masturbates, the blood pressure becomes greater and greater, only the blood isn't flowing at a normal rate to the brain. When he climaxes, the blood is at an incredibly high pressure, much higher than it would be under an ordinary climax. The result is an orgasm of massive proportions."

"And he almost died because of that?"

Doc nodded. "He could have. You can only limit the flow of blood to the brain for so long before there's damage due to lack of oxygen." Doc leaned back in his chair, recalling the *New England Journal of Medicine* monograph he'd read. "Some of the these boys hook the rope up to a drawer or a doorknob so both hands are free. They pass out from the lack of oxygen and literally hang themselves. Other times the metal prong gets stuck on the strap and after they pass out they're strangled to death.''

Jill stood up and walked to the window. She looked outside and saw Patty Graham walking out of Heller's Pharmacy.

Goddamn you, Patty Graham, she thought, for not having any problems today.

Still looking out the window, she said, "I don't believe you, Doc.''

She'd pressed the wrong button. Doc hadn't been sleeping well lately. There had been Dreiband's death, then finding the Conforte boy's body, now this. It wasn't the way he had envisioned semiretirement. Stitching up a cut here and dispensing antibiotics there was what he'd wanted. Why didn't they go to young Brownley or Michaelson? They were competent physicians and practically kids. Christ, they could use the business.

"If you've got another explanation, Jill, I'd like to hear it." She turned, surprised, and looked at him sitting behind his desk. Doc said, "You don't suppose someone creeped in the second floor window at your place, tied him up and—"

"Doc!"

He closed his eyes and pinched the bridge of his nose with this thumb and forefinger. It was an unforgivable thing to say to a worried mother.

He looked at her. "I'm sorry. I shouldn't have said that. I've had a rough week, Jill. Frank Conforte. I get no joy out of performing an autopsy on a young boy." He puffed on his cigar. "And I don't want to have to perform one on Evan."

He knew what he was talking about, Jill thought. It was awful, but he was right. And he was worried about Evan. He cared almost as much about her son as she did. He'd delivered him, hadn't he? Wasn't he responsible for bringing Evan into the world?

If what Doc said was true, then she had to face it and figure out how to save her son's life. Jill walked to the chair and sat down.

"What would make him do a thing like that, Doc?"

"You have to find that out. He's a smart boy, Jill. Maybe that's part of it. Maybe he got bored with normal experimentation. That's why a lot of kids turn to drugs, for instance."

Something in Doc's voice told her he wasn't convinced that was it. "What other reason?"

He stared at her for a second, knowing the boy had inherited most of his intelligence from his mother. Then he said, "Could be some sort of emotional stress."

"Emotional stress?"

Doc nodded. "Some kind of mental trauma."

* * *

Patrolman Gary Murchison settled in with the remains of the Sunday *Chicago Tribune* Koester had left in the office. The classifieds section was gone, and Murchison smiled at that. He knew the sheriff always liked to page through it and see how much municipalities around Chicago were offering lawmen. It was something that raised the hackles on his back.

"Twenty-three thousand a year for some kid fresh out of police academy. When I pinned on my first badge I got all of two hundred bucks a month."

Russell Patterson would allow, "That was a long time ago, Doug, back when hot dogs were a nickel."

And Gray would throw in, "I didn't think they even had hot dogs back then." Gary would laugh, but later Russell would tell him something like, "You shouldn't lay it on that heavy with Koester."

Up yours, Gary would think but not say. I'm not bucking for his job.

But there was something to Russell's warning. There was a look he'd catch every once in awhile in the sheriff's eyes that said, "Don't press me too hard, boy. You're liable to get a might more than you bargained for." And Gary was pretty sure Koester was the kind of guy who could deliver more than a person had bargained for, that he was the kind of guy who could grab your balls between his fingers and pop them like they were grapes.

He jumped as the phone jangled away his thoughts about Koester. "Sheee-it," he said just before he pulled the phone from the cradle. "Sheriff's office. Patrolman Murchison speaking."

"This is Father John Hines."

"Yes, Father."

"There's been a murder."

Later, Gary would be pleased with the professional manner in which he'd reacted, but for the moment he had to struggle to keep his voice calm. He reached for the pen and pad on the desk.

"Take it easy, Father. Who's been murdered?"

"George Hayward."

"How do you know?" Gary asked, scribbling on the pad.

"I saw him. I just came from his house."

"Where are you at now?"

"A Standard station near—"

"Chet's Standard. Okay, that's fine. You stay right where you are. I'll have a car over there in a minute."

Quickly, John said, "You'd better tell your people to watch out for Tom Conforte."

"Tom?" He let the pen drop. "How come?"

"He was at George Hayward's house when I got there."

It was Tom Conforte's hand that John felt on his shoulder and, looking at George's mangled body, he was primed to have the wits scared out of him. That was very nearly what happened. He jumped forward, away from whatever ghoul was about to seize him.

The only direction to leap was toward the corpse on the foyer floor, and in doing so he kicked into George's body and stumbled face forward over it. It was cold and moved in a way living things didn't move—heavily.

He slipped, tumbled and rolled across the body, his mouth paralyzed with fright. When he looked back he saw Tom Conforte standing in a crouch.

"Father Hines?" Tom said.

Feeling came back to his face gradually, and he became conscious of how hard he was gritting his groin muscles to keep from urinating on himself.

"Damnit," he said aloud, allowing himself the luxury of a curse to take the edge off his panic. "What are you trying to do, Tom?"

"I'm sorry. I didn't mean—"

"Didn't mean to what?" John snapped, standing up. "You creep up behind a man when he's just discovered a body and..." John's words trailed off as the thought struck him that he could very well be looking at the person who had murdered George Hayward. If that was true, then he was not exactly dealing from a position of strength.

"He's dead," Tom said, lowering his eyes to George.

"Yes, he's dead."

Tom looked back up at John. "Guess you must think I killed him."

"I didn't say that."

Urgency crept into the boy's voice. "But you're thinking it, aren't you?"

"No," John said with some assurance. "I don't think you killed him."

"I'll bet."

John worked to take the upper hand. "This man has been dead for some time. If you killed him you surely wouldn't stay around here."

That made sense to Tom, but his defenses went right back up. John was on their side. Even though he wasn't as old as Koester and Elmer Fortmann and the rest of them, he was still on their side. He'd say anything. He'd try to trick him. Maybe not to hurt him, but to save himself he'd sure try to trick him.

"You've got blood on your robe," Tom said.

John looked down and saw the splotch across the front of his robe. He was surprised it was there, even though he'd all but wrestled with George.

"It'll come clean."

"Just like me, huh?"

John could bear the tension between them no longer and blurted out, "Did you kill him, Tom?"

Tom looked down at George again, then back up to John as he said, "Naw. But I would have."

"Why?"

"I think he killed my brother."

John felt his head begin to pound again. The boy was unbalanced. The pain of finding his younger brother stuck in a hole out in the woods like some dog's bone had brought him close to the cracking point. John had to be careful with him.

Tom dug his hands into the pockets of his jeans. "And if he didn't kill Frank, I'm pretty sure he knew who did."

"What makes you think so?"

He shrugged and very casually said, "Just a hunch."

John laughed. It was one of those times where you wished you could reach out in the air, grab it and stuff it back in your mouth. He couldn't help it. The insanity of the situation called only for two responses—laughter or screams.

A hunch. The boy had said it almost as an afterthought, something as important as that with a dead man lying on the floor between them.

Tom was staring at him evenly, his eyes more hollow suddenly. He was measuring him, trying to guess if John would turn and bolt back through the house and try to make it to the rear door or stand and fight him. 50-50, Tom thought. And that was about his chances of beating the priest in a fight. The priest had about 20 pounds on him and most of that, he guessed, was muscle. But Tom was younger and faster and in condition from playing football.

Maybe it wouldn't come to that.

In that moment when the priest had laughed, Tom wanted to lurch toward him and bash his head in, the same way he had wanted to bash George Hayward's head in when it dawned on him that George might know something about his brother's death.

That had come to him just as he was about to fall asleep the previous night. There was no great reason for him to think such a thing. George had barely known Frank and only had a nodding acquaintance with his parents. Still, something insisted that George was involved with his brother's death. He lay in bed for hours, mulling it over.

It didn't matter. He didn't have to think about it or find reasons or logic. He just knew it to be so. For half an hour he thought he might be losing his mind. He was bright enough to understand the impact finding his brother's body had had on him and his parents. He knew people could crack under that kind of thing.

This thing about latching onto George Hayward was pretty scary. It was the kind of thing crazy people did. Only he knew he wasn't crazy because he knew he was right. George had something to do with Frank's death—somehow, some way.

When dawn came he got dressed and rode

out to George's house and found him where he lay now, with his head bashed in. And Tom knew, more than ever, that he was right, that George had something to do with Frank's death. Well, he'd paid for it. God had struck him down.

None of it made any real sense, and that was why he had to tell the priest it was just a hunch. He would have punched him out for laughing, only he could understand it. If it didn't make any sense to him, how could it make any sense to anyone else?

John turned toward the door that opened onto the living room.

"Where are you going?"

"To call the sheriff," John said over his shoulder.

"You don't want to do that."

John walked two more paces before he heard the sound of the hammer being cocked. Wisely, he stopped and waited for Tom to tell him what to do.

"Turn around, Father Hines."

When he did, John saw the long-barreled .38 Tom had pulled from his waistband. The boy held it without shaking, in a confident manner that told John he knew how to handle the weapon.

"What are you going to do with that, Tom?"

"That's up to you."

"Put the gun down."

"I know how to use it, Father."

"I'm sure you do."

"I'm not going to let Koester lock me up."

"No one's going to lock you up."

"You don't know Sheriff Koester."

"Did you kill George Hayward?"

"I already told you . . ."

John turned from him. "Then you've got nothing to worry about." John walked toward the living room, determined to tough it out. When the footsteps echoed swiftly in the foyer, it dawned on him that Tom Conforte was running toward him. John managed to partly turn around before the blow fell. He could see the raised barrel of the .38 and nearly blocked it.

There was pain.

Then everything went black.

Doug Koester examined the cut phone cord in George Hayward's living room. Then he looked at John and asked, "He say anything about where he might be running to?"

"No."

"I don't suppose you'd tell me even if he did confess to killing George."

"He didn't. You don't seriously think . . ."

"Don't know what to think right now. It's way too early." The sheriff walked back to the foyer, John following. "All we know for sure is that he was in the same room with the deceased, he had a gun, and he assaulted you."

John began to feel some of what Tom had been talking about. Maybe the sheriff wouldn't come right out and say he thought

Tom had killed George, but he sure thought it. On the other hand, how could he blame him?

John looked at the body on the floor. It was absurd.

"Sheriff, this man's been dead for days. Why would Tom come back here if he killed him?"

Koester shrugged. "Sometimes the stereotypes hold true. That's how they become stereotypes. Besides, we don't know for sure how long he's been dead."

Irritated, John said, "You've been here for fifteen minutes and looked at everything except the body."

"It ain't going anyplace," Koester said. In truth, he'd learned the investigative technique from Thomas Noguchi's book, *Coroner*. The former Los Angeles County Coroner always checked everything else at the murder scene first, leaving the body for last. It was important to look for physical clues before you became involved with the body itself.

He decided against explaining it to the priest, who had him more than a little pissed off right now. It was really none of his fucking business. What had him even more peeved was that Hines immediately assumed Tom Conforte was innocent. Wasn't that just like a preacher?

If someone wanted to bet with him about the boy's guilt or innocence, Koester would have passed on the bet. He'd been honest when he'd told Hines it was too early to tell, but the Sheriff knew Hines thought he'd already made up his mind and had condemned him for it.

Russell Patterson was down in the basement checking things out. Koester had called him in after Murchison had told him what the situation was. Maybe the college boy could earn his keep for a change. Russell had picked up the priest on his way out to the house. Koester wanted to drive directly there.

Now he bent to examine George Hayward's body. He ignored the smell, looking at the wounds around his face. He noted George's right hand was missing. The stump was a congealed mass of drying blood and bone.

"Yep. He's been dead for a couple of days, all right. You say you stumbled over him, Father? That's how you got the blood on your robe?"

"That's right."

The only thing that bothered the sheriff was the eyes—or at least where the eyes had been. Aside from that it wasn't any worse than what he'd seen during the war.

He was still looking at George when he asked, "How'd you get that dent in your car?"

"What?"

Koester swung his head around to look up at John. "Front left fender's bent pretty bad. How'd that happen?"

"I ran off the road last night. Hit a bridge abutment."

"The roads are pretty slick around here," he said, turning back to the body. "Mind telling me where you were going?"

"I wanted a Sunday paper," he lied.

Koester nodded as though it wasn't important. He was about to ask Hines another question when Russell walked into the room. He was wearing a beat-up pair of corduroys, a red flannel shirt and hiking boots. Koester's call had caught him sleeping, and he hadn't had time to get into his uniform.

"Pretty bad down there, Doug. A lot of blood."

"And a hand?"

"And a hand." Russell glanced toward the priest. "There's blood all over his electric saw."

"I thought there would be."

"Must have been someone he knew."

Koester stood up and looked at his deputy. "How do you figure?"

"Well, the door wasn't jimmied, for one thing. And the saw. If there was a fight, somebody wouldn't have the time to turn the damned thing on and drag him over there."

"Unless they killed him first, then drug him to it and put his hand through the thing."

Russell frowned. "And then dragged him all the way up the stairs?"

"You can't look for logic with a psycho." Koester sucked in on his cigar, exhaled and said, "But you're right about the way it happened. Blood splatters on those stairs are random. If somebody drug him upstairs the blood from his hand would have left an even trail."

"Then why'd—"

" 'Cause you were right for the wrong reasons." Koester walked toward the door that led down to the basement. "Russell, go out to the car and call in for an ambulance."

"What about the phones?"

Koester shook his head. "Tom cut all the wires before he left. Probably wanted to give himself some extra time and make the Father here have to run out to Chet's to call us."

John said, "Those wires could have been cut before."

Koester stopped by the door and looked at John. "Yeah, and I could be Ronald McDonald. But I ain't and they weren't." Then he turned to Russell and said, "Call the state police. Tell them to put out an all-points on Tom Conforte."

CHAPTER 8

Tuesday morning Sheriff Koester found out Evan Gregory was in the hospital. He knew he'd have to talk to Jill before he could see him, but he decided to run over to Doc Brannigan's house first. He wanted to know why the boy was admitted, and a phone call to the hospital only had gotten a bullshit response from the nurse on duty—something about how she'd just come on and wasn't quite sure why Evan was there.

Doc offered him coffee, but Koester passed on it. He wanted to keep it business. Brannigan sensed that was why they were sitting in the tiny office in his house instead of the living room. It was a work office, the walls lined with bookshelves containing

medical volumes, but it was a retreat as well.
A desk as weathered as the physician himself
took up about half the room. A straight-
backed chair, an old floor lamp and an ashtray perpetually brimming with cigar butts
completed the decor. It was a room Doc had
figured to wind out his remaining years in
dispensing sage medical advice over the phone
and leafing through medical journals.

It wasn't to be so.

"There's been a lot of work for you and me
lately, Doc."

"The kind of work I don't need," the old
physician observed. "I had a couple of
reporters from Milwaukee banging on my
door yesterday. Wanted to know about Frank
Conforte. I guess they'll be back, what with
George dead and Tom missing." He drew on
his cigar and asked, "You think the same
person killed Frank and George?"

"Don't know. Maybe, maybe not. I don't see
much of a connection between them. And the
methods were different."

"You think Tom killed George, don't you,
Doug?"

"Could be." Koester leaned back in the
chair. It was hard to keep things strictly
business with a man as cordial as Brannigan.
He made you let your guard down. "God
knows he had a motive."

"He did?"

"At least he thinks he did." Koester crushed

out his own cigar. "Father Hines told me Tom thought George had something to do with his brother's death." Quickly, he added, "That ain't for release, Doc, you hear?"

"I hear."

"I heard Jill Gregory's boy is in the hospital."

"Yep."

"How come?" Koester asked, hoping that imparting the privileged information the priest had given him would induce Doc to return the favor.

It was a vain hope which Koester knew from the start.

"A medical problem."

"I didn't think he was in 'cause he wanted to see the circus."

"How come you want to know?"

"Do I really have to tell you?"

"You bet."

"Because Evan Gregory spent most of his Sundays over at George Hayward's place, that's why."

Doc pouted a lip in thought. "You think he might know something?"

"Might. Anyway, I'd like to talk to him, and it'd help if I knew the reason he's in the hospital."

"He fell down and—"

"Come on, Doc. I'd rather you didn't tell me anything than to hand me a line of crap."

Brannigan leaned back, and the chair

rocked away from the desk. He weighed telling Doug Koester the truth. He had the right to withhold medical information if he had a mind to, and Evan's case was certainly sensitive enough for him to think about it. But Koester had a legitimate reason. Someone had died—been murdered.

So he told him.

Strangely, it was harder for Koester to listen to that explanation than it had been looking at George Hayward's body. It turned his stomach sour to picture what Doc was talking about. Freakiness always nauseated him.

After Doc had finished, Koester said, "Then it's all the more important that I talk to him."

"You know you're going to have to ask Jill's permission."

Koester nodded. "And I also know she'll be more likely to give it if you tell her it's okay."

"I'll do that, Doug. But I want you to do something for me."

"Sure," Koester said, figuring Doc wanted him to avoid talking about what had gotten the boy in the hospital. "What?"

"I want you to tell him you know why he's in the hospital."

Doug's jaw hung open for a moment. "What?"

"Don't try to con him, Doug."

Koester folded his arms across his chest. "Now wait a minute, Doc. I ain't no psychologist, and I'm not too good with kids in the first place. I can't talk to him about something like that."

"Just tell him you know why he's there."

"That doesn't have anything to do with why I want to see him."

"Don't be so sure. If he saw something at that house auto-asphyxiation could be an emotional release for him. It might fit if there was something he saw too awful to accept."

"You mean that?"

Doc nodded.

Koester said, "That's not why you want me to tell him I know, though."

"No, it's not. Evan's my patient, and I want what's good for him. What's good for him is to realize he's not going to be able to hide this thing. He's got to know that people know. That way he'll be free to talk about it later."

"I don't know, Doc."

"Tit for tat."

Koester stood up and said, "You old coot. You should have run for office like I told you twenty years ago."

Jill agreed to let Koester talk to Evan. Doc had actually talked her into it quite easily. Telling her it was best for Evan was about all that needed to be said. But Jill had insisted on being there when Koester arrived and on being in the room with Evan when the sheriff talked to him.

Koester decided to get the worst out of the way fast, so he said, "Evan, I want you to know I know why you're in the hospital."

The kid looked tiny in the hospital bed—a face in the middle of a snowdrift of sheets. Jill had told the sheriff her son wasn't eating well.

Evan looked at him with genuine surprise. "You do?"

Koester nodded.

He looked to his mother. "Did you tell him, Mom?"

"No, honey. Doctor Branni—"

"Then I don't want to see that buzzard again."

"Evan."

But Evan already turned back to Koester. "I know about George getting killed."

Koester wasn't surprised, but Jill asked, "How did you hear about that?"

"I heard one of the nurses talking about it."

"Evan," the sheriff began, "when was the last time you saw George?"

"Saturday."

"You were at his house?"

Jill said, "It was Frank Conforte's funeral and Evan was too upset to—"

Koester silenced her with his hand. He asked Evan, "Was anyone else there?"

"No. Just us."

"Did he get any phone calls while you were there?"

"I don't think so."

"How come you didn't go over there on Sunday? Don't you usually—"

"Evan didn't go to church Sunday," Jill interrupted. "He wasn't feeling well and I—"

Koester looked at her again and she fell silent. He turned back to Evan. "When you were there on Saturday, was George acting . . . odd?"

"What do you mean?"

"Nervous, angry. Anything like that?"

Evan shook his head. "He was like he always was.

"Did he drive you home?"

"Sure."

"And what time did you get home?"

"Around six."

"That was the last time you saw him?"

"Yeah."

Koester walked across the hospital room and looked out the window, down into the parking lot. After a second he asked, "Do you know Tom Conforte?"

"Sure."

"Did you see him on Saturday?"

"No."

"You're positive?"

Jill inched forward in her chair. "If he says 'no' he means 'no.'"

Koester nodded. Then he looked at Evan Gregory. His eyes had a sunken look to them, probably from being confined to a hospital room. Places like this weren't good for kids.

Koester fought against what he wanted to ask the boy. It was all the worse because his mother was there. He didn't want her to be in the room, but it was the only way she'd agree to him seeing the boy.

Then he plowed ahead.

"How did you get along with George on Saturday?"

Jill perked up her ears and cocked her head, not quite sure she'd heard Koester's words right.

Evan shrugged. "Just like always."

Koester tried a disarming smile, but knew the boy could see straight through him. Kids were like that. "You didn't have an argument with him or something?"

"An argument?" Evan glanced at his mother.

"Sure. You know, friends fight sometimes."

Jill stood up, taking a single step toward the sheriff. "What are you talking about?"

But Koester looked at the boy, at his face. He was searching for something. He didn't know exactly what it was—maybe a twitch at the corner of his eye or the beginning of a smile on his lips. He'd know what it was if he saw it. He didn't have much time. Jill wasn't going to put up with this shit too much longer. He damned sure wouldn't if he were in her place.

"Maybe you broke something," he hurried, "or dropped something. And George got mad at you, started shouting at you. Hell, you'd be scared. Anyone could understand tha—"

Jill stepped between her boy and the sheriff, as if blocking a bullet fired at her son. Her nostrils flared, and she held her hands up as if she was going to strike him, actually hit him.

"Get out of here," she hissed.

"I got a few more—"

Jill pointed a crooked finger at him and said, "You get out of here right now, Doug Koester. And if you come back I'll see to it the mayor takes your damned badge away."

That was not too likely.

But it was equally unlikely he'd get anything out of the boy. It was a long shot that Evan had anything to do with George Hayward's death. What he'd really wanted to do was shake the kid up a little. The fact was Evan Gregory was probably the last person, besides the murderer, to see George Hayward alive—and he knew something. Koester could tell that. Maybe George had said something to him, given him a clue that he knew someone was after him. The kid would be afraid to talk about it out of fear the killer would come after him. That was how Koester figured it.

But the boy was cool. Maybe he was a little bent, too. Anyone who'd sit in their bed and jack-off with a noose around their neck—and that was what he'd done—had to be a little off.

Doc was right. The kid might have done something like that because of something he'd seen, something too awful for him to accept.

Something like George Hayward getting his hand sawed off at the wrist and his face pounded in with a fucking hammer would be pretty awful.

Without a word, Koester turned and left the hospital room.

Alan Landano sat in the third seat of the first row, listening to Miss Neilson telling the news to the class.

"We don't know how long Evan's going to be in the hospital, but I think it would be nice if we let him know how much we miss him. Don't you agree, class?"

Most of the 13- and 14-year-old heads began to bob. One of the girls in the first row of the class waved her arm frantically.

"Yes, Amy?"

"Miss Neilson, how come he's in the hospital?"

"I didn't get all of the details from Mrs. Gregory, but I believe he fell on the stairs at his home."

There were a few painful "ooohs" from the class before the English teacher reached into the brown paper bag on her desk and pulled out the get well card. She held it up for all to see.

"I'm going to pass this around and I'd like all of you to sign it."

Alan wished he was sitting in the fifth row or even the second row. It would give him more time to think of an answer. He knew he wasn't going to get away with it because Marcie Conklin was sitting behind him and she had a crush on Evan. Besides, she was a troublemaker.

Sure enough, when he passed the card back to her Marcie looked at it and jabbed him in the back. She shoved the card over his shoulder and said, "You didn't sign it, dummy."

Alan tried to bury his face in his English book, but he knew Marcie wouldn't give up. He knew exactly what was going to happen. It was like watching something he'd seen all before.

She leaned closer, her voice more insistent. "Alan, I said you didn't sign the card."

Over his shoulder, Alan whispered, "Just pass it on, will you, Marcie?"

"But you've got to sign the card. We've all got to sign the card."

"I'm not signing it."

"Why not?"

"Because I'm just not and if you'd just—"

"Miss Neilson, Miss Neilson, Alan won't sign the card."

The teacher looked up from the compositions she was grading. She didn't particularly like Marcie Conklin. She didn't like snitches, even though they had their purpose. Brenda Neilson thought the girl must be wrong this time, though. Alan Landano was no troublemaker. He was one of her best students and got along with almost everyone in her class.

"Marcie, you don't have to shout."

"But he won't sign the card, Miss Neilson."

The rest of the students intently watched the exchange, their heads rotating from teacher to student as if it was Lendl and McEnroe.

"Take a look at the card, Marcie. I'm sure Alan's signed it."

"But he didn't."

She looked at Alan, who was reading and seemingly oblivious to the conversation. "Alan?" When he didn't look up she repeated his name a bit louder.

He looked at her with dread. "Yes, Ma'am?"

"Did you sign Evan's card?"

"No, Ma'am."

She was confused in that moment. It was not at all like Alan Landano.

Miss Neilson said, "Marcie, give Alan the card so he can sign it."

In an even voice, Alan said, "I'm not going to sign it."

Her eyebrows knitted as she tried to understand what was wrong. "Why not?"

"Because I don't like Evan Gregory."

"Alan, that's a very impolite thing to say."

"It's the truth."

She leveled her gaze. "Truth or not, I want

you to sign that card. Evan's in the hospital and you ought to—"

"I'm glad he's in the hospital, and I hope he stays there. I—"

The air in the classroom shattered as Brenda Neilson smashed her open palm down on the desk. Pain flared in her hand and sheeted up her arm, the way it did when she'd slap King, her German shepherd, on the flanks if he made a mess in the house. It was just as stupid. She never really hurt King by slapping him on the butt, and she hadn't thrown any fear into Alan Landano by crashing her hand on her desk. All she'd done was hurt her hand and that made her angry.

"That'll be enough," she said, standing. "I think you'd better come with me, Alan."

He glared at her, disliking the fact that she was embarrassing him simply because he'd told the truth. It didn't make sense, the way a lot of things didn't make sense.

"Where are we going?"

"To see Principal Fortmann. I want you to tell him what you told me."

A low rumble of "ooohs" swept through the class again, and Miss Neilson silenced them with a baleful gaze. "I'll be gone for five minutes," he warned, "and if Mr. Bateman across the hall tells me there was any commotion while I was gone, you can all plan on staying after school."

The classroom became a tomb and stayed

that way the whole 15 minutes Brenda Neilson was away.

It was strange how things turn out, John thought. He had dreaded moving to the small town because he thought it would have none of the excitement he'd known in Miami. Well, it had more than enough excitement, even if it wasn't of the type he was accustomed to.

He had that light-headed, giddy feeling that comes from a lack of sleep, and he realized how long it had been since he'd slept soundly. Sunday night was a complete loss and Monday he'd only caught a few snatches here and there. He would sleep tonight, though. He was beginning to get distance, and distance was what mattered. Even with only a few days since Sunday night, he was beginning to feel a little better. The experience with the confessional was starting to take on a dreamlike quality, as if it hadn't really happened.

Only it had happened.

Discovering George Hayward's body was almost welcome, he thought morbidly. It immediately distracted him from thinking about the confessional and what had happened.

Sheriff Koester gave him the third degree, and there had been Tom Conforte to think about. Later, he had called Warren and Molly to keep himself from thinking about his own problems.

But now, with time passing, he began to

think about it again. It was like a night-mare—the blinding rope of light lassoing him and pulling him toward the booth, the sound raging in his ears, the church all lit up in the middle of the night.

He thought it might have been some sort of hysterical reaction to his sinning with the girl in Millburg. Only that hadn't really been a sin. Sin or not, he was still feeling terribly guilty about it.

He'd spent hours in meditation and prayer, and all he could do was hope he'd been absolved.

Monday night he agonized over what it would be like hearing confession again. How could he go back into that box after what had happened? He didn't know if he had the courage.

But with morning light came bravery. Just because you suffered a heart attack, it didn't mean you could never jog again. Besides, he had to hear confessions. It was part of his duty. Monday morning never saw the queues that lined up on Sundays, but there were always a few older Catholic ladies who attended Mass every day and who went to con-fession often.

Halfway through the third confession he began to feel foolish. Thank God there was a screen separating him from Audrey McAlister because he'd actually smiled.

Though it was a smile of relief, it was more than that. He was laughing at himself. It was wood and nails. That was all. He was sitting in a box that was just another vessel of the Church. If it had any mystical qualities at all they were good qualities because the Church was good. He believed that in his heart and rethinking it strengthened him.

After he said Mass, John called Art's Electric Co. from the rectory.

"Sure, Father," the thick Midwestern voice on the other end said. "I'm free this afternoon. What's the problem?"

"I'm not positive, but I think we have a short somewhere in the church."

"Wouldn't be the first time."

John stiffened. "Oh?"

"Yep."

He pressed the electrician. "There was an electrical problem out here before?"

Now Art sounded less sure. "Don't recall what I found. It was a long ways back, when Father Nicoletti was there. I'll look it up in my records before I come out."

"Fine. I'll see you this afternoon then."

"See you, Father."

John hung up the phone and went to the kitchen of his house. He made himself a tuna sandwich drowned in mayonnaise. After he cut it he looked up and out the square window over the sink.

The wind was picking up, and a transparent haze of blowing snow hovered over the back-yard. Tall, naked trees swayed beneath the invisible force. He wished they were palm trees and felt no guilt about wishing so. Maybe before, but not now. Before it had been his wounded ego that was angry about being shunted off to the boondocks. But now he was a prisoner in a town where people were being killed and where a church harbored a Godforsaken monster disguising itself as a confessional booth.

So that was the truth of it.

The knock at the door startled him so badly that he pushed the dish with the tuna sandwich off the counter. He watched, idiotically, as it tumbled through the air. At the last second he made a stab for the falling plate and managed to bang his knuckles into the front of the cabinet.

"Damn!" he shouted at the same time the plate hit the linoleum and shattered.

The knock at the front door came again and he called, "Coming."

For a second he stayed in a crouch, undecided about trying to mop up the mess or going to the door. The mess could wait.

Jill did a little jig on the doorstep, trying to beat off the wind chill factor. The green jacket she had on was supposed to be filled with down, but it was cheap polyester down and the Wisconsin wind knew what to do with it.

She had tried the church first. Surprisingly, it was open, even though it was way past

Mass, but Father Hines wasn't inside. Jill almost left, but she remembered what he'd said.

"That's what I'm here for. Any time you need help or if you just want to talk, you feel free to call me or visit."

It was time to find out if he was conning her or he'd meant it. She had always been able to depend on Father Thyssen and Father Nicoletti and Father Dreiband, but she knew them better, too. She'd grown up with them.

Maybe she was being unfair. Maybe he was like them, too. Maybe all priests were kind and loving and willing to help. Maybe it was in their nature.

She'd find out soon, because she needed help.

The door opened and the look on his face set her off right away. She'd interrupted something. He was in the middle of something when this dumb, helpless widow who couldn't get her shit together had pounded on his door.

"I'm sorry, Father. I didn't mean to . . ."

Then he smiled an easy smile, and she felt less cold. He moved out of the doorway and said, "Come in, Jill. It's good to see you."

She walked tentatively into the house, glad to be out of the cold but still not quite certain she was welcome.

"I came at a bad time, didn't I?"

"Not at all. I was just . . . I just finished lunch." He closed the door. "Can I take your coat?"

236

As Jill unzipped it, she began to cry, almost with no effort. Tears tracked down over her rosy cheeks one after another, and it was a few seconds before John even was aware of her crying.

He'd hung her jacket up and was walking her into the living room when he heard her trying to catch her breath. That was when he looked at her and saw the tears.

"Jill, what's the matter?"

She shook her head, unable to talk for a moment, so John led her to the sofa where she sat down. He pulled a linen handkerchief from his pocket and handed it to her.

"Can I get you something? Some water?"

She shook her head. "No, thank you, Father." She wiped at the tears, trying to push them back up into her eyes. "I feel so dumb crying like this."

"Sometimes crying is good." He looked away for a moment, then said, "Would you like to talk about it?"

"It's Evan," she said, clutching the handkerchief and twisting it a bit. "He's in the hospital."

John's voice dropped as he asked, "Is it serious?"

She shrugged. "I don't know. I can't talk to you about that now." Her eyes hurt, and she clenched them shut for a moment. But that only made them hurt more. She thought she was going to cry again, but then the feeling passed. The warmth of the room helped. If she had to tell him about it out on the landing she knew she would have cried more.

But here it was warm, and she thought that maybe part of the reason she had been crying was because it was so damned cold out and she had such a useless damned jacket and she wished she had something warmer. Years ago, when she and Ned were first married, he used to cling close to her from behind, wrapping his arms around her and pretending to be a coat. But now she had to fight off the cold alone, and she was getting tired of fighting. It was a losing battle. Every year the winters seemed to get colder and she seemed to get a little weaker and now here she was breaking down and crying in front of the new priest.

Jill pulled herself together and said, "Ask Doc Brannigan. He'll tell you about Evan. I'll tell him it's all right to tell you."

John measured the woman as if searching for wind while sailing. Surely she was crying because her son was in the hospital. But if she didn't want to talk about it, then what had she come to him for? How could he help her if she wouldn't let go?

Cancer, leukemia? Those images visited him and he cringed at the thought, remembering how Evan had frolicked in his backyard the last time Jill had visited.

As if reading his grim thoughts, Jill said, "It's nothing fatal. It's bad, but not that bad. That's not even the reason I'm here, the reason I'm crying like a dumb . . ."

He took her hand, which was warmer than he'd expected, and asked, "Then why are you here, Jill?"

Anger flamed in her as she thought about the answer and pulled her hand from his. John was worried that he'd offended her by taking her hand, but she said, "It's that damn Doug Koester." She looked at the priest sitting next to her and said, without much regret, "You'll just have to excuse me for blaspheming, Father, but if ever a man deserved to be cursed it's that sheriff."

"What did he do?"

"He as much as accused Evan of having something to do with George's death."

He tried to imagine the sheriff accusing Evan Gregory of killing George Hayward and found he could not, not that Koester wasn't intimidating enough. He'd intimidated him, or at least tried to, when he'd met him at Hayward's house. But Koester didn't impress him as a fool, and only a fool would accuse a 13-year-old boy of murdering a man as big as George. Sheer size worked against it, if nothing else. A kid of 90 pounds doesn't take on a 235-pound man. And even if they did they didn't slice their hands off with a saw and then chase them around the house afterwards.

"Jill, are you sure of what you're saying?"

"I know what he asked and the way he asked it."

"The way he asked it? Then he didn't actually—"

"He didn't have to," she snapped. "I know what he meant."

"You should have heard the way he talked to me."

"He talked to you?"

"Of course. I phoned him from George's house when I was there."

"You mean you were there? With George dead and . . ."

John nodded.

She closed her eyes. "The last few days have been bad for me. I've been so caught up with Evan being in the hospital that I've lost touch with the world."

"And I think that's part of the problem. You've probably gotten yourself completely run down. A little rest and you'll be fine."

That was when the tears came again.

Tears were something John had difficulty with. He could handle counseling, problem-solving, working things through logically. And he could squeeze a donation to the church out of rich parishioners all right.

But condolence calls, giving comfort to the suffering and grieving, were difficult for him. Not because he was cold. Quite the opposite. He was so sensitive to their grief that their pain often became his pain. He could not remain removed from it, apart from it.

He was watching Jill Gregory with one part of his mind, but another part was bathed in a rainbow glow of understanding. That was it, of course! That was why the confessional had such an effect on him, why he had become aroused when he had heard the young girl's confession. It had to do with him, not the booth.

He had overly empathized. He had cared too much. He had allowed himself to be too impressionable. In trying to understand the girl's lust he had let it become a part of him.

John felt enormous relief swarm over him. It was so simple. It explained everything.

Everything except that light reaching out and pulling him toward the booth and what was inside.

John felt his skin chill. That was what really frightened him—the thing that was inside. What was it? Father Dreiband? Blood? Himself?

He shook off the feeling. There wasn't anything to be frightened about, because there was nothing inside the confessional except some wooden benches, a divider and a screen. What was inside was a place to perform the duties of his cloth.

He looked at Jill, remembering that he was needed and feeling ashamed that he was thinking about himself when there was a weeping woman sitting next to him on the sofa. He took her hand in his again, hoping it would stop her from crying, but it only made her cry more.

His heart began to pound as he watched the tears rolling down her face. Her eyes, large and still pretty, shimmered behind a wavering liquid pain. Her bottom lip quivered out of control as she said, "I'm so frightened, Father."

"There's nothing to be scared of."

"There is," she insisted between sobs. Her sentences came in jerky gasps. "Sheriff Koester hates me and Evan . . . Poor George dead . . . What Evan must think . . . Worried about my son . . . Some killer loose in Nettleton . . ."

He was stroking her hand, ministering to her fears, and all the while he felt the heat rising in him like the black hood of a big Buick roasting in the July midday sun. It didn't get hot on you all at once and you could never tell the exact moment it turned to fire, but if you happened to jump up on that hood in your bathing suit (like John had when he was seven) you'd get a lesson you'd remember all your life.

He would never know the exact second when he passed over from comforting Jill Gregory to something that was oh, so different. But once he was there he knew he was there.

There was a slipping, desperate last beat when he still had a chance to reach out and lock his hands around a branch and try to pull himself out. But it was so sweet to give in, oh, so sweet. Why not give in? Why not enjoy it? What was there to run back to? To a town where people cut each other's hands off before they hammered their faces in?

The resistance fought in him, trying to give him strength.

But his feet were leaden, and he realized it wasn't his feet, but his mind. Why think? What mattered was the continuous rise and fall of her breasts as she shuddered with sobs. They were small breasts, and they were firm and jutting out, and Christ, did he want to touch them. Through white cotton he could see the pattern of lace on her bra and knew what lay beneath.

He looked into her face and saw that she had been watching him as he stared at her breasts. Jill's lips were puffed, but he didn't know if it was arousal or the sobs that had puffed them. Maybe both. He could see her, but something hung in the air between them. Thick hot sensuality would not let him pull away because that last moment of resistance had passed. The strength had ebbed and in its place was only shared passion, and John knew that he had to have her and that she wanted him.

Their lips met and hers parted. He felt the swirl of her tongue as it passed over his lips. How could anything taste so soft and yielding? He kissed her face, the tears scalding against his lips and her arms laced around his neck, at once tentative and urging.

When they kissed again all pretense was gone. It was hunger and they hurried to devour each other.

John felt the throbbing not just in his groin but throughout every part, every nerve in his body. He was galvanized and being shaken by a force that dwarfed that which had grasped him two nights earlier in the church. There it had been a bolt shooting out toward him, but here it was a completed circuit and each was energizing the other.

As John moved his hands up the front of her blouse, her neck hinged back as though it had been snapped. He closed his fingers on her left breast and felt the low growl begin deep in her throat.

"Yes . . ." she gasped. "Do that. Touch me there."

And he did, moving his hand in lazy circles, feeling her breasts stiffen in his palm, feeling her nipples grow taut between his thumb and forefinger.

John closed his eyes as he felt Jill reach for him and begin to stroke him steadily. He opened his eyes and saw the look of carnal pleasure on her face at what she had discovered between his thighs. Then he closed his eyes and drew her against his body, wanting to touch as much of her as he could, wanting to possess her completely.

"So good," she groaned. "I need you, John. I want you now."

Her hand was on the buckle of his belt when Sheriff Koester knocked on the front door.

CHAPTER 9

An hour before Jill drove to the church, Tom Conforte was squatting behind a clump of bushes, slapping his gloved hands together in an attempt to drive circulation back into them. He was tired and cold and hungry. The night before had been spent in Stu Kopernik's barn, but it had been a full day since he'd eaten anything.

He had to get out of town, but he knew he couldn't use the Mustang for that. The word would be out on him, and they'd pick him up before he could get anywhere. He was also worried about the .38. He only had four rounds of ammunition, which wasn't going to do him much good if things got rough.

He squinted, watching Deputy Russell

Patterson's house for signs of life. There had been no movement during the half hour he'd been squatting in the bushes. The longer he sat there, the more certain he was of his plan.

He knew Russell well enough. The deputy was a councilman for the church, and Frank had been an altar boy. Russell would pick up his younger brother and drive him to the church a few times a week, so Tom used to shoot the breeze with him now and then, enough to know Russell worked the night shift and would probably be sleeping this early in the morning.

The green Bronco police car was parked on the side of the house. Inside were probably a couple of handguns, maybe even a riot gun, and plenty of ammunition. He'd tie Russell up, take a uniform and some ammunition, then use the Bronco to put some miles between him and Nettleton. It'd be 12 hours before Russell was missed. Tom figured he could make Canada in that much time. Along the way he'd abandon the police car and steal another auto. It was his only shot.

Wind whipped around the house and the five acres of barren land that surrounded it as Tom moved from behind the bushes. He walked toward the house, feeling the press of the .38 in the waistband of his jeans.

Inside the house, behind the curtains of the bedroom, Russell Patterson watched the youngster. He fingered the trigger of the gun cradled in his arms.

John was ten when his mother caught him "playing doctor" with Trish Rayburn in the den of their apartment in Baltimore. Caught was probably the wrong word. Actually, she'd stumbled in on them. The two children looked up with youthful terror as she wandered past the den.

Yvonne Hines was a good-hearted woman who loved her son. He had a destiny to fulfill. She felt that since he was able to walk. Her husband was an agent for State Farm, and life was good for them. When she first walked past that open door and saw an expression of supreme shock on the children's faces, she all but burst out laughing. She would have, too, if she didn't know how embarrassed they already were.

She did the best she could, quickly covering her smile and walking on down the hall. On her way back she checked in the den again and—everyone hastily dressed, now—asked if anyone would care for some lunch.

It happened so fast that John was almost convinced that she hadn't seen him. For a week he couldn't look at his mother, even though she tried her damnedest to pretend nothing had happened. In time he forgot about it, at least consciously forgot about it. He never thought about how fortunate he was to have a mother who had her head together. He never reflected about how a different kind of woman—a woman like Jill Gregory's mother, Sally—could have used the incident to goad and torment him, to scar him for life.

Now, as he straightened the front of his shirt and watched Jill hurriedly tuck her blouse into her skirt, it all came flooding back to him and he was sure that his mother really had seen him and Trish. He blessed her memory for the way she had handled it.

John brushed his hand across his face, feeling the flush of embarrassment still there. He couldn't look at Jill right now. What had passed between them would have to be dealt with at another time. What was important was keeping whoever had knocked on the door from finding out.

He glanced at Jill and her blouse, to make sure she looked presentable. Then he crossed the living room and opened the door.

Sheriff Koester nodded. "Morning, Father. Mind if I come in?"

The smile on John's lips felt false, like the smile he had forced when a major cocaine supplier in Miami had donated $20,000 to the church. Snorting his way to salvation!

"Certainly, Sheriff." John closed the door and said, "Mrs. Gregory is visiting me. Her son is in the hospital, I'm sorry to say."

Koester stiffened and touched the brim of his cap. "Yes, I know." He looked past John. "I'm sorry about what happened back at the hospital, Jill."

She turned away from him, looking to the fireplace.

"You have to understand we've got two dead people on our hands. I have to check out—"

"You have to interrogate my son like he's a criminal?" Jill shot as she turned toward him.

"You misunderstand. I didn't mean—"

"Yes, you did."

Koester folded his arms. His voice softened with sincerity. "If you took it that way, I apologize." He paused a moment, then added, "And I'll apologize to your son, too, if you like."

John felt the tension build between them. Then Jill backed down, maybe because she felt guilty herself. "Oh, forget it. Maybe I'm just nervous because he's in the hospital."

"I could understand that."

Jill picked up her coat and said, "Thank you for seeing me, Father Hines. I'll talk to you soon."

John looked at her for the first time since Koester had knocked on the door and was struck by how natural she seemed, as if nothing had happened between the two of them. He felt a slight chill creep up his back. He wouldn't want to play poker against this woman, he thought.

"I hope Evan is better. I'd be happy to stop at the hospital and see him."

They walked to the door, Koester warming himself by the fireplace.

"Doc says he should be able to go home tomorrow, but I appreciate your asking."

After Jill left, Koester said, "I guess she told you we had a run-in at the hospital."

"She mentioned it."

"Strong-headed woman."

"A lot of women are like that when it comes to their children."

"Wouldn't know. Essie was never able to bear."

"I'm sorry."

"I'm not. Not particularly. Don't think I'd be too good a father."

"That's an odd thing to say."

"It's the plain truth. I don't have the patience for children. Maybe it's because I've been in law enforcement for so long. You get used to things going by the book—regulations. Kids shouldn't have to grow up with all those regulations. They ought to be able to run loose for a little while." He shook his head. "My kids wouldn't be able to do that."

"Why not?"

"I wouldn't let them. I know I wouldn't."

"Can I get you some coffee?"

"No thanks. Got to get into the office. I just stopped by to ask you a question."

Koester peeled the cellophane from a cigar, bit off the tip, spit it into the fireplace and lit up. John smiled. The man had seen too many episodes of *Columbo*, he reflected.

"With all the excitement over at George's

254

place, I forgot to ask you why you were there."

"I went out there to see him about the confessional."

Koester faced his backside to the fire. "What about it?"

"One of the seats is in need of repair. I wanted him to have a look at it, since he built it in the first place."

"Why didn't you just telephone him?"

As if on cue, the phone rang. John picked it up. "Hello?" He listened, then said, "For you, Sheriff."

Koester took the phone. "Yeah?" It was Koester's turn to listen. After a moment he said, "I'll be there." He hung up and began buttoning his coat. "I have to go, Father Hines."

"Sounds serious."

"Maybe." As he walked toward the door he said, "We'll talk again."

John gripped the doorknob. "You don't believe me, do you?"

Koester stopped by the door and put his cap on. "Should I?"

"It's the truth. I went to George's house to talk to him about the confessional."

"I got a feeling you're holding something back. Don't know why, just yet. I will, though. You can make book on that."

Then Koester left.

Tom Conforte had only been to Russell's

house twice, once to borrow the deputy's shotgun for his father—Warren's was in the shop unexpectedly and he had duck hunting plans—and once to return it.

There was a door off the kitchen in back and that was where he was now. It wasn't locked. Tom wasn't surprised. Nettleton was one of those towns where not many people locked their doors. Anyway, who'd be dumb enough to try and break in on the town's deputy?

He eased the door open and stepped inside, closing it behind him. He looked down and felt a pang of guilt at the gray slush he was tracking on the floor.

He pulled the .38 as soon as he heard Russell say, "You want to be careful Tom. Real careful."

He looked toward the door that opened into the dining room. Russell's voice was coming from in there. There was neither fear nor anger in it. It was the voice of a deputy sheriff, all right.

"How'd you know it was me?"

"I've been watching you out there for twenty minutes. I wondered when the hell you'd come in."

"Well, I'm in."

"And you're armed. That's not good, Tom. You want to be thankful I'm not Sheriff Koester."

"That's why I'm here and not at his place."

"It'd be a mistake for you to think I'm a soft touch," Russell's voice answered.

"All I want is your car and some ammunition."

The deputy laughed. "Oh, is that all?"

"It isn't funny, Russell."

"No. You're right. It isn't funny. You've got yourself in a bad jam, kid. You can get out of it, but you've got to do it now, before it gets worse."

"That's just what I plan on doing."

"You're going about it the wrong way."

"It's my choice."

"Right. But it's the wrong choice."

"I want that car and that ammunition," Tom said, taking a step toward the open doorway.

"You show yourself in that doorway and the only ammunition you'll get is what's in my gun." When Tom didn't say anything, Russell added, "Ever see what a riot gun can do? I'm not talking about in the movies—*Dirty Harry* or that shit. I'm talking about for real, Tom. You'll spend your last seconds alive trying to stuff your guts back into your belly."

"I've got a gun."

"I know you do." Russell softened his voice. "Look, you've got to give it up now. Nothing can be as bad as what's going to happen if you don't." Sincere concern crept into Russell's voice now. "I know what you're going through. I knew Frank, you know. He was a good kid. But he's dead and that's it."

"I didn't kill George."

"I believe you."

"Koester doesn't."

257

Russell snapped, "What Koester believes doesn't mean shit."

"The hell it doesn't." He was going to slip on the goddamned linoleum floor. He was going to fall on his ass right in Russell Patterson's kitchen, and then Patterson would rush in with that riot gun and snuff him.

"He doesn't matter," Russell insisted. "Sure, he can take you down to the station and lock you up and question you. But if you didn't kill George, then that's that."

"I didn't."

"Then put the gun down and let's go talk about it."

"I've got to get out of here."

"It's too late for that," Russell said.

"What do you mean?"

"Look out the window over the dishwasher."

Tom turned, but slowly, glancing back to the doorway to make sure Russell wasn't going to try something funny.

Then he saw the two prowl cars parked out past the bushes he had been using for cover. Yeah, it was too late.

Like a kid, he asked, "How'd they get there?"

"I called them. You never had a chance of pulling this off, Tom. Now put the gun down and let's talk."

Tom took another step toward the doorway and he heard the slick, swift, clean sound of

Russell sliding the Remington into the ready position.

"Don't do it, Tom. Please," Russell said, really meaning it. "I don't want this to happen."

"Tom . . ." A metallic, but familiar voice echoed in the distance. "Tom, this is Dad."

"Shit," he moaned, the .38 suddenly heavy in his hand.

And then Russell capped it. His voice was gentle and pleading as he asked, "Do you really want to do this to your parents? Isn't it enough they've lost one son already?"

When Tom started to cry, Russell eased off the trigger of the riot gun. It was over.

At 3:30, while Tom Conforte was eating eggs and bacon and toast in his cell, Henry Landano was in a small office off the chancel talking with Father Hines. Neither of them knew that Tom Conforte had surrendered himself to Sheriff Koester that morning.

"It's not like Alan to cause trouble, Father."

"He doesn't seem that kind of boy to me."

Henry nodded, eager for encouragement. "He's always made his mother and me proud. Good grades and, of course, his being altar boy at the church and all."

John watched as the slight man fidgeted. He impressed him as a man not used to trouble and reluctant to ask others for help when it came.

To confirm John's thoughts, the man said, "I wouldn't bring this to you, except for what he told me." He smiled nervously. "Kids say funny things. Act funny. A parent can handle most of it, but with an adopted boy . . . We love Alan like he was our own, but we just don't know all there is to know about his background. You put most of it off to growing up."

John wanted to reassure him that everything was all right, yet he could tell how concerned the man was and didn't want to sound flip.

Henry shook his head. "But this . . ."

"Why don't you tell me about it, Mr. Landano. Sometimes if you share a problem it makes it easier."

"Yes. Alan's out in the church," he said, stalling the issue. "I hope you'll talk to him after we're through."

"Of course I will. Alan and I get along well. I'm sure whatever it is can be worked out."

"I wish I was sure of that." Henry said, "Well, I told you about how he wouldn't sign Evan Gregory's card."

John folded his hands, noting how it was with people who were troubled, how they always backtracked, how they'd do anything they could to avoid taking that final plunge.

"Yes, you did."

"Elmer Fortmann called me about it. We

know each other, play a little poker once in a while. He was pretty upset, and I can't say I blame him. Surprised me, I'll tell you that.''

John nodded.

Henry drew a breath and took the plunge. "So, when I got Alan home I asked him about it. He told me he didn't care about Evan. Told me the boy could die in the hospital as far as he was concerned. I can't believe he could say a thing like that, that Evan could just die and he wouldn't care.''

"That surprises me, too," John said and it did. The father was right. It didn't sound at all like Alan Landano, not the Alan Landano John knew. "Did he know about George Hayward?"

"I don't know. I suppose he could have heard about it in school. You know how kids are.''

"Yes." John tapped his finger on the desk top. "That could be part of it. There have been some bad shocks for the community lately. The Conforte boy and now Mr. Hayward. You never knew how it affects children.''

That was for sure, John thought, recalling his conversation with Doctor Brannigan at noon. It hadn't been easy to draw it out of the physician, and John thought part of it was because he was a clergyman. In fact, Brannigan had even told him he'd have to speak with Jill before he could give him the details.

But apparently she told him it was all right, because when Brannigan called back he told him the story, although haltingly. John found his sensibilities tested. It was one thing to read about a drug dealer who had donated $20,000 to your church being found in the trunk of a car with his hands cuffed behind his back and a bullet in his head a week later. It was something else to learn about a young boy tying a belt around his neck and . . .

But Henry Landano didn't know about the Miami coke dealer and he didn't know why Evan Gregory was in the hospital. All he knew was that his son wasn't acting the way a boy was supposed to act.

"But to say something like that about a schoolmate. It worries me, Father. I can't remember ever feeling that way when I was a youngster. Can you?"

"No, but these are different times. What did he say when you asked him about it?"

"He wouldn't say anything more." Then, hesitantly, Henry said, "Except that he wanted to talk to you."

"To me?" John asked, suddenly understanding that it was at Alan's insistence that they were here.

"Yes. He said he had to talk with Father Hines."

When they traded places Alan hardly looked

at his father. Now that Henry was out in the church and Alan was sitting across the desk in the small office, he seemed less upset than his father about the matter. The boy apparently had made up his mind about something.

"Alan, your father tells me you've had a problem at school."

"It's no problem, Father."

"Your father's concerned."

He frowned. "I know he is. I'm sorry about that, but it can't be helped."

"Why didn't you sign that get well card for Evan Gregory?"

"Because I don't like him."

"What has he done to you?"

"Nothing yet. But he will."

John leaned forward in his chair. "What are you talking about, Alan?"

"You'll have to find that out for yourself, Father. I can't tell you. I wish I could, but I can't. I'm too young."

"You can tell me whatever's on your mind. It won't go any further."

"Like a confession, huh?"

"Yes," John said, but he was struck more by the expression on the boy's face than his words. It was an expression that told him he knew about the confessional, and John felt the skin on the back of his neck tighten.

"Alan . . ."

"No, I can't. I'm too afraid. He's powerful."

"Evan?"

"Yes."

John leaned back in his chair, his hands suddenly damp. It was moving too fast. It was getting away from him again. It was getting past him. "I don't understand what you're talking about."

Then Alan said, "I don't want to end up like Frank Conforte."

It wasn't a boy talking to him anymore. It was a fugitive. He was frightened, but he wasn't a boy. He was a hunted man who was telling John that they were on the same side.

Alan added, "And I don't want to end up like Father Dreiband."

John leveled his gaze. "This is a serious matter you're talking about now."

"I know."

"Frank Conforte was murdered."

"I know, Father Hines. And he was this church's altar boy, just like I am now."

"Alan . . ."

"I can't say anymore. I'm taking a big enough chance as it is." Alan stood and John was surprised to see the boy was as small as he was. "If you want to know more you'll have to talk with Father Nicoletti."

"Nicoletti? The priest who was here before Father Dreiband?"

"Yes."

"What does he . . . ?"

Alan's voice was shaking. His voice sounded

like a boy's voice again. "I can't tell you any more. I just can't."

John stood and said, "All right, Alan. You can go."

CHAPTER 10

Cindy drove into Nettleton on Thursday morning. The news hit her hard, the way the news of a devastating climactic event hits people. People who were forced out of their homes and onto Red Cross cots in gymnasiums would be in a state of shock or panic or fear. It hit them hard, but they knew, in advance, that the storm was coming. It was only a question of intensity.

That was what it was like for Cindy Breslauer. Sitting in Benny's on Sunday night she knew something bad was going to happen, or had already happened, to George. What she didn't know was that he was already rotting flesh. Death is the great negotiator. You pawn off bad memories for the good, and because you make the deal you get to slough off a little of your guilt at having disliked someone who was now dead.

"The good that men do lives after them. The evil is oft interred with their bones. So let it be with George Hayward."

She smiled, knowing she'd gotten the quote ass-backwards and thinking George would have liked that since that was the position he preferred women in when he screwed them.

George had been a job, good pay, laughs, gifts, a chance to drive around in a flashy Cadillac and some high old times in the sack. So what if he was a little kinky? She wondered what she'd be like when and if she made it to his age, especially if she ended up being a fat slob like he was, which was a distinct possibility.

That was why she was going to the funeral. It had ended badly for them, but in all honesty she had to admit there were more good times than bad. She owed him her last respects. It was only right.

She recognized some of the people in the church as former customers at the woodcraft shop. To a few she nodded. It was a closed coffin ceremony, and Cindy had heard the reason for that. Actually, she was grateful. She had no desire to see George again, alive or dead.

The church was surprisingly crowded, so Cindy sat back, listening to a few speakers talk about how George had donated to this building fund and how he'd sponsored a little league team and what an all around great guy he was.

It was hot in the church, the heat really pumping away, and Cindy nearly dozed off. John's voice was like a splash of ice water on her face. She sat up with a jerk as she heard his voice. She was good with voices and recognized his immediately.

As she looked toward the altar she focused on him standing in his white vestments. There was not even a moment's doubt that it was the man who picked her up in Benny's, and it was all she could do to restrain herself from laughing. What a perfect priest to oversee George's funeral, she thought.

"You're Cindy Breslauer, aren't you?"
She turned at the question and looked at the heavyset man in the sheriff's uniform. She didn't know Koester by name, but she'd seen him around Nettleton. He was the kind of guy who gave what used to be known as bad vibes, the kind of guy you played it very straight with.

"Yes, I am." She watched as the six pall-bearers loaded the coffin into a waiting hearse.

"Going to the cemetery?"
She nodded.
"No hurry," Koester said. "You can follow me. I'll walk you to your car." As they walked, he said, "You worked in George's shop,

right?"

"That's right."

"And what else?"

Cindy glanced at him. He knew. "Do you always ask questions you know the answer to?"

Koester grinned. "Sometimes."

"Only when you want to catch people in a lie, huh?"

"Something like that." Koester nodded as Brad Hamilton walked past him. Then he lowered his voice and said, "You got nothing to worry about."

"I'm glad to hear that."

"Wasn't no woman that did that to George, poor bastard."

"Look, Sheriff, George and I were close. You know what I mean."

"Yeah, I do. I also heard you quit working for him. Why's that?"

"We had a argument. I suppose that makes me a suspect or something?"

"I already told you you got nothing to worry about."

"Then why are you—"

"Do you know a fella named Tom Conforte?"

She thought as they stopped by the car. "No, I don't."

Koester pulled a copy of a yearbook picture of Tom out of his pocket and showed it to her. "He ever come in the shop while you were there?"

"No."

"Don't answer so fast. Look at the picture. It could be important."

She looked at it more closely. "I don't recognize him. I'd tell you if I did."

"I believe that."

"Who is he?"

"A suspect."

"You think he killed George?"

"Could be. I got him locked up at the jail." He opened the driver's side door for her and said, "I may want to ask you some more questions. You mind?"

"Anything I can do to help."

"Good."

She got in and Koester closed the door.

Cindy had to hold the steering wheel hard as she drove the car. She knew her hands wanted to shake. Until now she'd only thought about the fact that George was dead. Now, having spoken with the sheriff, she realized someone had actually murdered George, a man she'd slept with. It could have happened any time. Someone could have broken into the house while she was there, in his bed, and killed both of them.

There were times you made eye contact with the people you were speaking to and times when you didn't. A funeral was one of the times you didn't, John felt. You didn't because you were speaking more to the person being buried than to the mourners.

Maybe that wasn't right. You could argue, he thought, that the mourners needed to be comforted. But he believed this was the last mortal contact the deceased would have and that even though his soul had already passed out of his body, there was still a small mortal spark that lingered for the final address.

John finished the prayer and nodded. The coffin was lowered into the grave. He'd been at funerals where it went badly. Grief could be either paralyzing or mobilizing. The grief-stricken could wail and scream, and he had presided over funerals like that. It could get to you.

George Hayward's funeral was different, partly because the man didn't have any close kin. A cousin from Chicago had come up, but he had told John they hadn't spoken for some time. Most of the 20 or so people gathered around were friends or business acquaintances.

After it was over, John looked around the circle. It had grown since the final service began, latecomers closing up the ranks. He smiled his benevolent smile until he saw Cindy.

She was looking straight at him. John felt his eyes grow large in their sockets as blood pumped through his skull at a furious pace. There was no question it was the girl, no question at all. He forced himself to look away from her.

Next he looked at Sheriff Koester. All he

needed was for the girl to tell Koester about him. He'd all but forgotten that she said she knew George. His mind had tried to wipe the whole incident out, but now it was back to haunt him, possibly to ruin him.

But it wouldn't go that way. When he looked at her again he knew that much. It wasn't threat he saw in her eyes or anger or even surprise. It was amusement. Just a faint flicker of a smile toyed at the corner of her mouth. She had a right to be amused, he granted. He was caught.

Cindy snared him just as he reached his car. "Uh, Father, do you mind if I talk with you for a moment?"

He turned to her, glancing around to see if anyone was in listening range. "What can I do for you?"

She laughed. "You already did plenty."

He shrugged. "Okay, you've got me. Where do we go from here?"

"Back to your place?" she grinned.

John smiled in spite of his discomfort. "I'm afraid not. I'm not going to apologize for what happened the other night, Cindy. I'm a human being and I had a moment of weakness. If you want to—"

"Hey, easy guy. I'm not asking for any apologies. Hell, I get a kick out of this."

"Obviously."

"It's no big thing. Don't worry about it. I'm just sorry it didn't work out." She pulled up on the collar of her coat. "I can understand what happened better now. Really, I'm not angry, and I'm not going to expose you or anything like that." She lit a Vantage and said, "Boy, that's really something about George, huh?"

"Terrible," he agreed, glad to be on a different subject. "You knew him well?"

"As well as a person can."

He nodded, understanding. "It was nice of you to come to the funeral."

"I'm a nice girl." Cindy leaned against the car. "You probably don't think so, but I am."

"What I think is that you're too hard on yourself."

After a beat, she said, "You're right about that. It's a bad habit. Maybe I'll get out of it someday, if I meet the right guy. Hard finding good guys nowadays."

"You won't find them in Benny's."

"No? I found you there."

"And look how it worked out."

"It could have worked out differently."

"No, it couldn't."

"Ah, I guess not." She dragged on the cigarette. "The sheriff talked to me. He said they arrested someone."

"Tom Conforte. Only I don't think he killed George."

"Neither do I."

"You know Tom?"

"No."

"Then how do you . . ."

"I don't know. When I looked at his picture

I . . ." Her voice trailed off and she looked away. "I guess I better get going."

"Cindy, I'm sorry about what happened."

"I thought you said you weren't going to apologize."

"I know."

"Forget it," she said. She held out her hand. "Friends?"

"Friends," John said and he shook with her.

When she turned from the car, the nausea swept over her like the flu. Only it came in seconds, not hours. Her stomach gurgled loudly and she frowned, putting her hand on it. When she staggered slightly, John moved closer to her and held onto her arm so she could lean against the car.

"Oh," she said, feeling her tongue thicken.

"Are you all right?" John asked, still holding her arm. She had gone white and looked anything but all right.

She nodded, having some difficulty speaking. The dizziness was clearing but she was still feeling bad. Not for herself, but for John.

"Cindy?"

"Be careful. He's right."

"Right? Who's right?"

"The boy. Alan."

John let go of her arm.

Russell Patterson broke away from the paperwork when the phone rang. He was grateful for the interruption. He didn't like working days. He was a night person. It was all Tom's fault, of course. He'd thrown his whole schedule out of kilter ever since Koester called him and told him to get his ass out to George Hayward's house.

Koester had put him on the day shift after that. It was the price of being Koester's right arm, he supposed. The sheriff wanted him working with him on the murder case. Of course, Tom Conforte didn't know he'd been shifted to days. On balance, Russell guessed it was for the best. If he hadn't been up and getting ready for work, he might not have seen Tom creeping around outside his place. The kid might have been able to get in the house without him knowing it and . . . Well, it would have ended badly, maybe for Tom and him both.

Yeah, it could have been a lot worse. Tom was sitting in a cell, and here was Russell filling out paperwork about the arrest. Technically, he was being held for questioning, but Russell knew damned well Koester wasn't going to let the boy out until he had made up his mind about him. If Warren Conforte pressed the matter, Koester would go ahead and book Tom on suspicion of murder. The sheriff didn't want to do that, and Warren didn't want it to happen either. So it was a stand-off.

"Sheriff's department," Russell said after he picked up the phone. "Deputy Patterson speaking."

"Russell, this is Father Hines."

"I hope you're in better shape than the last time you called."

"Yes, I am. I need to ask you a favor."

"Shoot."

"Can you tell me where I can find Father Nicoletti?"

"Nicoletti?" Russell kicked back in his chair, surprised at the question. "How come you want to see him?"

"I have to talk with him about a church matter."

"Well, he's over at Mercy Medical in Oshkosh, but I—"

"Thanks, Russell. I'll talk with you later."

"But—" Russell listened to the click as the line went dead. He thought about calling the priest back, but it sounded like he was in a hurry. He'd already be out the door. Russell made a mental note to talk with him about it later.

It was a 40-minute drive to Oshkosh. The road crews had the highway in good shape so John made excellent time. He tried to formulate the questions he wanted to ask, but found himself frustrated as he wandered down blind alleys. He gave it up halfway and turned on the radio, deciding to play it by ear.

A gas station attendant directed him to Mercy Medical. The five story building was imposing, much more than Community Hospital in Nettleton, John thought as he parked the Sentra in the lot.

The lobby was awash with visitors and a smoothly flowing sea of nurses in starched white. There was an efficiency here that came from having large amounts of money to work with. Even without seeing the laboratory, John knew their equipment had to be far superior to what they had in Nettleton, and his mind swept back, for a moment, to Miami and all it had to offer.

"May I help you, Father?"

He looked at the strawberry blonde receptionist and said, "Yes, I'd like to see Father Nicoletti, please."

"Of course. Just one moment."

John glanced at the small gift shop as the receptionist picked up her telephone. In a second she said, "Father Nicoletti is on the grounds in back. He's having lunch out there if you'd like to join him."

"Outside?"

She smiled. "He's an outdoors person. If you'll go through the double doors and turn right you'll find the exit at the end of the corridor."

"Thank you."

It wasn't as cold behind the hospital as John had thought it would be. The area, which had scattered benches, was protected on three sides by the jutting wings of the hospital, so it was shielded from the wind. Only a thin layer of snow lay on what was well-kept lawn during the rest of the year.

Besides Nicoletti there were only two othe

people in the courtyard—a man and his wife. He saw the crutches leaning against the bench the couple sat on. Nicoletti was eating lunch at a bench about 20 feet from them, his back turned to John.

"Father Nicoletti," he said as he approached.

The black-robed man turned to see who had called his name. He set his sandwich down and stretched to a towering six foot five inches. He was massively built. A great brown beard covered his cheeks and chin, and only when a broad smile broke did John feel at ease.

"I'm Father Hines," he said, holding out his hand as he drew alongside the bench. "I'm at Sacred Heart in Nettleton."

The smile lessened a bit on the man's face as he took John's grip in his own firm hand. "Sacred Heart. Yes. I heard about Father Dreiband."

"You were there before him, I understand."

Nicoletti nodded. "I inherited it from Father Thyssen. How does it go for you?"

"Not well, I'm afraid. I won't lie to you, Father."

"I'm not surprised. Tell me about it," Nicoletti said, motioning for him to join him on the bench.

There was much to tell. The murders, the confessional, the feeling John had had, almost from the start, that there was something very wrong about Nettleton and Sacred Heart.

He spent 20 minutes telling it all, urged on by Nicoletti's gentle prodding when it was needed. The man was a good listener, John thought, and probably a good priest, as well. He was right about the former, but terribly wrong about the latter.

After he had heard it all, Nicoletti nodded and said, "Nettleton is a difficult parish. It always has been. Father Dreiband wasn't the first to have problems there."

"What are you saying?"

Nicoletti looked off into the distance, contemplating whether or not to tell the story. He had known the priest would come to him. He was the only one left. It was only a matter of time until he tracked him down.

Then Nicoletti turned to John and said, "Do you know Jill Gregory?"

John's fingers tightened around the green painted slats of the bench.

"Yes, I know her."

"And her boy?"

"Evan."

"Yes. Evan. I know them, too," Nicoletti said, stroking his beard. "A troubled family. Father Thyssen told me as much. Jill had great difficulties when she was young. Her mother was a fanatic. It took her over the edge. She did things to Jill, as a child, that I will not repeat. Thyssen had trouble telling me about them, but he felt I should know since I was taking over the church."

A warbling siren punctuated their conversation, and for a moment they both listened to the disembodied howl. Then they saw the white ambulance as it rounded the building and pulled into the emergency entrance.

When it was silent again, Nicoletti said, "His telling me about her helped, but it couldn't entirely prepare me for what I had to face. I think Thyssen knew that. There were things he wanted to tell me beyond that, but he couldn't. He was a broken man."

"Broken?"

"Spiritually," Nicoletti said, folding his broad hands. "It happens."

"I imagine it happened to Father Dreiband."

"You're correct. A priest does not undertake suicide lightly."

"Were you talking about Father Thyssen when you said Father Dreiband wasn't the first to have trouble in Nettleton?"

"No." He waited such an unbearably long time to answer that John almost prompted him. Finally, Nicoletti confided, "I was talking about me."

"I see."

The man looked at him suddenly with cold eyes and said, "No, you don't. You will before you leave here. You'll begin to see, all right, but you don't see now."

John leaned away from him.

"I said I wouldn't tell you the details about Jill Gregory's childhood and I won't. Suffice it to say she put a great deal of trust in Father Thyssen. He was responsible for saving Jill from her insane mother, so it was only natural that she felt an abundance of esteem toward Father Thyssen and to the Church."

John nodded in agreement.

"When Thyssen suffered his eventual loss of faith and left the Church, Jill was devastated. I was a newcomer and it took her some time before she felt comfortable with me, but finally she loosened up. The Church held a strong, mystical attraction for her. In a very real sense, the Church was her father, her own having left her.

"She married Ned Gregory, but he was a rough, crude animal of a man. During confession she painfully explained how he brutalized her constantly, not to the point of sadism, but enough that she bore bruises from his drunken beatings."

John asked, "Could you get help for her?"

"You can't help a woman who does not want it."

"But he beat her."

"He also supported her. He put a roof over her head, food on her table and clothes on her back. Jill felt it was a trade she was willing to make. Perhaps if she had some marketable skills it might have been different, but I doubt it. She hadn't been raised to be an independent woman. So she settled for a person like Ned Gregory."

Nicoletti sighed and stared at the darkening skies.

"It wasn't easy listening to her confessions.

How many times did she break down weeping in the confessional? I can't count the number." He drew a slow, deep breath and said, "Then she came to me about the matter of children."

"About Evan?"

"Well, it was before Evan was born. Jill desperately wanted children. Partly because she felt it would save her marriage and also she felt it was her duty as a Catholic. When she told me about it we were in my office at Sacred Heart. The church was newly built back then. She sat across from me in the small, private office and said, 'I want to have children, Father Nicoletti.'

" 'And you should,' I answered. 'You will.'

" 'I don't think so. We've been trying for a long time. He wants to have children because he knows I want them, but I don't think we're able to.'

" 'Have you asked Dr. Brannigan about it?'

" 'She nodded, staring sadly at me. 'He said there's nothing wrong with me. It's Ned. But I haven't told him yet. It would hurt his pride terribly.'

" 'Do you know for certain that the problem is Ned?'

" 'I only know Doc said there's nothing wrong with me. Father Nicoletti, what am I going to do?'

" 'Keep trying. If it's the Lord's will it shall be.'

Nicoletti explained that it became an obsession with Jill. In the weeks and months ahead she poured her heart out in the comfort of the confessional. It became the consuming centerpiece of her life. A child was the answer to everything. Gradually, it became as important to Nicoletti. He knew her background from Father Thyssen and empathized and sympathized with her. More than that, he felt the woman might just be right, that a child *would* help to soothe her relationship with her husband.

In the sanctum of the confessional they shared that mutual desire for a child that would make everything right. After every confession of how she was angry at her husband for beating her, Jill would talk about how she wanted a child. And after every confession about how she blasphemed the Lord for making her husband sterile, she would tell Nicoletti how badly she wanted a child.

One day in April, after she had gone to confession, Nicoletti asked her back to the rectory for tea. It was a lovely spring day and a balmy breeze wafted in through the open window of the small, comfortable home. They sat on the sofa casually discussing the future, Ned and the child Jill wanted so badly. And this time Nicoletti just couldn't hold back any longer. He gave in.

They both knew it was moving toward this for months. For a long time the attraction was so strong Father Nicoletti had difficulty looking directly into her eyes, but it wasn't lust. It was a driving desire to help her. That was the true attraction.

Once they embraced, Nicoletti admitted, "I don't know if I can go through with this, my child."

"You have to, Father. It's the only way I can have a baby. If I have it with you, it'll be good and pure."

"No," Nicoletti objected. "It's profane. It's—"

"It's not profane for a priest to help someone, and I need your help. My baby will belong to the Church. No one will ever have to know. Ned will just think we finally succeeded."

Nicoletti looked at her moist pouting lips and the curve of her breasts, and suddenly he drew her into his arms, telling himself he was doing it for her. But he knew deep inside that that was only half the truth.

Ned Gregory was not fooled. In July her pregnancy became evident, and Ned confronted her with it on the day before the Fourth.

"Tell me who did it, you fuckin' slut."

Jill stared at her husband with abject horror. Her eyes shot wildly about the living room, looking for an avenue of escape. There was none. The brass lamp sat on the oak table next to the television, and she thought she had a shot a reaching it. But then what? Could she actually hit him with it? Wouldn't he stop her before she could? Ned was a big man, feared even among musclebound truckers. It was no match.

She tried to gauge her husband's anger, as she had tried to many times before. How far would he go before he hit her? He was pacing the room like a caged animal and that was always a bad sign.

But there was a new factor working here. She was with child now, and Ned knew it. Jill wasn't sure he would risk striking her because of the baby.

"Why don't you believe me?" she quivered, clinging to the useless lie. "It was us, Ned. We're able to have the baby. I thought you'd be glad."

"You really think I'm that stupid?" he said, whirling to sneer at her. He crossed the room and grabbed her, close to blows, but at the last second he backed off. He turned Jill loose and turned his back on her as he explained, "Last year, when I was on a run to Phoenix, I saw a specialist. He ran some medical tests." It was ordinarily something that he'd be embarrassed to talk about, something that would offend and wound his macho sensibilities, but he was so enraged it didn't matter anymore.

"It's me," he said, glaring at her again. "The doctor said it was me. You can't have children because I'm sterile."

"He was wrong," she bleated, knowing he was near the ignition point.

"Bullshit! Bull-fucking-shit!" He was

288

coming toward her again, his fingers stabbing at her. "You went out and got yourself knocked up, and I want to know who the bastard was." Ned grabbed her by the arms and shouted, "If you don't tell me I'll beat the crap out of you."

And as he shook her, Jill cried out, "The baby, Ned, the baby. You'll make me lose it."

"I don't give a shit. It ain't my blood." He balled his fist and cocked it back, about to slam it into her belly. "I'm gonna make you lose it unless you tell me. Right now, Jill, tell me or I'll do it. I swear I will. I swear I'll hit you and . . ."

As he drew his arm back farther, about to loose the blow, Jill saw her entire world teetering on the brink. She had gone through so much for the baby. It was all that mattered.

"Father Nicoletti," she screamed, tears spewing forth.

Ned held her in his grip, his fist still drawn back, his teeth bared. He couldn't move. It took awhile for it to register. Then the image of the priest fucking his wife flashed through his brain, and he pushed Jill aside like a dead animal. He turned and stormed from the house, not even hearing Jill's voice shouting at him.

Ned Gregory's Impala was hitting 50 when he went through the intersection at Maple and Grant. Arthur Dierke, who owned the pharmacy in town back then, never saw him coming. Dierke was the more fortunate of the two.

He died instantly. Doug Koester, sitting in his office half a block away, ran down the street and was able to pull Ned out of the smouldering Impala seconds before it exploded in a fireball, shattering store windows up and down the street.

Ned lingered in a coma for a week but never regained consciousness.

"The secret died with him," Nicoletti said.

"Evan Gregory's your son?" John asked.

Nicoletti nodded. "I told myself I did it to help her. I told myself a lot of things. I'm not sure what I believe at this point. I don't know how it would have worked out if Ned had come to the church like he'd planned."

John reached out and held the man's hand, hearing the tremble in his voice. "You can't blame yourself for that. It was what she wanted. You're a man and a man can only stand so much before—"

"It wasn't her fault."

"But—"

"It wasn't her fault," Nicoletti repeated. Then he said, "And it wasn't my fault. You know who's fault it was, John? It was the confessional's fault."

It was getting colder now and John thought it might snow again soon. He wanted to go inside, but the chilliness didn't seem to bother Nicoletti and John didn't want to admit that the weather bothered him.

"Because you heard her begging for a child in there?"

"No," Nicoletti said emphatically. "It's more than that and you know it." He leaned closer to John, almost whispering. "It's evil, John. It has evil powers."

John quickly pulled away from him. "Blasphemy."

Nicoletti shook his head. "No! It's the confessional that blasphemes. Haven't you felt it? Haven't you sensed its power?"

"It's just a small booth made of wood and . . ."

Nicoletti let out a long, high laugh that sounded like the screech of an El train that he once heard while visiting Chicago. He was afraid of Nicoletti at that moment.

Then the laugh was gone and Nicoletti spoke quickly, trying to force out the arguments that would convince him that he was right. "George Hayward made that confessional."

"I know that. And just because he's dead doesn't mean—"

"Do you think George made his fortune from that woodworking shop he had in Nettleton?"

"I don't know how—"

"Well, he didn't. He was a middle class laborer who did some carpentry work on the side. Just a regular fella, until he made that confessional booth." Nicoletti's eyes narrowed to pinpoints. "Then his luck changed. Oh, did it ever, my friend. The man could do no wrong—investments, gambling, real estate.

You name it, and George would turn a profit at it."

"So what are you trying to say?"

"I'm saying . . ." And then Nicoletti's voice slowed to a crawl. "I'm telling you that he made a deal."

"With whom?"

Nicoletti crumbled the paper around the remains of his sandwich, tossed it into the garbage container and said, "It wasn't with God, Father Hines."

"Father Nicoleeeeetti."

John turned to the sound of the voice calling for the man. A nun was standing by the open door of the hospital.

Nicoletti waved toward her. "Coming, Sister Agnes." He stood and said, "I can't talk any more about it."

"But—"

"It's tiring, John. You have to understand that."

John hadn't realized what a drain it was on the man. The color was gone from his face. He no longer had the ruddy, weathered look he'd had when he first arrived and saw him sitting on the bench.

"I know, but—"

"I'm sorry, John. I don't have the strength. I've told you things today that I've had bottled up for many years—partly to help me and also to help you. What I've said about the confessional is true."

"If it is true," John questioned, "then what

can be done? Should I destroy it, Father Nicoletti?"

Nicoletti laughed again · softly, not the dangerous laugh as before. It was the good-hearted laughter of a teacher amused by a naive student. He stifled his chuckles and turned serious.

"You can't destroy it, John." He took John by the arm and began walking back toward the hospital with him. "You can't even get close to it if it doesn't want you to. And, as you've already seen, you cannot stay away from it if it wants you near. It controls *you*. You don't control *it*."

"If I accept what you say as true, then what's the answer?"

"I don't know that. I'm sure it has something to do with faith. Much to do with it. That's why I could not stop it from doing what it would with me. I suspect Father Dreiband failed as well. You haven't succumbed yet, but you may. Even if you don't, I'm not sure you can defeat it. It may be that no human being can defeat it. The power it commands can only be challenged by Almighty God, and I'm afraid none of the priests of Sacred Heart have yet proved themselves worthy of his assistance."

"But we're priests. We're men of God."

"Are we? Were you a man of God when you felt the temptation sitting in the confessional and fell prey to it?"

"But I resisted. At the last moment I resisted."

Nicoletti nodded. "For now. But how long can you keep it up? Don't you think it will win in the end? It'll beg you to come over to its side and then you'll prove it right again." Nicoletti stopped walking and looked to the ground. "I think it may be a chess game between God and and the Antichrist. I'm afraid we make damned poor pawns, John."

Nicoletti patted him on the shoulder and walked toward the door of the hospital. He disappeared inside, but the nun waited, holding the door open for John. She was an older nun, older than Nicoletti.

As they walked down the corridor of the hospital, John said, "He's a remarkable man."

"Yes," she agreed. "He has strength to fight the inner battle he's waged for so long."

Even they knew, John thought, though he was certain they didn't know all the details. "Does he do anything besides his work with the hospital? Is he affiliated with a church in town?"

The nun stopped abruptly and looked up at John. "I don't understand what you mean by that question."

John smiled. "Father Nicoletti. Is he permanently assigned to the hospital?"

"No, Father Nicoletti doesn't work for the hospital. He's a patient here."

John stared dumbly at the woman. "A patient?"

"Yes. He had himself voluntarily comnitted. He's been undergoing psychiatric reatment for the past thirteen years."

John closed his eyes, feeling a sudden need o pray.

CHAPTER 11

F ather Nicoletti was emotionally disturbed. That was the diagnosis the psychiatrist in charge of his case told John. Outwardly he seemed normal enough, but there was a conflict going on inside the man. When John asked the doctor what the conflict was about he was met by silence.

After a lengthy moment, the doctor confessed, "I have no idea."

"How can you have no idea?" He glanced at the framed diplomas behind the doctor, hanging on the wall. There were enough there to tell him the man knew his field. "He's been a patient here for more than a decade and you don't know what his problem is?"

"He refuses to talk about it."

It was a simple answer, but it was an answer John appreciated. He had no intention of talking about it to the psychiatrist himself.

"I get the feeling," the doctor said, "that he's staying here for sanctuary."

It was dark when John got back to Nettleton. He felt drained from the meeting with Nicoletti. How much of it was true and how much were the ramblings of a lunatic? Nicoletti didn't seem like a lunatic. Had he actually made love with Jill Gregory? Was Evan their child?

It was easy to discount. Nicoletti had spun a good story about the confessional, but then John had told him about his experience with it first. Perhaps the man had merely seized on the threads of information and woven the story, playing on John's fears. John had no intention of becoming Nicoletti's roommate at St. Joseph Hospital.

John parked in front of the church rather than in the garage behind the house. He had no illusions about what he was going to do. He felt primed. He had to find out. If Nicoletti was right, then the confessional would know that he knew. If he was wrong there would be nothing. It was that simple.

The church was hollow and seemed to be waiting for him. Darkness surrounded him except for the faint pavement lights around the altar. He genuflected, then walked cautiously toward the confessional. Abruptly, his steps turned forceful, in an attempt to prove to himself there was nothing wrong. It was only wood.

John stopped before the booth, then walked to it and opened the door.

It was like bursting open the escape hatch on a jetliner cruising at 30,000 feet. The force sucked him inside with sudden and immense power. He was lifted off his feet, the air surging around him in a roaring rush. John tried to scream for help as he toppled through the air, but he could not. He was in a vacuum where no screams could be heard.

And then there was pain.

It was a throbbing pain in his knee. When he landed in the booth he'd struck his knee square against the hard edge of the bench. He closed his eyes against it, still unable to cry out. John lay on the floor of the confessional, almost in a fetal position, cradling his injured knee.

When he opened his eyes it was to total darkness and he realized that the door of the booth was closed tight. He could hear his own labored breathing now, and he drew some relief from the return of sound.

"Damnit," he said under his breath, trying to straighten his leg. His foot brushed against the door, and he had to restrain himself from kicking it. It would be a stupid act, but worse than that, he was afraid it would accomplish nothing except to prove he was trapped in the confessional.

He lay there, trying not to think about what had happened, about how it had happened. He knew it would mean admitting Nicoletti was right, and if that were true then he was in the arms of his enemy even now.

"Are you okay, Father?"

Startled, John angled his head upward, toward the voice coming from the other side of the screen. His sweating hands still wrapped around his leg, he asked, "Who is it?"

"You know who it is."

"Evan?"

"You got it."

He moved around in the cramped quarters of the booth, which wasn't designed for sitting on the floor. His leg ached as he eased himself up onto the bench. John's back rested against the unyielding wood and he breathed deeply, trying to collect himself, knowing Evan was waiting.

Finally, he asked, "When were you released from the hospital?"

"This afternoon."

"Where is your mother, Evan?"

"Home."

"She allowed you to come to the church by yourself?"

"She brought me here. I told her to."

"You told her to?"

"That's right." Evan laughed and said, "You sound scared, Father Hines."

"Why should I be scared?"

"You tell me. Hell, I'd be scared."

"Don't profane in—"

"I'd be pissin' in my pants if I were you."

Angrily, John said, "Your mouth is foul. You've sinned."

"Don't try that stuff with me, Father Hines. Let's talk about how you've been fucking my mother."

John leaned away from the screen, the moral offense of the boy's language physically sickening him. He tried to organize his thoughts and said, "You should still be in the hospital."

"Hah! Don't want to talk about that, huh?"

"Your mother and I have met and talked a number of times. What you're suggesting is—"

"Okay, okay, maybe you haven't actually put the meat to her yet, but you want to, don't you, Father Hines? And I'll bet you're gonna, too. Just like old Nicoletti."

John pushed against the door of the confessional, panic overflowing. He was trapped in the box, being suffocated. He had to get out, away from the madness.

But the door wouldn't open and Evan was laughing. He leaned back in the seat and shouted, "Stop it! Stop your laughing!"

And Evan did stop. He said, "You can't get out of here, Father Hines. Not until I want you to. Nicoletti was right about this place, ya know."

"You don't know what you're talking

about."

Evan filled his voice with mock fear, sing-songing in a comical imitation of Nicoletti. "It's evil, John. It has powwwwwers. The confessional blaspheeeeeems. Haven't you felllllt it? Haven't you sennnnnnsed it's power?"

John's voice cracked as he asked, "How can you know what he said?"

"Goddamn, you're slow. Haven't you been listening to me?" And then he repeated it, without anger and in a matter-of-fact tone that frightened John more than anything he'd heard so far. "Nicoletti was right."

John sat on the bench in the dark, sweating profusely. Abruptly, he reached for the screen, but when he touched it Evan said, "You don't want to do that."

John held his hand on the screen dividing their faces for a long moment.

Evenly, Evan said, "I'm telling you for your own good, Father. You don't want to open the screen. Trust me on this one. You'll save yourself a lot of grief."

Finally, John took his hand away from the screen. "What do you want, Evan?"

The boy's voice perked up, filled with friendliness. "Hey, that's what I like to hear. Now we're talking turkey."

"What do you want?" he repeated.

"Just a little conversation every now and then, that's all. I like you and I like to talk.

I like this place, too. So we can meet here and shoot the shit, ya know."

"Not like this. I won't talk with you when you use language like this."

The warmth was gone from the boy's voice then. "You'll meet here whenever I tell you to, Hines. And you're gonna do whatever I tell you to."

"I won't—"

"Yeah, yeah. I know. I heard all that before. Sure you won't. Not right now you won't, but you will in the end. You'll come around. It'll be easier when you do. We'll get along good then."

"I don't understand what you want."

"Let's start by you humping my mother."

John turned away from the screen, coughing, feeling the spit in his hand. His eyes began to tear, and another seizure of coughing hit him as he thought about the base words being uttered in his holy vessel of the Church.

"Aw, come on, Hines. It's not like you don't want to. Don't make such a big deal out of it. What the hell were you feeling her up for if you didn't want to bang her?"

John swallowed the phlegm and asked, "Did she tell you this?"

"Yeah, she told me. And Nicoletti called me from his padded cell after you left and filled me in on your conversation. I got people all over the place who—"

"Enough!"

"All right. Don't get so shook. Christ, you make such a big deal out of everything." After a second, Evan said, "We'll keep it simple. You just fuck Mom and fill me in on the details later. That'll do for openers."

The air was stifling and John knew he couldn't take much more. He was going to pass out and that was something he didn't want to do. It would leave him vulnerable to—vulnerable to what?

He didn't know. But he did know he had to have all his faculties about him. He had to stay alert.

John said, "How can you ask such a thing?" He shook his head, mulling it over. He waited a long moment. Then, when there was no answer, he asked, "Evan?" Still no answer. "Evan?"

John leaned forward and pushed his hand against the door of the confessional. It swung open easily. He stepped out of the booth and looked at the door next to his. It was still closed. John gripped the handle, turned and opened the door. The booth was empty. He stared at the emptiness, then felt the pain begin to flare in his knee.

He had the Sentra up to 65. Speed was important. Getting far away from Nettleton was important. It came to him when he woke in the morning that distance might diminish its power. The confessional was capable of drawing him to it. He should have seen that from the start, that night he'd felt compelled to look inside for the first time. It hadn't been John's wish. It had been the confessional's.

The sickening feeling that he was being used descended on him. He'd always been so proud of the fact that he was in control—in control of his faith, of his manly impulses, of his congregation. Now he was in control of nothing. Now he was wheeling madly out of control—into the control of another force.

It was like a magnet, and its power was getting stronger. Even Evan said as much. "You'll come around. It'll be easier when you do. We'll get along good then." He sounded so sure of it.

As he drove, John knew he was grasping at straws. Maybe distance didn't have anything to do with it. Maybe distance didn't matter. Maybe the thing could reach out to Milwaukee or Chicago and pull him right back. Maybe it could reach all the way down to Miami.

He glanced at the speedometer and saw it inch past 70. It occurred to him that the confessional could have instigated his getting transferred from Miami in the first place. Maybe it knew all along. It wanted a weak priest, someone it could work on. He fit the bill for that one, didn't he?

"Where are we going?" Jill asked.

She was afraid. John could hear it in her voice when he'd called her in the morning. He'd waited until ten o'clock, when he was sure Evan would be in school, and when he'd told her they had to meet, he could tell she knew it was about Evan. He wasn't sure how much she knew or how involved she was in it, but her fear came across the line.

"Just a little further."

"But where are we going?"

"Here," he said, deciding they were far enough away from the town. He took his foot off the accelerator and when the car slowed he eased it onto the shoulder. John put it in park and turned off the ignition. He leaned back in the car seat and tried to relax the muscles in his neck.

It was no use. They'd tightened up on him and locked. He'd risen in the morning with the feeling that eagle's talons were clutching the back of his neck and maybe they were. He'd talk to her in a second, but all he wanted now was a few moments to try and ease the tension from his neck.

"I don't mind telling you've got me plenty scared, John."

He turned to look at her scrunched in the passenger seat. Her pink ski jacket was bunched up and made her look something like Mae West. Matching mittens were clutched together in her lap as she stared out the window at traffic whizzing mindlessly by the car. Every once in awhile she'd shiver as a semi roared past and buffeted the car.

He said, "I'm scared, too."

She turned from the windshield, looking at him. "What are you scared about?"

"Evan."

Her bottom lip quivered and he wondered if she was going to cry or laugh. She did neither, though. "I'm worried about him, too, but I don't see why we have to drive out here to talk. Doc Brannigan said—"

"That's not what I'm talking about, Jill." He appraised her questioning stare. Could it be she didn't know anything about it? Yes, it was possible. "Did he tell you he came to the church last night?"

"Of course. I drove him there. He wanted to go to confession." She shrugged. "I thought it was a good thing. He said he wanted to cleanse himself. It sounded pretty healthy to me."

"What he told me wasn't healthy."

"But you knew about—"

"Not that."

Concern showed at the corners of her eyes. "What did he tell you?"

"He . . . he thinks you and I are having . . ." John's voice trailed off when he saw she understood. A sense of relief washed over him as he watched Jill turn away, her mittened hand balled up by her mouth.

She was ashamed, and that was the one reaction he'd prayed for. It meant she didn't know about it. He saw her shoulders begin to shake, and for a suspended moment he was afraid she was laughing. But she wasn't. She was doing what he hoped for. She was crying.

He reached out and touched her shoulder,

feeling the cold material of the ski jacket. "Jill . . ."

She shook her head, still crying. John reached around and turned her toward him, smiling. "I wouldn't have told you, except—"

"No, I'm glad you told me. I'm just trying to think if it was something I said or did."

He wiped at her tears with his fingers and thought that she looked beautiful like this. John pulled her closer, wrapping his arms protectively around her. In a moment she was sighing and calming down. She looked up at him, and he kissed her gently on the mouth. Her lips were wet with tears and he could taste the salt.

Her hands tightened on his forearms, and he moved into a more comfortable position as a semi jolted the car.

"I need you," she whispered when they broke the kiss. "I want you so badly, John."

"I know. But we've got to talk more."

"I don't want to talk," she said. "Not right now. All I want is for you to kiss me and hold me."

And he did. He closed his eyes and let the passion roll over him like a gentle wave. He wasn't on a highway shoulder any longer. He was away from everything, on an island somewhere with Jill. Warm winds were blowing, and they had only each other. No Evan. No church. No Nicoletti. Just each other.

He didn't want to open his eyes. He just wanted to stay like he was with his arms around her and her arms around him and their lips pliant and molding.

But the air was bothering him, intruding on their passion. He tried to remember if he'd left the ignition on, if exhaust fumes were seeping into the car. That would be dangerous with the windows rolled up like they were.

But it wasn't exhaust fumes.

It was a bad smell, and the taste was suddenly just as bad. Jill's lips were slipping off his, sliding away as though they were greased. He moved to the left, trying to touch her lips with his again, but they were just too damned slippery and the taste was awful.

And he remembered where he had smelled the mouldering odor before. His eyes whipped open, and he saw George Hayward grinning at him. John licked at his lips and tasted the corpse's blood on his mouth. He began to scream and pull away, but it was no good. George had him in his arms and wasn't about to let him go.

He looked worse now than he had looked in the house, because time had passed and he was rotting. The holes where his eyes had been hammered in had turned black, and the edges were circled with greenish moss from the grave. When John brought his hands up and tried to push the thing away he felt the splinters of bone from George's shattered face as they cut into his hand.

And then George exhaled.

In that moment John nearly passed out.

Maybe he actually did. The fetid, revolting breath of the dead savaged him. It was thick and vile, a smell that carried the decay taking place within his body.

John buried his face in George's shoulder, anything to get away from the stench. And in his heart he prayed that when he looked up again it would be Jill.

But it wasn't.

It was George, with his mouth open and breathing on him. Most of the thing's teeth had fallen out, and inside John could see that his tongue had turned black as the sockets where his eyes had been. But the tongue wiggled lewdly at him, and John watched, both petrified and nauseated, as two long worms slithered out from under the tongue.

As he began to throw up on George, the wild idea occurred to him that this might revolt the creature enough to make him let go. But he was wrong again. George's grasp never slackened as the vomit cascaded across the splintered forehead, dripping down into the open cavity when the shriveled remains of his brain rested.

All at once George pulled him to his chest and began to stroke his head. John felt the thick ooze of blood spread across his hair and he turned to see the stump where George's hand had been, only it wasn't blood. It was embalming fluid, and it was green rather than red. The struggle had freed it from inside George, and it was flowing out like paste.

And then John was screaming, beyond hysteria, and he was sitting up in the bed, clawing at the sheets and the pillows and the memory of George Hayward. It was a long time before he realized the phone was ringing, and even after he had, he didn't answer it.

CHAPTER 12

Alan Landano didn't want to go out to recess the day Evan came back to school. He knew what was waiting for him. As it was, he didn't have any choice in the matter. He was in Mr. Burnside's arithmetic class before recess, and Burnside wasn't one of his admirers. The math teacher had heard about Alan's refusal to sign the get well card for Evan Gregory, and it hadn't set well with him.

When Miss Neilson had told him about it a few days earlier in the teacher's lounge, Burnside had suggested, "The boy should be sent for counseling."

"To his advisor?" Miss Neilson asked.

"No. For psychiatric counseling. I don't think that's rational behavior he's exhibiting."

"Oh, I wouldn't say he's—"

"I'm serious, Brenda. It's one thing for these kids to have their little quarrels. Quite another for them to say they wish a boy to stay in the hospital."

So now, when Alan was alone in the room with Burnside, the teacher felt little sympathy.

"But can't I just stay in here, Mr. Burnside?"

"No. I have a stack of tests to grade and I don't want you here."

Alan held the sides of his desk. "I won't make any noise. I promise."

Burnside crossed his arms in front of him. "Frankly, Alan, I don't want you in my classroom at all. I've heard about your behavior and it sickens me. I can't do anything about keeping you out of my class, but I'm certainly not going to have you hanging around here between periods."

Alan stood. Burnside had gone back to grading the papers, but as the boy walked past his desk he looked up. A thought struck him, and he tingled at the idea of putting pressure on the brat.

"I expect you to go outside to the playground, Alan. Don't hide out in the corridor. My window overlooks the playground and I'd better see you out there."

"But I told you I don't want to go out there."

Burnside nodded. "I'm sure you don't, but you made your bed. If the other students judge you harshly I don't blame them. I'd better see you out there when I check on you or I'll report it to Mr. Fortmann, and I think another unsatisfactory report to the principal will be enough to have you suspended for awhile. I know I won't miss you."

Alan trudged out of the classroom.

Mike Kopernik saw him coming first. He called to Chucky Hamilton, and they both watched attentively as Alan walked down the stairs from the back of the school. There were more than 40 children in the playground, but Alan felt as if he were alone. Word had spread quickly and he was left out on a limb, unable to explain his feelings.

Alan wanted to be by himself and headed toward a secluded area. He rounded a corner that led him to a quiet alcove, but Evan was waiting for him. Alan was startled to see him standing there, but not really surprised.

"Hi, Alan. Glad to see me out of the hospital?"

"So what am I supposed to say?"

"Nothing, you little bastard. I'm the one who does the thinking and the talking."

Alan backed away from the stocky boy and jumped when he felt Chucky lock his arms around him from behind. Mike was laughing and shouting, "Hit him, Evan. Bash him hard."

Evan cracked a smile, angry with himself or grinning. He wanted Alan to be as frightened as possible because having someone scared helped build the energy in him. "Shut up," he said to Mike. He looked at Alan and asked, "How come you didn't want to sign my card?"

"Because I don't like you. Did you want me to lie and pretend I did?"

"It's not a question of liking me," he said, advancing on the captive boy. "It's a question of respecting me."

"I don't respect you either."

"Boy, that's just not too smart, Alan. You could end up getting hurt, hurt real bad. Maybe even like Frank Conforte did."

"I suppose you had something to do with that?"

"Maybe. It just could be."

"You don't scare me, Evan. You're just—"

Evan's fist silenced him as he drove it deep into Alan's belly. Alan hadn't been ready for the blow and it completely knocked the wind out of him. He tried to double reflexively, but Chucky held him up, thrusting his stomach out for Evan.

Mike screamed, "Hit him again, Evan! Hit him again!"

And Evan did. And then he hit him again and again and again.

Maybe it had only been a dream, but John knew there was some truth in it, too. And what had happened before that, in the confessional with Evan, was no dream. That was real. The boy was connected to the confessional, and he

had the sickening feeling that there was more
to it and that it involved Frank Conforte and
George Hayward and Father Dreiband. John
knew he had to get to the bottom of it and fast,
because before long *he* would be in it. He was
already in it. Its hold was getting stronger.

When he pulled to the curb in front of
Brenner's Grill, Jill came out. She was
wearing a white waitress's uniform, and when
she got in the car John saw that it was heavily
starched.

He started to drive.

"You sounded serious on the phone."

"I am serious," he said. Then he added, "I
hope I didn't get you in trouble for taking time
off from work."

"No trouble."

He drove toward her house, listening to her
directions. He didn't want them to be at the
church when they talked.

"You drove Evan to the church last night?"

"Yes. He said he wanted to go to confession."

Dear God, it's starting again, just like the
dream.

As he stopped for a traffic light he looked
at Jill, half-expecting to see George Hayward's
corpse reaching out for him. He pulled away
from the light and said, "Jill, do you understand what's happening here?"

"What do you mean?"

"About the confessional," he blurted.

"What are you talking about, John?"

"I visited Father Nicoletti yesterday."

"Oh?"

He heard the shift in her tone. It was like a machine clicking into a different gear.

"I'm sorry, Jill. I wish I had time to be tactful about this, but I don't. I don't think any of us has time." He paused a beat and said, "He told me about the two of you . . . about Evan."

She had her hands in her lap, twisting them together.

"It's true, isn't it?"

She didn't answer.

"You shouldn't feel guilty about it. I don't think it was your fault."

She looked out the window, her voice shaking. "It wasn't my fault. All I wanted was a—"

"It wasn't his fault, either. Nicoletti said it was the confessional."

She laughed bitterly. "That's as good an excuse as any."

"You don't know the whole story."

He pulled the car into her driveway, went inside and spent the next hour trying to tell her what had happened and not sound like a madman at the same time.

When he'd finished she said, "If you believe that then you belong with Nicoletti." Jill paced the small living room. "Just because a man under psychiatric treatment tells you a wild story . . ."

"Haven't you heard anything I've told you?

didn't you hear what I said about Evan last night?"

"I don't want to talk about it."

He walked to her side. "We've got to talk about it. We've got to decide what to do."

Then she whirled on him and said, "There's nothing to do. I don't want to do anything. I don't want to talk about anything. All I want is for you to make love to me, John. I want to feel you inside of me. God, I want you to fuck me."

The thick mental haze cloaked over him. It was palpable, something he could physically sense. It wasn't a part of him. It had never been a part of him. It was something from without that was threatening to push into his body and take him over.

When he nodded, Jill thought he was agreeing, but he wasn't. He was nodding in understanding. It was a part of him all right. It was a part that he'd successfully repressed for so long. If the confessional had done anything it had just lifted the repression and made his inner self more accessible, and if he acceded to it he had only himself and his lack of will and his lack of faith to blame.

Jill was in his arms and he was holding her, and he knew George Hayward would not come this time. He followed her to the bedroom and slowly stripped the waitress uniform from her. She stood before him, wearing a white garter belt and nylons. He caressed the smooth expanse of naked flesh above the tops of the stockings, running his fingers beneath the taut elastic straps that cut into her thighs.

Her hands traveled across his chest, toying with his nipples until they were erect, her tongue sweeping across his neck arousing him.

His hand snaked upward and discovered the moist prize waiting for him. And then his fingers were in her and he was no longer a priest. He was only a man.

". . . want you . . . I want you so bad, John." Her words were hot in his ear, and he responded, cupping each of her breasts and lifting them to his waiting mouth. He looked down and saw her hips undulating, and he carried her to the bed.

Jill stretched out on it, pulling her arms up and behind her neck. As her supine body beckoned him, John knew he'd crossed the last barrier. When he entered her he was startled to find it was without guilt. Her scalding insides had melted it away, and there was only lust and pleasure and the needy woman in his arms and beneath his body.

Their bodies worked as if one, Jill's legs latched up high around his hips. She met each thrust with a counterthrust, grinding her womanhood against his hard pubic bone to enhance her pleasure. Her nails raked down his back, leaving long red ribbons in his skin, and he stiffened as she bit into his shoulder.

As their pace quickened, Jill began to cry out with each penetration and withdrawal. Her cries roused John to fresh heights, and he knew he could not contain himself much longer. Her vaginal muscles began to spasm and the action was so unexpected that John felt himself come almost at once.

He spewed into her, the orgasm wracking both of them at once. And they screamed in that moment, the two of them, and John could no longer separate whose voice he heard. It didn't matter. In that moment nothing mattered. He clutched at that fleeting pleasure, a secret part of his mind telling him that it would be the last moment of pleasure he would know in his life.

It was 7:30 and it was getting dark in Millburg. Cindy Breslauer had just put a Stouffer's Turkey Tetrazzini in the oven when the current pulsed through her. She was struck blind by the power of it, and for a full ten seconds she danced spasmodically in the kitchen to a beat she could feel but not hear.

Her arms flapped and jerked at her sides as the spasm wracked her body. Inside her head she could hear bones throughout her body snap in response. Like the keys of a piano, the discs in her back tinkled one by one from the shock of it. Her unseeing eyes bulged in the sockets and her nose began to bleed. Spittle dripped down out of her mouth.

Surprisingly, there was little pain, just the

feeling of being gripped tightly. The worst discomfort was in her chest because she wasn't able to breath. She wasn't close enough to consciousness to feel the blood flowing from her nose, so she wasn't aware of it.

Then it was over, and her feet kicked out from under her as she tumbled to the kitchen floor. The bruise on her leg would turn blue within the hour, but it didn't matter since this was the last day of her life. Sprawled on the floor, she tried to gather her senses and gradually felt pain flooding over different parts of her body.

Her back hurt her the worst. Each time she moved, the aftershocks worked their way up her spine. Cindy wiped her hand across her mouth, terrified at seeing the amount of blood coming from her nose. She pulled a roll of paper towels from the countertop and watched it fall and roll across the kitchen floor. She crawled to the yellow towels, tore a handful off and wiped it across the blood.

She rolled onto her back and looked up at the naked 75 watt bulb. "John," she said. "Oh, John."

Sheriff Koester was waiting for Russell to get into the office. His deputy had gone back on nights now that Tom Conforte was in jail. There was going to be an arraignment, but there was something about it the sheriff didn't like. It was a gut feeling, and Koester trusted his gut feelings. He knew there was a new generation of cops coming who put more trust in computers and other electronic gadgets, but he felt law enforcement would lose something when the last of the cops who trusted their guts were gone.

Koester's gut told him Tom Conforte hadn't killed George Hayward. It didn't jibe. There'd been three brutal deaths in Nettleton in the past six months—Father Dreiband, Frank Conforte and George Hayward. When Frank had been discovered it occurred to Koester that one connection between the boy's death and Father Dreiband's was the church. Frank had been an altar boy for Dreiband and now they were both dead.

George Hayward had broken the connection, if there was one, in Koester's mind. Oh, he attended Sacred Heart and he'd even built the confessional for the church, Koester recalled, but that wasn't enough.

Only later, when he was interrogating Tom, did it hit him that there *was* another connection to the church. Father Hines had been present at the murder scene. Koester didn't buy the story the priest had given him about calling on George about some repairs needed on the confessional. Koester's ten-year-old grandson in Dubuque wouldn't have bought that story.

But the connection was there. The church loomed in his thoughts, and as it grew more important he began to regard Tom Conforte's innocence as more likely.

He was reaching for a fresh cigar when the door of the office opened and Cindy Breslauer rushed in. Koester started to get up, remembering the girl from the funeral.

"Howdy," he said.

"Sheriff, I don't have a lot of time. You've got to listen to me."

Koester grinned. "I'd be happy to listen to you. Have a seat."

She looked past Koester, at the cell where Tom was being held. "I don't want to sit. We don't have time."

"What's so important?"

"We've got to get to the church."

He stopped unwrapping his cigar, his eyes on the girl. "The church."

"Yes. Father Hines. They're coming for him."

His enemy was near. John could feel it breathing down on him, closing in on him, as he rummaged past the tools and dirty rags in the garage. Nicoletti had warned him there was no way to stop the confessional, but he had to try. It was either that or give in. There was no escape.

He found it. John hefted the five gallon gas can from the dark corner of the garage. He tried not to think about Jill Gregory or how he'd made love to her, but the vacant look in her eyes came back to torment him.

She laid there in the bed long after they finished making love. John thought she wa sleeping, basking in the afterglow, but when he looked up at her he saw that her eyes were open. She was staring at the ceiling, only she wasn't seeing anything. She had dead eyes, except that her body was breathing.

"Jill," he said, his naked body still sticking to hers. "Jill, are you all right?"

She didn't answer, though, and even when he shook her she didn't respond. He drew his legs under him on the bed, shaking her harder. Still she stared at the ceiling and John began to fear for her sanity.

What have I done?

Nothing broke the spell. John tried talking to her, sitting her up and getting her on her feet, but she was completely limp. Looking at her body on the bed, he wondered why he was so surprised about it after what he'd done to her. He'd destroyed her faith for a second time.

It didn't matter that she was a willing participant. He'd executed her all the same. The Church was the parents she had always needed. When her parents had failed her, when her marriage failed her, there was always comfort from the Church, from the confessional, from Father Thyssen. And then from Father Nicoletti and Father Hines.

He spent half an hour in the bedroom trying to rouse Jill, but it was futile. He covered her with the blanket and told her to get some rest, certain she could not hear him. He'd have to call Doc Brannigan and tell him about it. He'd have to get out of the house, because Evan was coming home.

John carried the heavy gas can into the empty church. He kept his eyes on the floor. He didn't want to look at the confessional. He didn't want to give it any edge.

When he got as close as 15 feet, he heard the creak of the hinges on the confessional door as it slowly opened. John tried not to look, but the movement caught his eyes and it wasn't only the movement of the door. He looked up and saw the carved figures on the front of the booth beckoning to him.

It wasn't dark in the church, now.

He could see clearly.

And the figures were alive and cackling and frolicking on the front of the booth. Their faces were twisted into snarling smiles and their wooden hands begged him to come to them. Their voices came at different pitches, their words unintelligible. But their message was clear and John felt himself seduced by it. There was a world of such pleasure, pleasure he could not dream of, even beyond what he had felt in Jill Gregory's bed.

The demons knew that pleasure. Their high cackles hinted of the debauchery, and their laughter was a promise that John could share in it if only he was willing.

And he was willing.

The gas can thudded on the floor of the church and he walked past it, toward the confessional.

* * *

Sheriff Koester was out of his chair, the cigar forgotten. It was too much of a coincidence, this latest connection. He scolded himself for having let the girl off so easily when he'd questioned her at the funeral. She knew a lot more about what was going on then she'd let on.

"Slow down, Cindy," he said. "You just tell me what you know."

"I know John Hines is in mortal danger. You've got to help. I know if we don't get there—"

"In danger from who?"

She turned from him, knowing her precious seconds were being used. "Can't we talk about this on the way to the church?"

"Does this have something to do with George Hayward's murder?"

She looked back at the sheriff. Maybe it was a way to get him to listen to reason. She could try to make a trade. "Yes."

Koester nodded. "Now we're getting someplace. Go on."

"John'll tell you about it."

"I want to hear what you know first."

"I'll tell you when we get to the church."

It was a lawman's voice that said, "You'll tell me what you know right now and don't give me anymore shit. If you got information in a murder investigation you'd better fork it over, lady."

Her mind raced for an answer as another

sheet of jolting awareness stunned her, making her close her eyes and stumble back against the desk. Koester thought she was going to faint and made a grab for her, but she startled him, throwing her arms out far to the sides for balance. He backed away from the woman, thinking she was having an epileptic seizure.

The power was stronger now, even stronger than it had been in her kitchen. Nettleton was the center of the evil and she was tuned into it, locked into it, and her awareness of things that were to be and things that had been was never stronger.

As she concentrated, she found she could exercise some control over it. It had never been strong enough for her to analyze it, but now it was here and she was able to look at the awareness and try to adjust it.

When she lurched against Koester's desk for support, the first thing she saw was Tom Conforte standing by the bars of his cell.

"He didn't kill George Hayward," she said.

Koester looked at her, struck dumb by what he was seeing. No amount of police work had prepared him for what was happening. He had a sickening feeling that the girl knew what she was talking about. If there was justice in the world she would know what she was talking about, because she was paying a heavy price for the knowledge.

Koester reached into his pocket, took out a handkerchief and held it out to her. "Here."

Cindy looked at it and asked, "What's that for."

Koester said, "You're bleeding . . . from your ears."

Cindy put her hand to the side of her face and felt the trickle of blood as it coursed down across her cheeks. Again there was no pain, but the damage had been done.

"It doesn't matter about that. What matters is getting to the church."

"Look," Koester said, taking her by the arm and leading her to a chair, "you and I have got a lot of talking to do before we're going anywhere."

"Noooooo!" she shrieked, catching Koester completely off-guard. He'd expected a weak young girl who was devastated by some ungodly disease that was making her hemorrhage from her ears. What he got was a powerful shove against his chest that toppled him backwards against the cell bars. Koester was about to regain his footing and come for her when Tom Conforte's arm wrapped around his neck.

Koester struggled, and if Tom had only grabbed him he might have had the strength to break free of him. But too much was working against him—the way Cindy had surprised him, how he was off-balance from striking the bars, and most of all fear. Fear sapped the strength from him, and he was disgusted because he was a man who rarely knew fear in his life.

He did now. He knew it intimately.

Then Koester blacked out.

Cindy stared at Tom Conforte, who let loose the sheriff. She watched as the big man dropped to the floor of the jail.

Tom held the stare with the girl for a moment, then said, "I don't know how, but you know I didn't kill George."

Cindy nodded.

"You said something about the church."

"Father Hines is going to die—worse than die, if I don't get there fast. It may be too late already."

"You're going to need help." Tom looked down at Koester and said, "The keys to the cell are on his belt."

He was inside the confessional. John sat there in numb fear, part of which was because he didn't remember getting inside. That meant it was getting stronger. It could make him black out for short periods while it did what it pleased with him. It wasn't necessary for there to be a snake of light anymore to pull him into the box, and John knew he was near the end now.

The door was closed and he was sealed in.

It is a crypt.

He sat there waiting for it to begin, like a dumb animal being led to slaughter. There was no getting out of the chute. It was over.

No, it's playing tricks on me, John thought. I'm not thinking that. It's trying to make me think that. It's not over. Nothing's over unless I want it to be over. I'm a priest, a man of God.

Evan's laughter came low and strong like the roll of a tidal wave across the ocean. "Your God's deserted you, Father Hines. And do you know why? Because you deserted Him."

He turned toward the screen. "I have not deserted my God." And he began to pray desperately, with all the passion he had.

As he prayed, Evan said, "How was my mom's pussy, Hines? She fucks like a bunny, doesn't she?"

He ignored the words, filling the booth with his prayers.

"Words won't work now, Hines, and that's all they are—just words. They're empty. God was watching when you pinched her nipples and when she sucked your cock and when you filled her with cum. Fill her to the rim, Hines. Fill her cunt to the rim."

Then John broke off the prayers and shouted, "That wasn't me. That was you."

"Bullshit. You fucked her."

"You made me."

"You wanted her. You wanted her the same way Nicoletti wanted her. So you took her, you fucked her and no amount of copping out is going to change that."

He was right, John thought. It wasn't prayers he was saying. It was only words. And as he thought that, he wondered if it was Evan making him think the thoughts, if it was the confessional or if it was really him. If it was him, then it truly was over because it meant he'd lost his faith, the same way Dreiband had lost his faith.

"What do you want?"

"I want you," Evan said, the noxious odor seeping through the closed screen. It curled in the air, green and sickly, and John felt himself about to wretch. He gagged, choking.

Evan laughed again and said, "You'll get used to it. You'll be surprised at what a man can get used to. Dreiband got used to it."

"Why me?"

"Because you're so fucking holier-than-thou. You and your religion and all the bullshit that goes with it. You're a joke, and I'm going to deliver the punch line."

John felt tears tracking across his cheeks and he cried, "What do you want of me?" He turned his head from the question, because he knew that just asking it meant he was crossing over the boundary. But he also knew that asking the question would bring relief from the stench and from the evil presence and from the terrible weight that pressed in on him from all sides of the booth.

The air was still heavy with the green fog, but it was less revolting now. The rats clawing inside his guts had pulled their paws away for a moment. The revulsion he felt receded ever so slightly, and the thing that was Evan said, "See how much better it can be? It doesn't have to always be bad like it was a couple of seconds ago. I can be a goooooood boy."

John found he could breath, and he gasped at the foul air, stretching his legs to ease the cramped muscles. His face was wet with tears, and he sobbed as he begged, "Tell me what you want."

"Well, let's see. Why don't we start with something simple. How about that little bastard Alan Landano."

"Alan? What about him?"

"The little brat wouldn't sign my get well card. That's not very nice, is it, Hines?"

John leaned against the back of the bench, the waves of nausea still sweeping over him. He stared at the door but knew it was a waste of energy even to think about escape. Besides, it could get inside his head. It would know what he was thinking even before he thought it.

"You could do me a real favor if you'll kill the kid."

Even with all that had happened, John wasn't sure he was hearing correctly. "Kill him?"

"Sure. The punk doesn't deserve to live after the way he snubbed me. You agree, don't you?"

John was about to protest when the fury came back into the booth, suffocating him, crushing him in a green grasp of putrid air that sickened him. The rats were clawing in his belly again, and his face contorted in pain as he tried to bear the agony. But it was unbearable. He knew there was only one escape, only one way to make it stop.

"Yes! Yes, I agree with you."

And again the pain subsided. He'd stopped weeping, though his eyes still teared from the air. As the power ebbed John felt the last shreds of decency return to him. He could protest again. He could reason. He knew he wouldn't be able to much longer.

This last time, when the agony had begun, he had actually agreed with Evan. Not just in words, but in his mind. Alan *did* deserve to die if he had snubbed Evan that way—and he'd kill him. In that moment of supreme pain he would have killed him. He would have done anything to ease the torture.

But now, with it subsiding, reason came back to him. How long would it be before reason was gone altogether and he agreed with Evan even when there was no pain? Not long.

"We're gonna get him, Hines. You're gonna do it for me. Just the way Dreiband did it for me."

"Father Dreiband," he said, everything crystallizing in that one moment. "He killed Frank Conforte. You made him do it."

"I didn't make him do it. He wanted to." Evan chortled. "In the end he fuckin' begged me to let him kill the boy, just the way you're gonna beg me."

"And afterwards? What about then? He killed himself because of what you made him do. He lost the Kingdom of God because of you."

"Up his ass."

And then the door of the confessional slowly creaked open. Light cracked into the booth, illuminating the green, seething haze that surrounded John. Bit by bit the door opened further. Finally it was open enough for John to see out into the church.

Alan Landano was standing in one of the pews.

Through the screen on the confessional, Evan said, "Let's get the show on the road, huh."

John squinted, peering through the haze. Alan was just standing there, but there was something wrong with the altar boy. It was his face. John sat straighter in the booth and tried to get a better look at him. His face was puffed and bruised and cut. His eyes were glazed, and he stared straight ahead.

"What did you do to him?"

"I beat his little ass," Evan answered.

"Then in the name of God why don't you kill him yourself? Why make me do it?"

"That's good. I like that. Kill him in the name of God. But you're gonna do it for me, Hines. It's poetic justice. A priest killing his altar boy. It'll bring you and me together—forever."

He had had enough of a rest. He had regained as much strength as he could hope for and with his last ounce of resolve he cried,

"Nooooo! I won't do it. I won't kill that boy."

"Oh, but you will," Evan said, and then John brought his hands up and clutched his head. The fog had closed in on him, circling his head and pounding against his eardrums until they were ready to burst, and he screamed aloud as his right eardrum *did* burst. Blood began pulsing out of it, and he shrieked hideously.

"You'll do anything I tell you," Evan said.

The rats were lower in his stomach now and they were moving down and he could feel their razor claws as they reached down into his rectum and sliced away at the tender flesh there. He screamed over and over as the blood poured down out of his rectum, soaking his trousers. John looked down and saw his hands, and he tried to clutch them in prayer. As he did they began to swell, his fingers puffing grotesquely, the skin turning yellow and beginning to peel away as if they had aged 100 years overnight.

"I told you you'd beg me," Evan snickered.

When John felt the force pushing him out of the confessional, he clung to the bench, knowing that if he left it he would kill Alan Landano. His only hope was to remain in the box he so hated. But it pummeled at him, like a salvo of sledgehammers, each blow more painful than the last, and he knew he could not resist for long.

Out in the church Alan Landano stood in the aisle, his face bruised, not caring anymore. He had always known it would come to this, but his mind wasn't thinking that. He wasn't thinking anything. He couldn't hear John's screams of pain or smell the vile stench from the confessional or feel the mortal danger he was in. He was beyond all that, far beyond it.

"It's over!" Evan shouted. "It's finished, Hines! Do as I tell you!" And each word Evan spoke through the screen was punctuated with another searing jolt of evil trying to pry him from the booth—the rats, the stench, the pressure, the pain in his ears, the blood.

It's so easy. Just do what he says. Just do it and it'll be over. He'll make it stop. Just do it, John. Do it. Do it. Do it.

"Don't do it, John," the voice said, cutting through his agony.

He forced his eyes open and looked at Alan, thinking the voice had come from him, but it hadn't. It had come from Cindy.

John saw her in the distance, standing by the open door of the church. She came in with someone else. Tom Conforte, he thought, only it couldn't be Tom because he was in jail. As she walked down the nave he saw the blood caked on the side of her face.

"Get out of here," Evan shouted to her through the door, and as he did John felt some of the pain ebb again. "You fuckin' slut," Evan spat, turning his attention on her. "You got no business in here."

Tom looked at the unfolding scene and the green fog spewing out of the box's open door. He heard the pounding voice that seemed to

341

be a boy's voice but couldn't belong to a boy. He saw Alan Landano standing in the aisle not far from Cindy, like an animal waiting to be slaughtered.

"It's your fault he's here," Evan cried. "You let him touch you. You seduced him in the first place."

"No," Cindy cried again. "Not me. You." Yes, she was able to control it now. She wasn't going to black out. She could see things that were going to be and things that had been and she could stay awake.

"Kill him," Evan said through the screen. "Kill him now before it's too late."

John shook his head. "No, Evan, No!"

And just before the final agony began, Cindy screamed out, "It's not Evan in there. Evan's at home with Jill!"

John turned in that last moment of control, grasped the handle of the screen and ripped it back. The eyes stared at him from the dark on the other side of the booth. They were yellow and green and rimmed purple. The face was not a face at all, but merely skin turned inside out, the tissue pulsating and pliant as raw meat. Things skittered across the skin that John had never seen before—small, long-legged creatures that had no form but emitted vapors of stink. One of them spat a bit of slime through the open screen, landing on John's robe, where it hissed. Then the thing turned tail and bored into the face of the Antichrist until it was below the surface and had disappeared.

The Devil's mouth was a perfect O, hardly moving as the words came forth, and as He spoke John felt the rancid breath born in the charnel pits of Hell and knew he could resist no longer. He knew it was over.

"Kill him now," He ordered. The voice was no longer disguised as Evan's, but was low and filled with malevolence.

As John turned to leave the booth of his own will, without being pushed, Sheriff Koester roared into the church, his long-barreled .38 drawn. He kept low, the weapon clutched in both hands. Just behind him Russell Patterson followed with a riot gun in his arms. The first thing Koester saw was his escaped prisoner, and he kept the weapon trained on Tom Conforte for a moment. Then other things came into focus.

Russell was standing at the rear of the church, still holding the gun, but listening to the voices inside him that told him a gun was of no use in this situation.

"What in God's name?" Koester said.

Cindy grabbed Alan by the shoulder and pushed him toward Koester, shouting, "Get him out of here."

The sheriff took hold of Alan's arm and began to pull him, no longer concerned about Tom Conforte. He was backing away and had gotten three paces up the nave when it began.

Koester's hand remained stuck on the boy's arm as he shook. For all the world he looked as if he was about to dance. But when his neck snapped back and bones began to splinter, Cindy and John and Russell and Tom knew it wasn't a dance he was doing.

He raised his arms out to his sides, as if he was doing exercises, and they began to rotate. Koester started to shriek, and the cry reverberated in the hollow church, bouncing off the walls.

He was whirling around then, faster and faster, with a deftness one would not expect out of so large and old a man. His feet spun with him, the screams rising to a crescendo as the pressure in his head exploded. His eyes were the first to go, bursting from their sockets and pulling long strands of tissue after them. Twin geysers of blood followed from each cavity and were soon joined by the spray of scarlet from each of the sheriff's ears. The rivers of blood shot through the air, landing on row after row of pews.

And Koester spun like that for a very long time because there was a full five quarts of blood in the man and Satan wanted him drained completely as he had had Father Dreiband drain Frank Conforte's blood when he killed him. Koester spun on and on, long after he was dead. At last the sprays of blood slowed, dripped, then stopped altogether, and Koester slumped lifeless to the floor of the nave.

Cindy and Alan and Tom stood not far from him, each drenched in Koester's blood. Tom wiped furiously at his face, sickened from the taste of it on his lips, knowing that he was about to be pushed over the edge of madness.

At the rear of the church Russell Patterson was standing with his eyes closed. He had dropped the gun and stood now with his hands cupped over the back of the pew. It couldn't be happening, he told himself, and as long as his eyes were closed he could somehow maintain that myth.

In the booth, sitting beside him, the Antichrist rasped, "That's how the boy will die if I have to kill him, Hines. Only he'll die much slower. I may string it out for an hour or two. Maybe even a day. A week? I don't know. Depends on how the mood strikes me. But I'll take my time and he'll be aware of every second of it, I promise you that."

John slumped back on the bench, too weak to answer. He knew the Antichrist could push him from the booth in this moment and then he would kill Alan, but it didn't want that. It wanted John to kill the boy of his own free will, as Father Dreiband had killed Frank Conforte. It wanted Alan dead, but it wanted John's soul more.

"He'll suffer bad, Hines. You want that to be on your head along with everything else?"

John looked out across the pews at Alan Landano. The boy had begun to whimper now. He was crying, the tears mixing with the blood

that covered his face. "I don't want to hurt!"
Alan whined. "Don't let him do that to me,
Father Hines. Please, Father. Pleeeeeease!"

"He doesn't have to hurt," the Antichrist
whispered to John. "You can get it over in a
second. Get Koester's gun. Take him out with
one shot, then we'll get on with the business
at hand."

He was right, John thought. Alan was going
to die anyway. It was John's fault. He'd led
him to this. All that was left was *how* he was
going to die. Better for him to die quickly,
with a minimum of pain. And as for John's
immortal soul, it didn't matter. He'd already
lost it. This was a last chance to do a final
good deed. Let the boy die without pain.

John stood and walked from the booth.
Behind him he heard the sputter and bubble
of the seething creature in the booth and he
knew that it was waiting, watching with
relish, ready to collect a soul that was long
overdue for delivery.

John walked through the putrid fog toward
Alan, and when he was less than six feet away
Cindy felt knowledge flowing through her
body. She was weakened from it this time, her
legs about to collapse. But she smiled with
ecstasy, at last understanding where the gift
came from. She felt the sticky flow of blood
down between her legs as her body buckled
under the power of the knowledge, and she
wept for herself and for John Hines and for
what they might have had if only he weren't

a priest. She even wept for poor George Hayward, that sick and twisted man.

Then she looked at Alan standing beside her, turned back toward John and stopped him by saying, "It's not Alan, John."

Something clicked inside his head, and he knew that she knew what she was talking about. He'd been had. He was going to be had. It was the sting of all time, only she was going to bust it before it came down. John listened to her.

"He's tricked you. You don't care about this boy. It's not Alan. Do you understand? There never was an Alan. It belongs to him," she shouted, turning to strike the altar boy about the head. She hit him over and over, drawing no pain or reaction from him.

Alan turned slowly and looked up past her pounding fists. He drew his lips back over his teeth, and as he did the corners of his mouth ripped easily apart. The skin continued to recede, pulling back over his jaw, at the same time lifting up over his nose, his forehead and his scalp, pulling back the bushy head of blonde hair with it.

John watched as the boy put his hands out toward Cindy, and as he did each of his fingernails popped off. The tissue beneath was red and raw, and then the skin on his fingers peeled back, exposing first white tissue, then bone.

The part that had been his face was changing, enlarging into a triangular lump of what might be flesh. Drool oozed down over where its lips once were. From the cavities where the ears had been crawled swarms of the same insects John had seen boring into the face of the Antichrist. Freed, at last, they began feasting on the face of the beast.

As the thing grew it tore loose from the clothing, and John saw that its entire small body had the same inside-out skin that the Antichrist was made of. Great spikes of teeth grew out of its mouth before John's eyes, and now he could hear its snarls.

It leaped through the air with a crude grace and landed on Cindy's chest, knocking her to the floor. Tom backed away and stumbled dumbly into one of the pews. At the rear of the church Russell was kneeling behind the pew, staring over the top at a memory that would be seared into his brain for all time.

John felt the release. She was right about it not being Alan, about Alan never having been. It wasn't an altar boy to be killed; it was a creature to be destroyed. He turned and ran toward the altar, bounding up the steps, past the sanctuary rail, past the sanctuary, onto the high altar.

His hands locked around the bronze crucifix and pulled on it. When it gave a little, he pulled harder, feeling the bolts begin to weaken. The roar behind him from the confessional was a cry of anger that rolled around the church with an avenging ferocity.

But before the Antichrist could put his

anger into words, the crucifix came loose and John held the heavy cross in his arms. He lugged it down the wide steps of the high altar, the foot of the cross dragging on the floor. For a moment he thought he would fall, but then he heard the death screams of Cindy Breslauer and the gurgling sound the Antichrist's creature made as it feasted on her flesh and blood.

He found new strength in his rage and pulled the cross along with him. Bolts of blue flame erupted from the confessional, terrible in their heat. One traveled a foot over Tom's head, and he stumbled to the floor of the church, the skin on his face already searing from the burn.

Another bolt fulminated down a pew, igniting the wood as it did. This time the bolt was coming for John, but when it got close he bent and pulled the crucifix high over his body. The bolt angled off to strike the beamed ceiling.

When he looked up he saw the monster squatting on top of Cindy, devouring her, its slithering head burrowing further and further into her neck as its claws cut cruelly into her shoulders. It reveled so intensely in this pleasure that it never heard John coming up behind it nor the wails of warning from the Antichrist.

Only when John groaned from hefting the heavy bronze cross over his head did the beast turn and look up from its prey. It looked up higher, above John, its eyes locking on the crucifix, and that was when John saw fear in its eyes. He cried out in holy vengeance as he brought down the heavy weight of God on the thing from Hell.

As the cross impacted with it, the Antichrist's servant pitched its voice from the agony of the holy metal. Its skin burned and boiled as the cross lay on it. It rolled onto its back, trapped under the weight of the crucifix.

From the confessional the Antichrist groaned, and John recognized the sound as something amazingly close to grief. For a split second he wondered if the creature was capable of compassion for one of its own. But he pushed those thoughts from his head, knowing they would weaken him.

Beneath the smouldering cross, the creature tried to move away. Already it was off Cindy. The thing that had savaged her now talked in Alan Landano's voice.

"It's me, Father Hines. He's fooled you. She was wrong. He only made you think I was bad. Take it off of me. Let me live, let me—"

But John stalked it and pressed down harder on the crucifix that pinned the beast, commanding, "Back to the Hell you came from!"

And then it retched one last time, gurgling deep in its throat. Cindy's blood belched from its mouth, and it went limp. Steam rose up from the beast, and John watched in horror as the insects about its face became airborne and flew toward the confessional, where they settled on the face of the Antichrist.

His hands still on the cross, John turned his attention on the confessional. He waited. He didn't know what to expect, but he sensed the creature had weakened. It had been surprised by all of them. It had not expected courage from a girl who was a slut. It had not expected faith from a priest who had slept with a woman.

The fog drew feebly back into the booth. John listened to the sputter of power from within. The smell wasn't as bad now, and he found strength in that.

"Go," John said. "It's time for you to leave. There's nothing more for you here."

He waited for an answer, but none came, only the hissing and sputtering from within the confessional.

With irony in his voice, John said, "I've killed it the way you wanted. Only it wasn't Alan I killed. It was something you spawned and that's not a victory for you. It's a victory for God." His voice rose as he found strength surging through him. "For Almighty God!"

John thought he heard a new groan from the confessional, and this time it wasn't one of grief, but one of pain. His voice was powerful now, resonating like the avenging angels he knew hovered just overhead. "It's a victory for Our Lord, God of the Host! For Jesus Christ, Son of God! Get out," John cried, advancing

on the confessional, his hands surrounded by
a pure white aura. "Leave his holy place, foul
being. There is nothing for you here! Leave!"

When it began to howl the cry of a wounded
animal, John knew for the first time that he
was gaining the upper hand. He crossed
himself and said, "Thank you, Lord God, for
standing by my side during this trial."

Again the Antichrist screamed, and John
held his hands out toward it, commanding,
"Leave now!"

The green fog sucked completely back into
the confessional. Abruptly, the door slammed
shut and the entire booth began to rock on its
foundation. The cry of the Antichrist wailed
through the church, echoing the sorrow of its
defeat, the agony it suffered at having missed
claiming a soul belonging to one of Christ's
captains.

The blast knocked John from his feet, the
entire side wall of the church being blown out
from the explosion. Dust and bits of wood
rocketed through the church, falling on top
of John. As the cold, purifying air from out
side bathed and cleansed him, he knew it was
as he had said—a victory for God.

He got to his knees and stared at the hole
where the confessional had been, where the
Antichrist had sat as if on a throne, doing
battle with him. He could see out into the
parking lot beyond, where pieces of the wall
lay.

There was no trace of the confessional.

A hand latched onto his shoulder and helped him up. He turned and saw that it was Russell Patterson. The deputy was trying to say something, but he was still having trouble forming the words.

John stood and walked to where Cindy Breslauer lay dying in the rubble. Her neck lay open where the creature had feasted on her. Blood still flowed from the wound, and for a moment John thought she was already dead.

But when he bent and took her hand she managed to open her eyes. She smiled softly and John said, "Take it easy. We're going to get help." He signaled to Russell, but Cindy raised her hand to stop the deputy.

Tom Conforte was by her side now as well. Cindy looked at Tom, then at Russell. Her voice cracked as she spoke the words. "Not him," she said to Russell.

He bent and said, "What? What is it?"

She swallowed hard. "He didn't kill George."

Russell focused on what she was saying, grateful for anything that could delay thinking about what he'd just seen. "Tom?"

She nodded weakly. "I killed him."

He arched an eyebrow, looking up at John. Then he turned back to Cindy. "Are you saying you killed George Hayward?" When she nodded again, Russell said, "That's a death-bed confession. It'll hold in any court in the country."

John told him, "Now go call for an

ambulance.''

After Russell left, Cindy grew peaceful. She stopped straining for breath. She was close to the end and found that a comfort.

She felt a last flicker of awareness, weaker than the others had been, more like when she could tell when the phone was going to ring or when a certain commercial was going to come on television.

"It wasn't Evan's fault," she said. She sighed, and John thought she was gone when her eyes closed. But she opened them again and gasped, "He didn't mean to do what he did. He was being used. He was just an instrument."

John nodded. "Like a pawn in a chess match."

"Yes," she said, closing her eyes. "They'll be all right, Jill and Evan."

John began administering the last rites, but Cindy touched his hand lightly and said, "It's all right. I'm not Catholic." Then she smiled, closed her eyes and died.

In the distance John heard the wail of the approaching ambulance.

CHAPTER 13

Months stretched out and with them came healing. Nettleton recovered. It wasn't easy, but it recovered. Sheriff Koester's death was mourned. Cindy Breslauer's brother flew in from Galveston for her funeral. Alan Landano's father showed a disquieting reserve at his adopted son's funeral, as if he knew something, John thought.

John presided at each of the burials, like a commanding officer burying his dead comrades. A gas leak was to blame, of course. The entire south wall of the church had been blown out, and what else besides a gas leak could do such a thing?

Russell Patteson was made Sheriff of Nettleton. John had the fender on the Sentra repaired, and Tom Conforte won a football scholarship to Notre Dame. That pleased Warren.

But Jill took the longest to mend. The events, both near and long past, had taken their toll on her. Cindy was right. She'd recover, but it would take time and it would take distance. She took Evan and moved out West. The June day she left Nettleton she looked pretty, and John hugged her as they said good-bye. There was no passion in the embrace, just friendship.

Evan understood less. He was leaving the town he'd grown up in and that saddened him. At the same time he welcomed it. The friends he had had for years were strangers to him suddenly. He felt differently about them, and they felt differently about him. Most of all, he felt differently about himself. A new town would mean a new start.

After John dropped Jill off at the train station, he drove to Oshkosh. He wanted to pay a visit to a friend. He was visiting Mercy Medical under better circumstances this time, much better circumstances.

John sat on the same bench where he and Father Nicoletti had spoken back in the dead of winter. Nicoletti's spirits were high this summer day. So were John's.

"Thirteen years is a long time," John said.

"No argument there."

"Are you afraid? About getting out, I mean."

"No. I think I'll adjust. I've probably go

some catching up to do on some things, but not that much." Nicoletti smiled. "I watch television, you know."

"What are your plans, Father?"

Nicoletti folded his large hands, basking in the warm breeze. "I've already spoken with the Bishop. There'll be an assignment for me. I'm grateful for that. It shows our church is open-minded. Just because a man's been ill doesn't mean he can't recover. Just because he's been spiritually paralyzed doesn't mean he can't be healed and made productive again."

John nodded. "I'm glad to hear that. Any idea where you'll be sent?"

"No. A small town, I hope. I like small towns. They have more of a sense of community than the cities."

"Yes, they do."

They were silent for a time, each with their own thoughts. A robin flew overhead, bringing a beakful of worms to her newly hatched. Squirrels cavorted across the verdant lawn. The sky was clear and blue and full of promise.

Nicoletti said, "You did a good job in Nettleton, John. Better than I could do. Certainly better than Father Dreiband did, rest his soul."

"Maybe I was just luckier."

"No. There was more to it than that. You were stronger than we were. Your faith was a rock. But . . ."

John turned to him. "But what?"

The priest drew a breath and exhaled it with conviction. He looked at John and said, "You must not delude yourself. It was only a momentary victory. The war between good and evil, between Christ and the Antichrist lives on. It will continue until the final victory or the final defeat. You were just a small hill to be captured. You managed to repulse Satan, but he'll move on, John, to another place and another time. Rest assured of that."

Nicoletti looked off into the distance and said, "Remember what I told you the last time we met? No one can defeat him. The best you can hope for is to keep him at bay. You've done that and you should be proud." Nicoletti frowned and added, "But heaven help the next man of goodwill who encounters him." He held John's gaze for a moment, then slapped both his hands on his legs and stood, his mood brightening. "But we shouldn't be talking of such dismal things on so fine a day."

John stood and walked with him.

"I'm going to take a stroll over to the little garden some of the patients have planted. Want to join me, John?"

"No, Father. I've got to get back to Nettleton. I only wanted to stop by and tell you how glad I was to learn you're leaving the hospital."

Nicoletti grasped John's hand and shook it meaningfully. "Thank you, John. I appreciate your coming."

"God bless you, Father Nicoletti. Let's keep in touch."

"Yes. By all means we should stay in touch." Then Nicoletti let go of his hand, turned and walked off toward the garden. John watched him go, thinking about how much wisdom and knowledge the man had to give to the new parish he was being assigned to and how fortunate the people were who would have him as their priest.

As Father Nicoletti walked he had an urge to look back one last time at John, but he repressed the urge. It wouldn't do at all. It would be pressing things. If he did, then John might see something. He might see the faint tinge of yellow and green deep within Nicoletti's eyes. He might smell the vile stench Nicoletti exuded but managed to keep just below the level of human smell. John might detect the tight little smile that played on Nicoletti's lips or hear the barely audible cackle that escaped from his mouth, even now, as he walked toward the garden.